More Praise for *Changers Book One: Drew*

"A fresh and charmingly narrated look at teens and gender."
—*Kirkus Reviews*

"Changing bodies, developing personalities, forays into adult activities—where was this book circa the early 2000s when I needed it? But something tells me my adult self will learn a thing or two from it as well."
—*Barnes & Noble Book Blog*

"The Coopers have a strong ear for teenager-isms, and the exploration of Drew's ups and downs is eminently believable . . . the slow build of a strong character—with the lure of something totally new coming up next—will leave readers ready for the next Change in this lineup."
—*The Bulletin of the Center for Children's Books*

"A perfect read for a young adult: warm and humorous without being superficial or saccharine, engaging real issues of teenage life with ease and natural grace, and offering an element of fantasy accurately reflecting the wonder and terror of growing up."
—*Chapter 16*

"'Selfie' backlash has begun: The Unselfie project wants to help people quit clogging social media with pictures of themselves and start capturing the intriguing world around them."
—*O, The Oprah Magazine* on the We Are Changers Unselfie project

"An excellent look at gender and identity and the teenage experience."
—*Tor*

"A must read for every teen."
—*I'd So Rather Be Reading*

"*Changers Book One* really stole my heart."
—*Bookcharmed*

"I was thrilled to discover a book that deals with issues of identity and belonging with so much heart and, more importantly, humor . . . *Changers* changed the way I think."
—Clay Aiken, singer/UNICEF ambassador

"Change. It's the one universal thing that everyone goes through, especially in high school. *Changers Book One: Drew* ratchets that up a notch and kicks open the door, with both humor and panache. Big questions and equally big highs (laughs) and lows (cries). And you thought high school was awkward before!"
—Kimberly Pauley, author of *Sucks to Be Me*

"Humor makes *Changers* a joy to read, and Drew the kind of character you'd want to be friends with in real life. I loved this book."
—Arin Greenwood, author of *Save the Enemy*

Praise for *Changers Book Two: Oryon*

"An excellent sequel . . . This installment raises the stakes, making the story not just about physical and emotional transformation, but about survival."
—*School Library Journal*

"Oryon's winning and witty narrative voice is consistently engaging . . . Oryon is African-American, and much of what he observes is about race . . . raises thought-provoking questions."
—*Kirkus Reviews*

"Addicting . . . as soon as I started reading I was immersed into the book, unable to put it down . . . The series is just getting better and better."
—*I'd So Rather Be Reading*

CHANGERS

BOOK THREE: KIM

BY T COOPER & ALLISON GLOCK-COOPER

This is a work of fiction. All names, characters, places, and incidents are the product of the authors' imagination. Any resemblance to real events or persons, living or dead, is entirely coincidental.

Published by Akashic Books
©2016 T Cooper and Allison Glock-Cooper
www.wearechangers.org

ISBN: 978-1-61775-489-0
Library of Congress Control Number: 2016935092
Illustration on page 256 by Alex Petrowsky

All rights reserved
First printing

Black Sheep/Akashic Books
Twitter: @AkashicBooks
Facebook: AkashicBooks
E-mail: info@akashicbooks.com
Website: www.akashicbooks.com

More books for young readers from Black Sheep

Changers Book One: Drew
by T Cooper & Allison Glock-Cooper

Changers Book Two: Oryon
by T Cooper & Allison Glock-Cooper

Game World
by C.J. Farley

Pills and Starships
by Lydia Millet

The Shark Curtain
by Chris Scofield

*For anybody who has looked in the mirror
and not recognized the person s/he sees.*

Before he became the one he was meant to be, before he lived through those four years called high school, those four years where everything he ever knew evaporated into air, where the ground dropped away, and he fell in love, and he lived through hate and violence and the loss of his best friend, and saved lives without even knowing how, and was rescued by a girl and a boy and words and music, and he did everything wrong until he got a few important things right, before he questioned what it meant to be special, what it meant to be anything, and harnessed his power, the power he didn't believe he had, the power others tried to take, before that and a hundred other awful, wondrous, ruinous, magical things happened, he was just a kid in Tennessee named Oryon.

SUMMER

ORYON

CHANGE 2-DAY 359

Is this working? ———?
I'm not sure I remember how to do this anymore, after what? Four months' hiatus from dutifully Chronicling every high school heartbreak and hangnail. (Not to mention all the useless thoughts and absurd fears that crossed my mind ever since being bestowed with the knowledge that I'm one of the rare, lucky Changers walking the planet.)

Pshhhst.

You want to know the biggest thing I've learned over the last two years? *Everything is temporary.*

Every. Thing. Is. Temporary. Life, love, strep throat, dandruff, icebergs, me.

I have one more week of being this *thing* Oryon, and then I'm going to be some other *thing* that turns up in my bed as mandated by the paperwork inside the packet that the Changers Council will drop off on that dreaded morning. Also known as: Change 3, Day 1. Not even a tiny bit psyched about that. Don't want to think about it right now. So I'm not going to. Why bother anyway? Because hey, *everything is temporary*, yo. Which is another way of saying, *you have no control over anything, ever*, so stop fooling yourself and sweating something you can't actually do anything about. Sounds comforting, right? In theory it should be. And yet in reality, I can't seem to *act* like I've learned this vital lesson about the leaf-on-the-wind, transitory nature of existence. Because, shit still matters to me.

Like, Audrey. Like, not being able to talk with Audrey since . . .

. . . Well, since *you know*.

We hooked up.

(Still can't believe that actually happened. I've played it over in my mind so many times it feels more like a scene from a favorite movie than my real life.)

Audrey. Sweet, beautiful, lovely—and probably deeply (and rightfully) *confused*—Audrey.

I still have no idea what happened after I disappeared on her. I've imagined every scenario in my mind. I know she was upset, like, jump-up-out-of-bed, gather-and-clutch-your-clothes-to-your-bare-chest-and-flee-the-apartment-before-running-haphazardly-into-moving-traffic upset. And she likely stayed that upset for a while. But did she ever try to contact to me when the rage dissipated? If it did dissipate. Which I wouldn't blame her if it didn't. I mean, she thinks I'm a psycho-liar-face-creeper who either bagged her best friend, or stalked them both, or some other stomach-churning combo of garbage-person scenarios.

I didn't reach out to her. *Couldn't*. What with the abduction. Followed by four months of reprogramming lock-down at the Changers "Restoration and Rehabilitation Retreat" (RRR), which buried me deeper underground than the *Titanic*'s colon. Even in federal prison you get to go out in the yard for a couple hours a week, wait in line for the pay phone every now and again. Not so much at the Changers Secure Housing Unit, where you can't even burp without someone checking a box on a clipboard, all under the guise of "restoring physical, mental, and emotional well-being to your many selves." And okay, sure, after the trauma of the whole Abiders kidnapping ordeal, I probably needed it. But the one-two punch of loss of control and the shredding of my dignity, such as it was, well, let's just say I now refer to that whole period of my putrid life as the "Tribulations."

That's another thing I learned: it helps to name things.

I wish I knew what to call my relationship with Audrey. I guess I don't have one anymore. Beyond the one in my imagination. Audrey lives in Memory Town now. What a dick-move on my part—to make her believe I loved her. I mean, it was the truth that I loved her. Like I've never loved anything or anyone. I *still* love her. I guess the issue was *who* exactly was doing the loving. I told myself it didn't matter. I let us both get swept up in the fever and just went with it like young people across millennia, continents, cultures, and galaxies do. Some guy named Anil and his girl Sujatha are probably curled up in the back of his dad's car on a steamy dead-end street in the outskirts of Mumbai right now. And a girl named Michèle and her crush Sophie are running down the steps of the Paris metro holding hands, their pink and blue hair catching the breeze from a train blowing into the station down below. Audrey and I were no different.

But I was. I was different. *Am* different. And I kept that to myself. What did I think was going to happen? What starts in a lie can only end in a lie. I set myself up to be the bad guy and *poof*, now I'm gone. For good. Never to be redeemed. *Later, Oryon.* Except for us Changers, there is no later.

Audrey didn't even get the pleasure of flipping me off in the hallways or watching her friends ice me out or having her missing-several-links brother splinter my tailbone one unsuspecting Friday after the football game. (Unless he was in fact one of my Abider kidnappers, but even then I can't imagine Audrey knew. She couldn't have. Could she?)

Bottom line—if I really believed everything is temporary, I wouldn't be obsessing right now, the first day I'm sprung from RRR. I wouldn't be sitting here thinking how horrible it must've felt (*still feels?*) for Audrey to have trusted me so completely and sincerely, only to discover me as a fraud. Or what she thinks indicates I'm a fraud. Which, I totally am the definition of.

As Nana would say, "A pig's ass is pork." Lies for good reasons are still *lies*. Any way you cut it, it looks bad for Oryon, who, come Monday morning, will vaporize and be replaced by someone else, the who of which hardly matters, because it won't be Oryon and Oryon is the boy Audrey loved.

Great, now it feels like I'm about to hyperventilate. *Breathe. Breathe.* Man, I'm still so messed up. It's crazy-making, this merry-go-round of thoughts and doubts and fears and what-ifs. Plus, I WAS FREAKING LOCKED IN A BASEMENT AND LEFT TO ROT WHILE MY BEST FRIEND DIED IN MY ARMS. Sorry, Changers Council, that ain't a stain easily bleached away no matter how much brain retraining or "life is a series of never-ending stories" continuum crap you lay on me.

Okay. I need to calm down. Get a grip already. Know what I can change and what I can't. I can't change how Audrey feels. I can't change what happened to Chase.

I *can* change how I respond right now. I can practice my "mindfulness meditation," one thing I got out of RRR that isn't the worst.

I am simply being here and now. Let's take inventory: I'm sitting on this old bed, in a new bedroom, in a new house, cardboard boxes filled with my familiar things all around me. Close my eyes. I'm simply breathing and sitting here on my bed, no big deal. *In, out, in, out.* I can hear the garbage truck rumbling on the street, birds tweeting in the branches outside the window, feel an itch stirring in the hairs on my forearm. I'm not going to scratch it. Just notice it's there, along with all of the other sensations in my body that are going on right now, pleasant and unpleasant. (Mostly unpleasant.) The rapid breaths I can't help, that come from somewhere in the center I can't quite reach, have no dominion over me. My dry mouth, a slight soreness on the left side of my throat every time I swallow. Nothing I need to do right now except breathe and be. *What's that?* Oh, it's the toilet running, which in only a few short hours in my new room I've noticed struggles to partially refill the tank every five minutes. There must be a slow, tiny leak somewhere.

Okay, so all that's happening. And so much more. And yet, also, really nothing.

I notice my breathing is slowing some now. Can't do anything but pay attention to it. *In, out, in, out, in, out.* Just for these five minutes I'm allowing Oryon/myself to be let off the hook. For everything. Nothing I have to do now but pay attention to the breathing, the panic subsiding. My heart isn't flip-flopping in my chest anymore. My crazy is chilling out. I'm the boss of my body. *I am the captain now.* Breathe: *in, out, in, out.*

KNOCK-KNOCK, my door is opening. (An actual door. Not a symbolic, spiritual one.) It's Mom, *knock-knock-entering* without waiting for a "Come in!" Per usual.

"Hey, petunia, you okay?"

Simply being is simply done. "Yep," I answer.

"Do you need anything?"

"Nope."

I glance up, notice again how Mom looks older. The events of the past few months registering on her face as years. She doesn't bother chiding me for the "Yep" or the "Nope." She doesn't bother with a lot of things like that anymore. The things that don't really matter when it comes down to life and death.

"Some ice water maybe?"

I shake my head. Smile with my lips closed.

"It's weird to be back, huh?" she asks quietly.

"But I've never been here."

"I know. I just mean back from the retreat," she says, pulling my old stuffed animal Lamby-cakes out of a box and propping him on my desk, his neckless head flopping flat to his shoulder. "I know everything is hard right now. I'm just glad you're home."

"It wasn't a 'retreat,' but yeah, me too."

Which wasn't entirely true. Because while I'm happy to be sprung from all of my former incarcerations, I would rather be navigating my way on the city bus to Audrey's house right this minute, trying somehow to make things right with her before I change again, instead of doing deep-breathing exercises in my bed with my mommy checking in on me every five minutes.

Sure, Mom's being totally thoughtful and accepting and nonjudgmental, all the things we talked about in family counseling during the triple-R sessions. (Dad's a different story, but whatever.) Thing is, I need a friend whose uterus I didn't come out of. One I can tell everything, despite how much trouble that could bring for not just me and my family, but for my entire Changers race.

"Want me to help you set up your room?" Mom asks,

scrambling my decidedly non-Changer-approved fantasies of outing myself to Audrey. "It'll go faster if there are two of us."

"I'm good."

Since the Tribulations, Mom's been treating me like a hollowed-out eggshell. Intact, but with its gelatinous guts having been sucked away via two tiny pinholes.

Or maybe that's just how I envision myself.

I know she's doing her best, that she's suffered perhaps the most through all of this, but I just want to be alone in this strange room, the fourth strange room in as many months. First the pitch-black Abider basement of doom. Then the impossibly bright urgent-care holding pen at Changers Central for the few days it took me to be rehydrated, renourished, and "stabilized" (ha!). Next it was the white, pristine "no triggers here, folks!" suite I shared with Elyse while we went through the RRR program together.

And now this bedroom, in a new house somewhere in the anonymous, weedy outskirts of Nashville, because "it was decided" by the Council that our old apartment in Genesis was potentially compromised—by my bringing Audrey there, and her brother maybe seeing me chasing Audrey across the highway like a scene from *Dog the Bounty Hunter*.

Yes, the *Boggle* board of my life has been jumbled yet again, this time more thoroughly, with everything about to settle into entirely new squares, spelling out entirely new words and stories. Starting with my name.

(It helps to name things.)

Miraculously, the Council didn't decide to switch my school. That particular risk-reward analytic came out in my favor. So, I'll get to see Audrey again. I will see her in a mere six days, even if it's from afar—and from behind the mask of yet another new classmate whom she will not know and likely not want to get to know after the last new kid she opened herself up to totally shattered her heart. Still, it'll be better than nothing at all. I can keep an eye on her, make sure Jason doesn't do something horrible, never mind that Kyle guy who was harassing her in my vision. Even if I don't find a way to tell her what happened to Oryon, the new me can stay by her side. Ride or die.

"You're going to need some school supplies," Mom says, interrupting my scheming yet again. "Make a list of the colors and ones you want, and I can grab them next time I hit the shop."

School supplies. I used to care about those. I actually spent time picking out the folders and the pencil holders, as if having the right folder or pencil holder would communicate something relevant about me and smooth my way into school society. Which it probably did. Because most students still care about folders and pencil holders, and they notice when a kid has a generic red one from the cheap place, and another kid has one with rhinestones in the shape of a kitten, and they make assessments about said kids based on those items and choices (loser, winner, friend-able, undateable, rebel), and they do this because they aren't preoccupied with, I don't know, *changing into a completely different human*, even though—spoiler alert—they are! Just not as obviously.

How's that for insight? Oh how the path to knowledge is strewn with large, bloody, severed chunks of ego. I am feeling just a tick pleased with myself. Warmed slightly by the irresistible cocktail of my cleverness and bitterness, and I absentmindedly decide I'll call Chase because he would laugh harder than anyone at my school supply riff, would nod his head and say he knew *exactly* what I was getting at, then probably ruin the moment by lecturing that I was finally "getting it" re: the hypocrisy of the Changer movement and the need for all of us to be out and proud and united and part of the fabric of daily life if we ever want to be completely 100 percent accepted and integrated into society, *blah blah*. The whole conversation plays out in my head in a matter of seconds, the way conversations with close friends always do. And it takes a beat before I'm reminded of the saddest thing of all. That from here on out, all my conversations with Chase will be in my head.

"Whatever school supplies are fine, Mom," I say.

ORYON

CHANGE 2-DAY 360

This must be what death row is like. Actually knowing the day you're going to cease to exist. You sit there as every minute, every second, every breath siphons away, aware this is the last time you will eat frozen chicken nuggets, a slice of terrible pizza, canned pear cubes in syrup; the last time you will do fifty push-ups; the last time you will have a headache; the last time you will dream about being a child at the park and holding your father's hand.

I know I shouldn't be so scream-queen dramatic, because unlike guys on death row (and they are like 99.9 percent guys—not exactly a ringing endorsement for the male persuasion), I get to have another life after this one ends. And then another one after that. And then I get back one of the four I've had over the previous four years. Some Changers and Touchstones I've met (Tracy!) are hella psyched about this whole process. *#Blessed*. What a unique life opportunity to embrace! Sorry, *lives* opportunities. "In the many we are one." *Blurgh*.

When I was Ethan, I didn't know I was a Changer yet, that in a matter of years, Ethan would be basically DOA. There was no goodbye. No processing. Maybe that was easier. Rip that identity off like the Band-Aid it was. *Bye, Oryon/Drew/Ethan*.

Wow, this is the first time I've thought about Ethan in

like, I don't know exactly. I nipped that in the nuts, didn't I? I mean, why think about him, about ever seeing him again, if I can never be him? At least on the outside.

Everybody—Tracy, my parents, my incarceration buddy Elyse—keeps telling me Ethan will always be with me, will always be a part of me. *Is* me. But I just feel further and further away from him and his life. He's a phantom. A guy I used to know. Maybe every kid feels this way. You get older, you see some stuff, and the person you used to be washes away like writing in the sand. Audrey probably doesn't feel like the same girl she was two years ago either. Likely I had something to do with that, for better and worse.

I'm realizing this is also the first time I've really thought about choosing my Mono. Probably because now there's a tangible choice, two different V's to choose between. I'm so sick of thinking and obsessing and being weighed down by my feelings, and yet I can't seem to stop thinking, obsessing, and plotting the if-thens ahead of me. Life just makes me do that. Which I guess is the point. But sometimes I wish I were a single-celled organism or something, with nothing to do or consider or decide or learn. A basic fungus, hanging out among all other fungi, every one of our cells exactly the same. *In the one I am done.*

Drew? That multicellular, multilayered V? I suppose I grew to love being her. Didn't want to change from her, now that I'm remembering. But I can sort of maybe see myself picking Oryon as my Mono. Wouldn't be the worst. Hey, perhaps when we're all grown up and graduated, I'll declare Oryon, and then go find Audrey—wherever she attends college, or on some crazy mission in South America that her family makes her do—so we can live happily ever after together. If she once had love for me, for Oryon, then maybe there could be love again.

If I really think about it, this love I have for Aud is really just an extension of the love I first felt for her as Drew. And it's probably the same for her too, whether or not she's conscious of it. She's got to sense it—like, a soul-connection or something. I mean, think about the greatest love stories of all time, when two people feel like they've known each other in previous lives. That's exactly what it feels like with me and Audrey. Only of course with me there actually *are* different lives at play. Even though Audrey doesn't recognize it.

But you know what? One day I'm going tell her, and everything will suddenly snap into place and make perfect sense to both of us. Right?

Meanwhile, *tick-tock, tick-tock,* I just keep checking the time on my phone, as every last second slips away on this death march toward Change 3. T minus 144 hours to execution day. No reprieve is coming for me from the governor, that I know for sure. May as well eat this overstuffed enchilada. The last one Oryon will ever enjoy. Extra guacamole, please!

What else? I have all my school supplies. They're just sitting there on my desk, taunting me by looking far more optimistic (even in all-business black) than I am about the start of the school year.

Scratch scratch at the door. It's Snoopy. Who, in truth, has been a little standoffish toward me since I got home from RRR. It's almost as though he doesn't remember who I am. Or more likely, as if he knows *exactly* who I am and how my stupidity is what almost got him his own seat on death row.

He's padding over to my bed, sniffing my comforter, eyeing me warily. I make the quintessential open-face, eagerly pat the bed, but Snoop doesn't want to jump up. Instead, he mopes back over to an open cardboard box, sticks his head in and noses around, then wanders back out my bedroom door.

Thank G for the little chip between his shoulder blades. Like the one in the base of my neck, come to think of it. Only his was a lifeline that brought my parents back from Nana's when the pound called and said they had Snoopy in custody, and that it's lucky he was microchipped, because as a pit bull, he wouldn't last more than forty-eight hours before being put down. "As sweet as he is," the animal-control officer had told Mom and Dad, "we just can't keep them around, for obvious reasons."

Them. For *obvious* reasons. A year as Oryon sure tuned me in more than ever to the ways bigotry blares from the spaces in between, the way crabgrass busts through the asphalt. I know now how narrow the margin of error is for anyone (or any canine) of difference. How once people decide something—*pit bulls = bad*—no amount of actual fact seems to scrub that prejudice away. Changers are right about one thing: the power of an idea is stronger than just about anything. The power of an idea can save a nation. Or kill a dog.

When I look at Snoopy now, I am filled with guilt and regret that I'm the reason he was within a few hours of being put down. My carelessness, my selfishness. The series of BS choices that nearly added up to total catastrophe. Sometimes, okay, *often* I get stuck in this obsessive mental loop. *If this, then that. If not this, then not that*. With Snoopy. With Chase. With Audrey.

Like, what if Drew had been put in a different homeroom than Audrey freshmen year? We might never have met. At least not like that. She never would've pointed me to the "right" (girls') bathroom in the hallway, never would've joked with me about Chloe's wretchedness, nor would I ever have ironically tried out for cheerleading, which is where we got so close. Us against the world.

And what if Mom and Dad hadn't changed the contact number for Snoopy's microchip when we left New York for Tennessee, and the shelter couldn't get in touch with my parents to let them know he had been picked up by the side of the highway, sans leash or collar? What if Mom got a flat tire, or was in an accident on the way home from Florida, and she didn't make it back by the deadline the shelter gave before Snoopy was going to be "terminated"?

And what if they never chipped him in the first place? I mean, the call about Snoopy was the first thing that tipped Mom and Dad off that something was amiss back home. A few unanswered calls to your teenager? That's expected, no need for panic at the disco. But when the shelter called, and they heard that Snoopy was found wandering free on the streets, they knew I never would've let that happen unless something was seriously wrong. I guess in a way, Snoopy being picked up by animal control was what helped the Council figure out that three of us Changers had gone missing. And . . .

Chase.

The ginormous elephant in the Chronicle I'm trying not to think about.

Chase.

Who is dead.

Dead because of me.

Even though nobody will put it that way. Nobody will come clean about the truth of what happened that day we got sprung from that basement. I couldn't get a straight answer out of anybody during RRR. Not Tracy, not my parents, not a single Changers counselor. Turner the Lives Coach made it very clear that Elyse and I should "bask in gratitude" that we'd been saved, thanks to Chase's brave actions, which was his "journey," and not for us to mourn, but to "accept and celebrate."

I knew Chase. Chase was not about his "journey." He was about fighting the fight. He was at the head of the parade, bearing the banner, representing for all of us other cowards too chicken to be honest. He wasn't about dying either. He would have said that crap was for the movies.

When I reflect on that time, on everything that happened, the rage fills me to my throat. Followed quickly by a sense of helplessness, a *hobbling*. So I shut it down. Put all the messiness in its respective boxes. Compartmentalize the eff out of my trauma. If I don't, I can't function. As evidenced by the first three weeks after the Tribulations when I lay in bed at Changers Central in a catatonic stupor, my mom and dad by my side, Elyse on the other side of the curtain, doing her own version of the same. Thank J for *Battlestar Galactica*. (Dad bought me the entire series on DVD, and I watched episodes back-to-back-to-back, breaking only for the bathroom and uncontrollable crying jags.)

The Council has advised that Elyse and I, the survivors, focus solely on our rehabilitation, our emotional recovery, and not fret about what happened, or how they will find and punish (or not) the perpetrators. *Shut up and be happy*, basically. We survived, we're conscious and up walking about, even if not everyone else got off so lucky. Look at what happened to poor Alex. Sure, the kidnappers didn't technically put him in that coma. But whatever happened amidst the fracas of the rescue certainly did. Yeah, the kid'll get another body come his Change 2, Day 1, but it worries me what's happening inside his brain, to his essential self inside the Alex shell, while he lies there in that bed at Changers Central, hooked up to beeping machines while his folks sit helplessly stroking his hand.

"Survivor's remorse," they called it at RRR. Told me I should abandon self-lacerating thought patterns because everything "is what it is, and is what it should be," and no amount of my hating life, or hating that I have lives to hate, is going to make reality different.

But.

They didn't see Alex. He was so scared. So small. He reminded me of Ethan. I was small then. I was scared. I was nothing like Chase.

Know-it-all Chase, always right about everything, always needing the last word.

Ah, yes. There's the irony. Which he would have loved, of course.

No matter who I am, it'll always remain imprinted on my brain. The first time I saw him at ReRunz. His smile curled at the corners. His confidence, unearned, but there nonetheless. I fell for him in that moment, before I knew he was a Changer, before I knew I was whatever I was. It was pure instinct, unfiltered, and that attraction deepened to love, and with love, respect; and before I knew it, Chase was my one true friend, the one who knew all the ugly about me and chose to love me anyway.

The end will also always remain imprinted. That same wry smile, maybe a little more world-weary, and on a different face, sure, but somehow essentially the same. And the "Fancy meeting you here!" slurred through bloodied, swollen lips, his head in my lap as his heart sludged up, slowing to a stop. I put my ear to his chest, hearing only three weak beats, sounding so far away. And then. He wasn't there.

I think I called his name.

I must have called his name.

Seconds later there was loud banging in the hallway, a vague smell of electrical smoke. I can't recall anything after that. Nor can Elyse. We've tried piecing it together, but neither of us can recollect much after Chase was thrown into the basement with us, bound and hooded. I try to concentrate. I meditate so hard, scanning the corners of my mind like some old, decommissioned hard drive. But all I can ever come up with is the door opening, the light searing into our pupils, noises, shouting, acrid, burning fog . . . and then waking up in a hospital gown at Changers Central, my alarmed parents pacing bedside, Turner the Lives Coach bending close to my eyes, the wooden prayer beads around his neck plunking on my chest like dropped marbles.

"Chase?"

Mom said it was the first word out of my mouth.

"He's awake!" she screeched, and immediately started weeping, draping herself over me like an emergency blanket as Dad jumped off a cot in the corner and raced around the other side of the bed.

"Thank God," Dad whispered into my neck. I think he was crying.

"I thought you didn't believe in God," I mumbled. I recall sounding so groggy to myself, my voice deeper than I remembered it sounding in my head before the Tribulations.

"Well, now I might need to reconsider," he said, laugh-crying. "Smart-ass."

"We were so worried," Mom managed through her tears.

"I'm sorry," I said. My head was so sore. It was then I noticed the searing sensation where the IV stuck out of my arm.

"Shhh, don't even say that," Mom said.

"You guys aren't angry?"

"Angry? Why would we be angry?"

But before I could formulate an answer, I nodded off again, too exhausted to press them about Chase, or Alex, or Elyse, or Snoopy's well-being, or where the hell I was. Nothing. Because immediately after I learned that Mom and Dad weren't upset with me, I was out cold again, for God knows how long.

ORYON

CHANGE 2-DAY 362

T-minus three days and counting.

Nothing to report beyond Mom remaining no farther than twenty feet from me at any moment, even checking on me when I'm in the bathroom for more than three whole minutes.

"You're constipating me, Ma!"

"It's only because I love you, Oryon."

Dad's been gone at Changers Central all day, every day, and into the nights, heading up an anti-Abiders task force. Even though the Abiders have been fairly quiet—well, at least they were quiet up until the Tribulations—Dad's terrified we're in the early stages of a concerted surge of Abiders' anti-Changers activities. But I think his obsession is solely because of what happened to me. You never *really* care about distant messiness until it floods your lawn like a ruptured sewer line. Either way, Dad is not standing for it, cannot just "move on," and will not forget for even one minute of one single day that this consortium of hatred and intolerance is roiling somewhere out there, operating in the shadows of society, and that no matter how much preparation or organizing we Changers do, there is no way to stop the next action or transgression on their part.

Despite all the talking and processing and counseling at the RRR, Dad just can't be happy that I made it, that I'm alive and well in his house, staring at him over our cereal bowls every morning. So he leaves the house early, funneling all of his rage and indignation about the Tribulations into "fighting for change, instead of sitting around waiting for it to happen." This morning I told him his ranting was starting to sound a little like Benedict and the rest of the RaChas, to which he replied that I didn't know "what the H-E-double-hockey-sticks" I was talking about, then grabbed the car keys and headed out the door.

I guess it's hard for him to accept the facts of what we're up against. It's like he refuses to acknowledge it as a reality, as opposed to a theory—as though ignoring the facts might actually make them not so. I think Dad thought it would be different by now, that there would be more acceptance in the world, and that at the very least, more progress would have been made in the years since he was going through his Cycle of V's. And yet here I am, living proof it hasn't. Maybe this whole Changers mission is a waste of time. Maybe Statics are getting worse on the whole, not better.

"Your father doesn't know what to do with his frustration," Mom says kindly as soon as we hear Dad's car pull out of the garage.

"He doesn't know what to do with the truth," I snap back.

"No, I suppose he doesn't," she concedes. "But not many people do."

Last week, Dad decided to take leave from work and assume a part-time position with the Council. He's not allowed to actually join the Council, as Changers by-laws state that nobody with a child who's still completing his/her Cycle is eligible to run. So many rules and procedures, I can't keep track. I'm even starting to forget the overarching mission of our existence. Mostly I just try to get through each day, like a simple bacteria just going through the motions until my brief time on this planet is up.

I kind of wish Mom would get busy with something too. I see her poking her head into my room in the night when I'm supposed to be sleeping. What does she think? Those Abider nut jobs are going to hunt me down, bust into our house, get past Snoopy, Dad's Taser (newly purchased), and scoop me up from my bedroom in the middle of the night?

Yes. That's exactly what she thinks.

I get it. But the Council assures us that whomever took me, Elyse, and Alex are so long gone by now, nobody's going to hear from them again. At least not in our neck of the Changer woods.

"All good in there?" Mom asks through the door for the forty-seventh time today.

"Yep," I murmur, trying not to sound as annoyed as I am.

"You know I hate the *Yep*," she chides weakly, her heart still not in it.

At least she's trying. Mom wants life to normalize. Like that's even a thing.

ORYON

CHANGE 2-DAY 365

So here I am, standing in my bathroom in boxers, shirt off, staring at Oryon in the mirror. Flexing my biceps, leaning in and inspecting the hairs on my chin. It'll all be gone tomorrow. Or maybe not. Maybe I'll change into some 1960s-looking dude with a full beard and mutton chops. Or maybe I'll change into a hipster girl with a bleached pixie cut and a walk like a giraffe. Maybe I'll change into the hottest dude in class.

Part of me still wishes I could simply stay Oryon. Oryon was cool enough. And cool enough is way better than gambling on what comes next. You know how people will stay with a boyfriend or girlfriend who's fine and all, but in the back of their heads they harbor lingering doubts, thinking maybe they could do better? (Memo to humanity: most of us can't.) Like that hippie song goes, *"Love the one you're with."* Not the worst advice. But I can't love Oryon enough to make him stay, or love myself enough not to care if he leaves. I'm an identity way station, and the next vessel is about to pull in.

On the eve of Oryon's dematerialization, I'm appreciating things about him as though I'm not him, but rather something else entirely, a creature stuck on the inside of the mirror looking out at him. His tightly curled hair, the distance between his eyebrows and hairline. His intense eyes, the warm color and smoothness of his skin. His famous lady-killing smile, which got him so many places. The way he walks through a room, the hint of rasp in his voice. I'm kind of loving it all right now, digging it so much more than I ever did because I know it'll be gone tomorrow. You don't miss water till the well runs dry. Or in this case, you don't miss your corporeal form until it's reassembled in some cosmic mixing bowl into something else entirely.

I guess it makes me think about appreciating stuff (well, people) more while you still can. Take Nana. She's still with us, but barely. I'm really happy Mom and Dad brought her back from Florida so she's closer, but because she's kind of out of it most of the time, it makes me feel horrible that I didn't spend more time with her when she was lucid. She knows so much, has been through so much. I took her for granted. Just like I did with somebody else ...

God, I miss him. A part of me refuses to accept he's really gone. So what if I'm stuck in the denial stage of grief? Not that those stages seem like anything more than BS made up to sell self-help books. Denial, Anger, Bargaining, Depression. I got them all. No start or finish. No checked-off box. Life's untidy that way. And I don't care if I ever get to the "final" Acceptance stage of grieving him. What am I accepting anyway?

Erggh. Mom just came in to tell me Tracy and Mr. Crowell are here.

Well damn, those two have reinvented the "honeymoon stage." The minute I saw her in the hallway, Tracy was practically floating a few inches above the ground, beaming so much I thought her head might split horizontally and unhinge at her jaw like a Muppet.

"You look soooo goood," she exclaims, letting go of Mr. Crowell's hand (for two seconds) to give me a hug.

I notice at once how she smells like cotton candy.

"You always look good, of course," she coos. "Not that looks mean anything. I'm just saying, you know, you look rested. Better than the last time I saw you."

"When I was bedridden? Good to hear."

Tracy continues to ogle me appraisingly as I shake Mr. Crowell's outstretched hand. He smiles his crooked smile. "How you doing, buddy?"

"Better, thanks," I say quickly and quietly, looking down at his suede bucks beside Tracy's pink espadrilles on the hardwood floor as she climbs up on her tippy-toes and nuzzles Mr. Crowell's neck.

"Do you kids want some tea?" Mom calls in from the kitchen.

"Nah, I should probably—" I start, while at the same time Tracy chirps, "Yes, Connie, that'd be lovely."

We stand there awkwardly in the hallway as Mom hollers, "Well, which is it?"

My neck flushes hot. I try, but I can't bring myself to make eye contact with Mr. Crowell. It's like I'm embarrassed by him knowing definitively what I am now. Every time he looks at me I can see him doing the math. What part was Drewy? What part was Oryony?

Ha, *Oryony*! How am I just now thinking of that? If Oryon were writing an autobiography, that would definitely be the title: *The Oryony of It All*.

The Oryony here being Mr. Crowell is, like, "normal," and didn't know this giant thing about me for the first almost two years of teaching me, and now he's suddenly been let in on the whole situation—and while it's rainbows and kittens that Tracy has found her Static mate, and Mr. Crowell is all cool with everything, I guess now I'll always feel sort of "less than" in his eyes ever since I was outed. Like I've been diminished in some way because he knows this "secret" about me, about my past lives. That I'm never truly who I seem to be.

I know it's probably psychological residue from the Tribulations, but it still feels wrong to have been unmasked in front of Mr. Crowell, who yeah, has been Changers Council–trained and vetted and approved before marrying Tracy, but is nevertheless, through no fault of his own, going to be new to all this alternate universe body-swapping chaos for a while. I mean, it's got to blow his mind on occasion. It still blows mine, and it's my everyday reality.

And while in theory I should be comforted by his knowing—the truth should set me free!—I'm not. Instead, I feel like an impostor. Or a freak. Or some cruel deceiver. With him I'll always be the *other*. I'll never just be the person(s) he knew before.

"What's the verdict, buddy?" he asks. About the tea, presumably.

Please. Stop. With. The. Buddy. Buddy.

Tracy catches my expression, which likely reads as terrified with a hint of rage. She exchanges one of those couples' predecided looks with Mr. Crowell, then drags me into the living room for a private chat, somehow managing to cleave herself from her new husband and be alone with me for a minute. (I swear I heard a suctioning sound when they separated.)

"How are you, *really*?" she pries, soon as we plop on the couch, her knee touching mine.

"Fine. Totally fine. Mostly."

"I want to believe that," she says, tilting her head like a dog hearing a distant whistle.

"You should," I reply, pulling my knee away, faking an itch that needed to be scratched under my thigh.

"Don't underestimate the level of trauma you experienced," she intones, dead serious. "I've spoken with Turner and a couple of the counselors, and if you feel like you need a little more time to recover, we can always do the homeschool thing until you're—"

"NO!" I shout.

Tracy flinches, her spine jacking straight.

"I mean, *no*," I say, "no thank you," making sure to sound calm and totally not hysterical. "Getting into a routine is probably the best thing for me."

I stare into Tracy's eyes, trying to be flat and emotionless so she doesn't smell my desperation. She does the dog-whistle head tilt again. Maybe she's receiving signals from outer space. Maybe the Council has her wearing a wire and she's double-agenting me as we speak, getting feedback through some invisible earpiece on what to say, like a hostage negotiator trying to convince some desperate schmuck with a shotgun to release more victims from the bank vault. I practice relaxing my face muscles. See? Not crazy. Not a killer.

"What?" I ask, super-duper chill.

"What, *what?*" she counters, eyes squinting now.

"I feel strongly that it'll be good to be back out in the world again," I say matter-of-factly. "The Council counselors told me that reengagement with others can be a huge aid to healing."

"It can also be avoidance behavior. A way to bury and distract from the pain instead of moving through it."

And? I think. Is that so wrong? Whole empires have been built on the sturdy back of mass cultural denial. In fact, one might argue "burying it" is a necessity for progress. You stop and consider anything for too long and you'll never want to leave the couch again.

"Trace, I'm going to make it," I say, smiling and praying I don't look like a cornered ferret.

For a moment, Tracy turns her chin toward the kitchen, where Mr. Crowell has obviously said something witty and charming to make my mom laugh really hard. Turning back to me, she is softer: "I was just ... well ... I really couldn't live with myself if anything happened to you again." She starts to tear up, reaching inside a pocket for a pink monogrammed handkerchief.

"It'll be okay," I say, patting her shoulder as she blots her eyes, taking care not to smudge her perfect liquid line.

"I should be telling *you* that," she snuffles, wiping away the tears, taking a deep breath, recomposing herself. "I am here for you. Know that. As your Touchstone. And your friend."

"I know that, Trace. You're a bad bitch when you need to be."

"Is that a good thing?"

"It's everything."

Soon enough it's quick hugs and kisses all around. Mr. Crowell pulls me into an awkward half-handshake/man-hug and mumbles, "Uh, guess I'll be seeing, uh, you in the a.m. . . ." and trails off into a nervous *cough-cough*. Tracy makes a plan with Mom to come and do the whole Y-3 initiation thing at our house the next morning, and I leave to return to my bedroom as Oryon for the last night.

I hear them chitchatting about me as I slink down the hall, but I don't really care what they're saying. I've had it up to my eyelashes with all the concerned, hushed whispers about my well-being. Bring back the contemptuous, free-floating neglect of high school already!

After deliberately skipping brushing my teeth—I mean, I'm getting a new body in the morning, why bother?—I log into Skype to see if I can catch Elyse before she goes to bed. It rings for a while before she picks up.

"You ready for this?" she asks, as soon as our video chat connects, busting out an old-school hip-hop move with her shoulders. She's wearing her PJs, the same flannels with punk rock fish on them that she wore when we roomed at the retreat.

"One thousand percent."

"Yeah, me neither."

"Well, that's settled," I pronounce.

"I like Elyse," she sighs.

"Well, you can always pick her at your Forever Ceremony when the day comes."

"I most likely will."

"I wish we were in the same school," I say. It's probably the hundredth time I've had that thought. I like Elyse too.

"Can't have too many of us in one place. Be, like, an *infestation*."

"In the many we are . . . problematic," I snark. Elyse laughs, and it makes me feel good inside for a second.

"My mom's sweating me," she says quietly. "Can we catch up tomorrow after school?"

"Totes," I say, the finality of the moment clocking me like a line drive to the skull. This will be the last time we'll see each other as Elyse and Oryon. Externally anyhow.

"Good luck with the whole Audrey thing," Elyse adds, being supportive, if not totally approving.

"Yeah, we'll see how that turns out."

"If she's as great as you say she is, then it'll be cool."

"I guess," I reply, wondering if anyone on any planet could be *that* cool.

"And if she's not, whatever. You are too awesome for drama. Remember that."

"I'm full up on drama for a long time," I sigh.

"Word to your mother."

Then a *click,* and she is gone. Forever.

Me too, come to think of it.

FALL

KIM

CHANGE 3-DAY 1

Yeah, so.
Uhhhhmmmn . . .

Is this supposed to be some sort of morbid joke, Changers Council? I guess I sort of thought that since I just went through the Tribulations, had to be sequestered at Changers Central for the remainder of my sophomore year and on through summer . . . you know, that you might've considered taking pity on me and given me an "easier" V this year of school. Make me a Hemsworth. Or even one of the lesser Wahlbergs.

But no. I am not a Hemsworth. Or a Wahlberg.

Nor am I a Latino goth girl with heavy eyeliner, in faux-dalmatian-fur creepers. Or a Southeast Asian–looking athletic girl with French braids and lululemon capris. Or a white guy with big tanned muscles and a loose, striped surfer tank top. Or a black girl with tiny ankles, in a giant sweatshirt she's wearing as a dress. Or a lanky, pale white dude with acne and red hair that matches his checked flannel shirt.

These are just the first five people who come to mind.

Why? Oh, only because they are just the first five people I ran into today. No, I mean actually RAN INTO, as in collided with in the hallways at school—and this was before I even made it to homeroom. Why did I run into five people before the first bell? Because gravity. More precisely, because my *center* of gravity is so different from Oryon's, from Drew's, from Ethan's, from anything I've ever known, that I actually lost my balance and/or tripped five different times while rushing through the hallways trying to make it to class on time, like a rogue bowling ball with shoes. That are tied together at the laces. And made of solid lead.

I'll just come out with it: *I'm fat.*

I know you're not supposed to say that sort of thing. Microaggressions! Body shaming! Even the word *fat* is verboten. And sure, it should be when you're talking about other people. But I'm talking to myself, about myself, so I can say whatever the hell I want to say about my fatness. Which is not inconsiderable. I'm beyond chubby or big-boned or husky. I'm a full-on plus-sized, ample, rotund, zaftig lady. Gravitationally challenged. My thighs touch when I walk. Their whole surface. I suppose they would chafe if I were able to walk long enough without toppling like a stoned toddler. Something to look forward to.

I know as a Y-3 Changer I'm ostensibly meant to have evolved beyond all superficial thoughts and temporal concerns, but nobody else around me seems to have, so why should I? That's the thing about being fat. People feel like they have the right—the moral imperative—to remind you of your fatness. As if you'd forget. (If this is my Y-3 lesson, I knew it already, Council. Every kid knows it.) At any rate, my fatness is all I can seem to think about right now, on the afternoon of my first day of being Kim Cruz. The five-foot-two, 170-pound Filipino-looking girl with the "pretty eyes" and "sweet smile," as determined by Miss Jeannie while snapping my photo for my student ID this morning.

"Now be a doll and say *cheese* for the camera," she cajoled in response to what had to be a "suck-it" frown sprawled defiantly across my face during registration. "Show me your sweet smile."

"I'm okay," I say.

"Come on, you gotta work what ya got," Miss Jeannie prompts (subtle fat-shaming dig number 1), tapping the old eyeball camera atop her computer with a long fake nail with an American flag painted on the tip.

I shake my head. (Even shaking my head feels different now, like I could feel it in the rest of my body, an echo or something.) A few beads of nervous sweat creep down my spine as I press my back closer against the white backdrop.

"Awww, so pretty in the face." (Subtle fat-shaming dig number 2.)

I yank my sweatshirt down over my chest and stomach (for the twentieth time already that morning) and stand there, working no expression at all. What I want to say is, *May want to check your own scale at home, lady,* but I somehow manage to bite my tongue, mostly out of grudging respect for her, knowing that it wasn't Miss Jeannie's fault that I've hated every single thing about myself from the second I opened my eyes this morning. Plus, I wasn't about to add to the fat-ism in our culture.

"Posture, dear, a straighter spine gives a thinner line." (And there's the hat trick!)

I grit my teeth and smile, my eyes shooting daggers into her soft, folded neck.

"You going to join the Mathletes, sweetie?"

Really? *Really?*

And that was the best part of the school day.

The worst was Audrey. More precisely, my invisibility to her. Which. How could you miss me, right?

Even though I sat right next to her in Honors English (filled with relief that, yay! she's still here) and made a point of saying a super-welcoming *hello* to her in the second floor girls' bathroom, and then again as I cruised by her table at lunch giving *Can I join you?* energy to her and Em, who also didn't even look up at me. They were both absorbed in the usual post-summer catch-up, feverishly talking over each other, and it was abundantly clear that I had no place joining that conversation, nor even a place at the table, at least not by their thinking.

They weren't cruel or anything. They didn't make snide remarks or even roll their eyes. They just ignored me. I was a plastic straw wrapper, a swiveling office chair turned into a corner, dirty popcorn under a theater seat. I was the detritus of peripheral vision. I didn't register. Which was a whole new kind of horrible. Also, possibly, now that I'm reflecting on it, worse than hearing pig noises when you walk past.

I thought Audrey was different. The kind of person who would never write somebody off because of her size or looks or whatever. The kind of person who was tuned into everyone and everything, who celebrated difference. I mean, she had a crush on a girl, Drew! She slept with a black boy, Oryon! How bigoted could she be? But Drew was pretty and part of her clique, and Oryon was confident and good-looking, even if he was a little nerdy. He had swag, and Kim, by any measure, taken in any universe, does not.

Crap, never mind Audrey. If I'm honest, *I'm* not the person I thought I was either. Because I'm more than happy to take part in shunning *myself*.

I can tell you RIGHT NOW who I'm NOT going to pick as my Mono after graduation. Wanna guess? Kimberly Cruz. Yes, even though I've been her less than twenty-four hours, I know deep in my "big" bones that this is not the life I intend to choose for myself. Why would I? The world is cruel enough. I'm going to pick a Mono that basically turns me into a walking *Kick me!* sign for all eternity? A short, minority female who struggles with her weight? Oh *yeah*, sign me up. Why not give me a stutter and a limp while you're at it?

Not that there's anything wrong with being "of size." Of course not. But I mean, my breasts are ginormous. Heavy. In the freaking way. And, after a few hours in Mom's joke of a bra, painful. Like two sacks of flour stitched to my pectoral skin. Talk about too much of a good thing. There is no way I'm surviving 364 more days of bearing the weight and weirdness of these things. I can't believe millions of ladies spend hard-earned coin to get surgery to make their boobs as big as these. Willingly. Why? So dudes will look at you? Here's a tip ladies: dudes look anyway. Been on both sides of the mammary lens, and I can vouch for that essential truth.

Dang, my spine is killing me ...

What else? Okay, back to this morning. Oryon's boxers were practically cutting off my circulation the moment I came to. I had to sprint into the bathroom to tear them off me, but on the way I guess I lost my balance (preview of coming humiliations) and smashed into the doorframe, jamming my middle finger knuckle, which popped loudly and is now purple and swollen. So everywhere I went today, I was subtly giving people the finger (preview of coming worldview?) because I couldn't fully bend it down into a relaxed position.

Right after the finger pop, Mom and Dad raced into my bedroom, Mom trilling, "Let's see you!" I could hear

Snoopy's jingling collar in all the hysteria and crazy energy going on around him.

"No!" I screamed through the bathroom door.

"Okay, in a minute then."

"Go away!"

"Kimberly Cruz. Sixteen years old—ooh, that's right! You can get your driver's license this year!" Mom read through the door from the Changers Council packet.

"Kim Cruz?" I whined, looking at her, at myself, in the mirror.

"Come on," Dad said agitatedly, "I've got to get out of here, and I want to meet this new V."

"I'll just see you after school," I tried.

"Well, I can tell you're a girl," he said. "So, that's—"

I burst through the bathroom door with a bath towel wrapped under my arms, covering most of my body.

"Whoa, hello there," Dad said, masking shock.

"I know," I said, and collapsed onto the bed, where Mom immediately crossed to me, draped her arms around my neck, and squeezed tight.

"You're beautiful," Dad soothed, but I could tell even he was alarmed by what had developed overnight under his roof.

I started crying. Desperate, no-way-out sobs. With a bucket of estrogen mixed in (again). God, I hate estrogen.

"Why don't you try your breathing exercises?" Mom said calmly, slowly rubbing my back and exchanging a knowing look with Dad that neither of them thought I could see through my wall of tears.

"What's the problem?" Dad asked stupidly.

"Really?" I shot back, looking up at him like, *You did this to me.*

"This is going to be a really educational year," he said reflexively, sounding like Turner the Lives Coach during a Changers Mixer keynote address. "You're going to grow by leaps and bounds."

"Oh, I think I've already grown by leaps and bounds."

"I don't want to hear any of that smart-aleck attitude," Dad said, now tipping into full disappointment in me.

I turned to Mom. "Why aren't you saying anything?"

"What's to say?" she asked.

"Seriously?"

"Ory—Kim! That's enough," Dad said. "Don't—"

"Speak to your mother that way," I interrupted, finishing his sentence. "Yeah yeah yeah. But you have to admit this is a rough card I just got dealt."

"Why? Because you're a little heavier than you're used to?" Mom asked.

"A little?"

"You're actually quite lovely to look at. Empirically. Your lips are perfection and your skin is beautiful. You're not exactly a walking horror show, Kim. Much as you may feel like one now." She pushed the hair out of my left eye and tucked it behind my ear. It fell out and went back over my eye, a black curtain I was more than happy to duck behind. "In any event, you have to get ready for school," she added, standing up and slapping her thighs. "Let's see what we can come up with to get you out the door. And we'll head to the mall later."

"Oh yay. The mall."

Mom chuckled despite herself, and Dad came over and awkwardly mussed my hair, sort of like he would when Ethan was around, then leaned down and planted a kiss on my forehead. "I have to get on the road. But you're going to do great. No different than last year. Or the year before. You got this."

I didn't bother arguing.

In Mom and Dad's closet were three garbage bags full of clothes from ReRunz. Tracy had dropped them off this time around to make my transition less stressful, what with the Tribulations lurking in the back of my psyche. There were boys' clothes in various sizes, girls' clothes in the same range. A pile of more gender-neutral offerings, and because it was Tracy, a whole shopping bag of accessories including scarves that smelled like the Civil War. I'd yet to inhabit an identity where I wanted to wear accessories, but I guess a Touchtone can dream.

I riffled through the options, but nothing felt right. The stuff that fit was boxy and itchy, made me look like the whale in *Moby-Dick*. Or wait, is Moby-Dick the name of the whale? I can never remember. Anyway, all the clothes I liked were too tight in the middle, or choked my arms like fabric boa constrictors. I found a big, off-the-shoulder knit sweatshirt with an old-fashioned motorcycle on it. It was cool enough and it didn't make me feel like a ham. I put on one of Dad's gym shirts underneath, and a pair of his sweats, which were not made for any woman's body, let alone mine. It was shaping up to be my best high school fashion debut yet.

I pushed my boobs into Mom's largest, most stretched-out jog-bra (now I know how sausage gets made), then jammed my feet into a pair of Drew's old Converse. As I stood to appraise myself in the mirror, I heard a buoyant, "Helloooo! Guess whooo?" wafting in from the hallway.

"In here!" Mom yelled to Tracy, while I mouthed *Noooo!* As if I could stop her.

CHANGE 3-DAY 1

"Where's my favorite Changer-in-waiting?" Tracy said, as her head popped in, followed by two giant mocha Frappuccinos from Starbucks, with extra whipped cream on top.

"Well hello, gorgeous," she said casually, acting as if seeing Kim Cruz in the former body of Oryon *Small* (oh the continued Oryony!) was something she'd expected all along.

"Don't even," I snipped, looking back at myself in the mirror.

"Your favorite," she chirped, offering me the drink.

"Like, two years ago," I snarled, being a professional brat, as I struggled to untie the knot in the drawstring of my dad's gray sweats. "Oh good, extra whipped cream. That'll help."

Tracy slurped some white foam through her straw and set my frappe atop Mom's dresser.

"Your hair is so shiny. And those *lips*. Like a film star in the forties."

"Right?" Mom chimed in. "I was telling her."

I tried to look at my new lips, but my gaze kept dropping to my stomach, my thighs, my boulder boobs.

"How's it going?" Tracy asked, 95 percent directed at Mom.

"So great," Mom mumbled sarcastically.

"Well, let's get this show on the road," Tracy said, fishing through her purse for the magnetic fob which initiates Y-3. "You applied the emblem?"

"Nooo," I moaned. In all my self-loathing, I'd forgotten the damn flesh-branding part of the morning. "At least there will be plenty of real estate to choose from."

Mom shot me her "enough" look as she emptied the packet from Changers Central. Out slid the dreaded lipstick tube from hell.

"I can't use the fob until the brand is in place," Tracy reminded us, loving nothing more than following procedure.

"I got it," I said, snatching the brander out of my mom's hands and heading into the bathroom to be by myself. I locked the door behind me, checking twice to make sure the latch was secure.

I popped off the cap and was planning on just going for it and getting the grisly task done without thinking too much or anticipating the pain of the burn. Only problem was... I couldn't reach the area where the thing is supposed to go on my butt cheek. I put a foot up on the toilet and twisted around, but I could only get the device perpendicular against the skin where it would probably be visible above my waistline. I tried propping up the other leg and reaching for the other cheek—but that one was even less flexible.

Lovely. Not humiliating at all. I can't even handle my own business in private.

"Mom!" I yelled, angry as hell, but it came out in a way that sounded like I was crying. "Can you come in here?"

I cracked the door, and she slipped in, giving her best accepting and calm "whatever" shrink demeanor. I held out the brander.

"Do you need help?" she asked.

"OF COURSE I NEED HELP!"

"Okay, okay." She took the tube, holding back every shred of mom-ness in her, which likely wanted to smack my butt as much as brand it. I turned around, pulled down Dad's sweats. Mom quickly uncapped the weapon of mass excruciation, took a deep breath, which prompted me to take a deep breath, and... O-M-JESUS!

That smell alone, like my own skin getting roasted on a spit. And the pain. Criminy. When I'm a full-grown

Changer, my first order of business is going to be joining the Changers Council and decreeing the elimination of the whole bass-ackwards emblem ritual. I mean, what are we? Medieval savages?

And yet, having my ass flesh seared by my mother in a cramped bathroom was a bounce-house party compared to what going to school was going to be like.

"That wasn't so bad, was it?" Mom asked.

"*You* do it."

"I would if I could," she said, almost wistfully. "*Believe* me."

"I doubt it."

She took a deep breath, took her time exhaling, and then: "When you have a child, you'll know exactly what I'm talking about."

"What if I don't want to have kids?"

Before Mom could answer, Tracy asked from the other side of the door, "All good to go?"

"Just finishing up," Mom said, giving me the eye and then cracking the door and moving aside so I could get by.

"Cool beans," Tracy said, prepping the fob.

"*Cool beans?*" I repeated. "So I woke up in a different decade, as well as a different body?"

Tracy ignored me, pushing her thumb into the top of the gadget, which caused it to beep three times, glow red, and then turn blue. All clear. Mom tried to be helpful and started to hold up my hair to reveal my neck, but I batted her hand away. I wanted to do something on my own.

I slowly pivoted and turned my back to Tracy, collecting my hair. It was the first time I'd really touched it since waking up, and I noticed immediately how thick it was, and straight, and very, very smooth. It was shampoo-commercial hair. In fact, if a guy were feeling this hair, he'd probably be way into it . . .

How gross is it I'm thinking that stuff—about *myself*?

"Okay, here we go," Tracy said, brushing aside a few errant strands with her left hand and holding the fob up to the back of my neck with the other. I felt a little buzz, heard a beep, and then a few quick clicks at the base of my neck in the usual area of my Chronicling chip. A vague, distant buzzing sensation seemed to be radiating down my spine. "Finito!"

"Cool beans," I muttered, releasing my hair.

As I swiveled around to face her, Tracy placed both of her hands on me, squeezing my shoulders like she was testing for ripeness. She looked directly into my eyes. I tried to squirm away, but she was determined.

"What?" I said exasperatedly.

"I'm so proud of who you're becoming."

"You mean this V?"

She didn't say anything, just bored her pupils laserlike into my eyes.

"You wouldn't be so proud if you knew what I was thinking inside," I added.

"I mean *you*," she said quietly. But the moment was lost on me.

After school, Mom made good on her promise (threat?) to take me to the mall. Spoiler alert: shopping as a person of size in the land of skinny jeans and crop tops is even more torturous than you think it's going to be. Especially when you look at yourself in the mirror and cannot find even a single thing to like about what's staring back at you. Not the curl of an eyelash, a shiny strand of hair, a patch of soft skin. Nothing.

In the car on the way home, Mom suggested maybe my day was so horrible because of my attitude going into it, my attitude toward myself, toward Kim.

"Oh great!" I hollered from the passenger seat. "BLAME THE VICTIM!"

"I don't think that applies in this instance," she said sharply, "but I do know that how we feel about ourselves can color every aspect of our existence. Surely you've picked up on that in the last couple years, no?"

But I wasn't having the discussion. Not then. Maybe not ever. Mom doesn't have to go through school as Kim. If she did, she wouldn't be peddling her "Big Is Beautiful" BS.

So, after what was left of any lingering self-esteem was pummeled into a fine powder by the dressing room lighting and the repeated apologies of the shopgirls that they didn't "carry my size," I bought some black PF Flyers (can't do Converse, there's no arch support, I noticed for the first time) and six extra-large black T-shirts. Two pairs of stretchy black pants, tapered at the ankle, one pair of tight Lycra jeans which Mom basically forced me to buy because she said it "showed off my figure" and (paradoxically) made me look trimmer. Whatever. Most importantly, I got a bunch of jog-bras that held my shit in, tight. And some XXL waffle-knit cotton boxers, which were the most comfortable things I tried on the whole excursion.

Looking at all this black crap sprawled out on my bed, it sinks in. This is really happening. *I* am happening. This is who I am now. A plus-sized street mime, apparently.

I don't feel like doing anything I'm supposed to do. Not reading and memorizing the Kim Cruz portfolio from the Changers Council, not organizing my binders for class, not playing a game, listening to music, nothing but flopping onto the bed and putting a pillow over my face to muffle the sensations and sounds of the world. But I can't even get into bed because it's covered with the trappings of Kim Cruz, and I don't feel like putting any of these clothes away in my closet, because that would make it real. Kim would be moving in for good. Here to stay.

I feel like disappearing. To a better time. I want to be Oryon again, the cool-nerd skater-boy in the band. The boy Audrey liked. Not Kim, the girl Audrey ignored, the sort of person I probably wouldn't notice either. Or if I did, I'd feel a bit sorry for. Pity plus neglect. What's worse than that?

Meh.

Meh meh meh meh . . .

Skype is calling!

Elyse's ringtone. At least somebody still loves me. Only because she hasn't yet laid eyes on me . . . I can't get to my laptop quick enough to accept her video chat—can't wait to see what V she got. Nor can I wait to talk to the only person I actually feel like talking to right now.

"I can't see you. Turn on video. Let me see you!" I hear, the second our audio is connected. The voice is a little deeper, but still sounds like a girl. I toggle my video on, and then suddenly her video snaps on, and there she is: I am gob-smacked. And instantly consumed by jealous rage. She looks exactly like Rihanna. But with pale blue eyes.

"Ahhhhhhhh!" we scream at the exact same time.

"Wow," I start. Because I don't know what there is to say; nothing will come out.

"What do you think?" she asks, turning her face side to side.

"Wow. I mean, what do *you* think?"

"I think I lucked the hell out, is what I think," she says,

leaning into her camera, presumably to get a closer look at me, in my (strategically) dark room. "And . . . that you are probably hating life right now, and also hating me, because you're thinking I won the V lottery, and you ended up with the booty end of the Cycle."

"Uh—"

"It's okay, I'd feel exactly the same way about you if the situation were reversed," she says.

"I—I . . ." I don't know how to respond. Candor feels too treacherous, but then again, she's asking me for it.

"I mean it. I totally get it," she prompts.

"It's just . . . you're the first person who's actually been straight with me about it. About what I am, you know? My mom, dad, Tracy. Nobody will admit that this V sucks."

"I feel ya," she says. "Honestly, though?"

I nod my head, move closer to the camera to give her the chance to see me in the light.

"It's nowhere near as bad as I know you think it is."

"You swear?"

"I swear," she says, completely sincerely, which makes me almost believe it. "What's your name?"

"Kim," I say. "Kim Cruz."

"Like Tom or Penelope?" she asks.

"Cruz like Penelope."

"Not bad," she tries.

"What's *your* name?" I ask.

"Destiny White."

"You've got to be kidding me. Who's your manager?"

"Ha ha. It's Destiny with a *y*, but just to be annoying, I'm going to tell people it's pronounced Desteeni, with an *i*, like in martini."

"Wow, that *is* annoying."

"But a girl this pretty?" she says, narrowing her eyes and flipping her hair like a diva.

"You're a bona fide trap queen."

"What's good, Kim Cruz? What's good?"

We laugh for a few beats, and then she asks, "So, how'd it go?" and sits back in bed and listens to me complain about my morning, my day, my life for twenty minutes straight, after which I talk about Chase, *again*, and how meaningless everything feels, and how it all makes me feel even worse for still caring about meaningless stuff.

"You can't help it. The external will always exert itself on the internal," she says kindly. Though, in truth, hearing Elyse's perceptive brilliance coming out of Destiny's mind-numbing gorgeousness is discombobulating. It's like getting Freudian therapy from a lingerie supermodel.

Even so, after unloading my baggage on Elyse/Desteeni/the luckiest girl in all of Tennessee, I feel the best I've felt all day. Not that I'm looking forward to tomorrow. I didn't fall and get a head injury or anything. But I feel a little more accepting of what *may* happen, at least. Thank Gods for Desteeni.

CHANGE 3-DAY 2

When I arrived at school today I was informed that I'd been transferred to Mr. Crowell's homeroom class. Tracy had decided it would be best to have an ally with eyes on me as much as possible, so she schmoopy-schmoopied her husband into working some behind-the-scenes clerical magic and presto change-o, I'm right back where I started with Chloe, Jerry, Audrey, and the rest of the gang.

Mr. Crowell had also obviously been informed of what my new V was, because when I walked in with another (legitimate) transferred kid, he beamed as if he was seeing a double rainbow. "And you must be Kim Cruz!" he gushed, patting my upper arm a beat too long. An intimacy that did not go unnoticed by the rest of the class who, like all animals in the jungle, are sensitive to any whiff of disturbance in the status quo.

"Why don't you take that seat right in front? Or would you prefer the back row? Really, wherever you like. We want you to be as comfortable as possible here at Central and especially in our happy little homeroom. Right, class?"

Nobody answered. They just stared at me like, *Why is Chubbers getting special treatment?* Mercifully, as I said, there was another transfer to the class, a guy named Kris who was dressed in silver Burberry sneakers, drop-crotch jeggings in neon yellow, and a sheer silver blouse. No joke. An actual blouse, like something my mom would have worn on a date when she was in graduate school. Kris and I gave each other the once-over, and knew undoubtedly what the whole class must be thinking in that moment: *The freak show has rolled into town.*

Difference was, Kris seemed to embrace his divergence, whereas I was standing there in my all-black-everything puddle of shame, laboring to disappear even as I tried to catch Audrey's eye. She could not have noticed me less. Maybe I should have worn neon-yellow jeggings.

"Now Kim, you've recently moved here from Maine, where you went to a small Quaker school. Fascinating," Mr. Crowell read from his clipboard, chewing over the "fascinating" way too conspicuously, like I was his own personal science project. "And Kris, Kris with a *k*, not a *c*, you're here, looks like you were homeschooled before coming to Central. Well, this will be a real departure from that, but in a good way, I'm sure."

Kris raised his eyebrows theatrically, like, *Really, bitch?* but I could tell he wasn't about to get into it in front of the rest of the zoo animals, who don't even know they live in a zoo.

Kris and I found empty seats, which turned out to be next to each other in the back row. As we passed Chloe, she couldn't resist shaking her head disgustedly, and her minions giggled a little, as they do.

"Girl's eyebrow game needs some surreous werrrk," Kris whispered to me as we sat down, nodding in Chloe's direction. He wasn't wrong. She looked like she'd overplucked them, then drawn a thin line back in with black pencil. She resembled a spooky puppet from a horror movie, the kind that sits up by itself once the lights go dim and cranks its neck to glower at its next victim, which, not for nothing, was exactly what Chloe and the Chloettes were giving me in that instant: horror-clown death-stare realness. Like their very proximity to somebody like me might damage their popularity stock—not to mention their sexy Q rating.

Audrey wasn't glaring, of course. But she had changed. She'd let her edgy short hair grow out into a bob, and she had highlighted blond streaks throughout. She was wearing a version of what all the Chloettes were dressed in—tight jeans, a boxy top that managed to be oversized and still show slices of midriff, and pricey sneakers or Tims. I remembered DJ last year making fun of rich white girls who wore Tims to "be street." The Audrey I'd known would never have cared about fitting in with Chloe, let alone dressing like her, but then again, the Audrey I'd known was probably so irrevocably damaged by her "Miss Independent" experiments with Oryon/Drew that she'd started to see the upside in conformity.

She still looked pretty.

At lunch I ended up sitting with Kris. Well, he sat with me. Which I guess if I'm being truthful, I wasn't thrilled about at first. Not because Kris wasn't potentially awesome. But because the last thing Kim Cruz needs is the outest pal in the history of gay. If I was trying to skate by in the shadows for my junior year, having Kris shine his blinding *Yaaas, queen* light in my direction wasn't much going to help my plan.

"The band break up?" he asked, as he slid next to me and began meticulously unwrapping his meal of Greek yogurt and a starlight mint.

"Pardon?"

He tilted a shoulder toward my black ensemble. "The mourning attire."

"Ah. Yeah. No. I'm in mourning for different reasons."

"No doubt. Like, this whole life, right?" Kris waved his hands as if presenting the entire cafeteria on a platter. "Please welcome to the stage . . . the worst of humanity."

Just then a disquieting cackle emanated from Chloe's table, and I reflexively turned in their direction . . . And, *WTF?* Audrey was sitting with them, the whole gaggle shrilly erupting at G knows what. I didn't see that one coming.

"The best part of homeschooling?" Kris started, cutting his eyes toward the Chloettes. "No bitch squad."

I laughed, but felt a knee-jerk reflex to defend Audrey. "They can't *all* be bad," I said weakly, to which Kris responded by cocking his head and making googly eyes.

"Stay tuned," he warned. "This ain't no Quaker-honor-your-feelings school. Those girls are sharks. And you, my dear, are the seal. Hope you're a fast swimmer." Kris took two spoonfuls of his yogurt, then wrapped it back up, shoving it deep into his lunch bag and tossing the whole wad into the trash. He stood up, fixed his hair, and popped the mint in his mouth, cracking it between his back teeth. "See you around, K."

"Yeah, you too, K."

"Ha! One more K and we got ourselves a reality show."

"Or an abominable racist social club," I deadpanned.

"Or both!" Kris added, laughing as he walked away, stomping so the buckles on his sneakers jangled loudly enough for people to notice. I watched him as he passed my lunch table from last year. You know, the unofficial a.k.a. official "black table."

DJ was at the head, cutting up with some of the guys, looking handsome and confident as ever. Maybe a little more muscular, an inch taller. I repressed the urge to wave hello to him, though knowing him, he'd probably just wave back if he'd actually caught the awkward new girl waving at him like old friends.

"Fly wheels," DJ said over a shoulder to Kris as he sashayed by. Without even a trace of sarcasm or animosity in his tone.

Later, at home on Skype, I ask Destiny if I'm the seal.

"The what?"

"The seal. The sad, pathetic creature whose fate is to be bait for more majestic animals with better skin and tighter abs and rows and rows of razor-sharp white teefs."

"Oh that. Definitely," she snarks. "Where is this coming from?"

"The mirror."

"Girl, enough. I can't do a whole year of you hating yourself because you don't look like one of Taylor Swift's ponytail posse."

"Easy for you to say. You're breathtaking."

"Okay. Maybe. But then what?"

"Who cares?"

"Kim, you know better than that. Besides, being hot can be a liability too," she says, sitting back on a fluffy pillow. "Everybody wants my attention, but they don't really want much else. I've become one-dimensional. A conduit for them to feel something about themselves, not about me."

"High-class problems," I say.

"I'm serious."

"You've determined all this in a mere forty-eight hours?"

"I'm a good little Changer, with one more V under my belt than you, not for nothing. And yes. It ain't that complex math."

"Well, here on the other side of the equal symbol, it doesn't feel so simple."

"I know, it sucks. But it could be so much worse. I mean, we almost didn't make it—"

"Okay okay!" I interrupt, not wanting to be reminded of the Tribulations, and Chase, and Alex, and those less fortunate than us. All of which I've managed to replace with the new Tribulations, a.k.a. being Kim Cruz.

"Oh, and another thing: my teachers assume I'm dumb," she says.

"There is no way you read as dumb. You're one of the smartest people I know."

"Trust me. When even adults are thrown by the way you look, it leads to all kinds of compensatory behaviors."

"That's grody."

"To the max."

"Still beats being the seal."

At that, Destiny claps her hands together like flippers and honks, her mouth yawning open and shut as if catching sardines.

"You even look sexy doing that," I grouse.

"It's my seal of approval," she says, laughing and honking.

We make a plan to get coffee together on Sunday, at the end of Hell Week One. Just fifty-one more to bear—well, for me at least.

CHANGE 3-DAY 3

Three days as Kim Cruz, and I have to say, I'm getting the knack for maintaining a low profile. In class, I am the big black-clad blob that hovers in the back row, hunching over my desk and praying for the TARDIS to appear and whisk me away to another time. Amazingly, everyone seems happy to let me do this. Ain't nobody got time for drawing out the shy weirdo. Which is fine by me. I am viewing this year as a prison sentence, and I will serve my time, quietly and without ruckus. Nothing to see here, folks. Keep moving.

Mr. Crowell is the one pesky fly in the ointment. He seems to think he's an extension of Tracy, and as such, I am somehow his charge. He keeps giving me the curious-puppy-dog eyes in homeroom, and asking me way more than my fair share of questions, which if he had any memory of his teenage experience in homeroom, he would know only makes my existence more of a misery. I need to somehow communicate to Tracy (and thus him) that this isn't a case where if I just "put myself out there," the gang is going to discover how amazeballs I am and shower me with respect and acceptance. This is high school. Not the Special Olympics.

After homeroom, I try again to connect with Audrey. I can't help it. To me she is worth the risk. I figure the old her has to be buried underneath her cutesy hair and glitter lip plumper. She can't have been subsumed completely by the bitch squad.

"Hey!" I say with . . . not much of a plan past that.

"Hey?" she answers back, checking me out for about two seconds before finding something to fiddle with in her backpack.

"You look f-familiar to me," I stammer. *Stupid.*

"Oh. Well. I mean, I look like a lot of people."

"No you don't," I reply too quickly.

Audrey lifts her chin from her bag and takes me in again, intensely this time. I stare back into her eyes, willing her in my head to see who I really am.

I'm Oryon! I'm Oryon! You loved me. You said so. You know me! How can you not know you know me?

"I'm sorry. Who are you again?" she says finally, seeming annoyed now.

"I'm Kim. From homeroom. Kim Cruz." *(And your best friend Drew, and your first love Oryon, but whatever.)*

"Kim. Good to meet you." She extends a hand to shake mine, looking over my head as she does, as if searching for exit doors. "I'm Audrey. Anyway. I really need to get to class . . ."

"Me too, same," I say, but she has already begun walking away. And unlike when I was Oryon, she doesn't stop and take one last look over a shoulder to see if I'm watching her go.

CHANGE 3-DAY 5

Oh splendor and wonder. Light of all lights, joy of all joys.

Today was Central's first football game, which brought with it a heavy case of PTSD. From my aborted, futile stint as a cheerleader when I was Drew, to the psychotic bullying by Jason when I was Oryon on the JV squad. Never mind when I was public enemy number one, pelted with corn dogs and slushies after being nearly choked out by Jason and Baron, his partner in idiocy/latent attraction. Yeah, I said it.

Just seeing the players in their jerseys (like I had been) and the girls in their cheerleading minis (still baffling how that survived the fifties) in the hallways and at the mandatory pep rally made me feel queasy and angry and fundamentally *other* in a way I really didn't need.

"God, sports are dumb," Kris said at lunch when he plunked down his Greek yogurt cup across the table from me. "On the plus side, they allow you to see just who the morons are. It's like a douche filter. Not that I mind the uniforms. Those can stay."

I considered telling Kris I had been a cheerleader once, but figured that would invite a lot of questioning I neither had the stomach nor will for, so instead I asked what he was into, since it clearly wasn't athletics.

"Theater, baby!" he answered in a long trill. "Not to be a total gay cliché. But it's kind of why I wanted to go to a regular school. You auditioning for the play this year?"

"Uh, no."

"Shy?"

"Talentless."

"I doubt that. You look like a woman with hidden depths to me. I bet there are lots of things you rock at."

I smirked at the *depths* part. Then, for some reason, I decided to confide in him. "I do play the drums. A little. I was in a band once."

"*Gurrl*, I knew it! My punk rock goddess. You have to be in the play with me. You can be part of the stage band! Total hotness!"

I considered the thought. Briefly. "How do you know for sure you'll get a role in the play?"

Kris bugged out his eyes like I'd suggested tomorrow had been cancelled.

"My mistake," I said, just as Michelle Hu rolled up on our table.

"Mind if I join?" she asked, politely smiling at me in a way I recognized from last year as Oryon. The "we're vaguely in the same tribe" smile. The "join us, or suffer a long, cold social winter on your own" smile.

"Pop a squat, cuteness," Kris said, before I could answer.

"I don't think you're ready for this jelly," Michelle responded, completely stone-faced, stepping over the bench seat beside Kris.

"Respect," he murmured approvingly, scooching over to make room.

Introductions all around (well, *re*introductions for me and Michelle, not that she knew it), and then Michelle proceeded to be as cool as ever. Funny, crazy smart. The type of exceptional weirdo who genuinely doesn't care about the lizard-brain concerns everyone else in high school seems fixated on. If I hadn't seen her two years in a row at school, I might've assumed Michelle was a highly evolved Changer, one who had it all figured out immediately after changing into her first V. I found myself wondering, again, why I didn't spend more time with her last year. And then I remembered: Audrey.

When you're in love, everything else falls to the wayside. Which I'm seeing now may have been a mistake. Because really, what did that singular pursuit net me? Depression. Exhaustion. A near-death experience, and not the groovy kind with the flashing white lights and long-lost relatives beckoning you home. My relationship with Audrey cost me a lot. Maybe even a best friend. Who tried to warn me before he died. Not about her, per se. But about my selfishness around her. I couldn't see the Changer forest for the Audrey tree.

It is a lovely tree . . .

While Kris and Michelle chitter-chatter, I glance over at Chloe's table, all of them in their cheerleading ensembles, high ponytails teased just perfectly in the back, swinging like pendulums as their heads swivel along to the conversation. Audrey turns my way and accidentally—I swear I don't mean to—my eyes lock with hers, and suddenly I'm right back to where it all began, our first lunch sitting across from each other as Drew and Audrey, at that very table, two years ago. How singular she was. And yet from the outside, this chick I'm looking at right now? Her I don't recognize.

Audrey's eyes dart away from mine, and she's back in the midst of whatever inanity is being discussed in that circle. Okay, I don't want to assume, because that's not what I'm here for, right? But I'm pretty certain they're not talking about climate change and the quest to maintain biodiversity in such a rapidly changing world.

My heart still pangs for her. But it's starting to feel more like regret than desire.

"So what do you say?" I hear Michelle asking me.

"About what?" I answer, clearly having missed out on whatever she'd asked during my trip down memory pain.

"Joining the Asian Cultural Club?" she repeats, cheery as hell.

"Is there a GAYsian Cultural Club?" Kris pipes in.

Michelle laughs. "I know, I know. It sounds unnecessarily self-separating, but the truth is, it's just an excuse to hang out and eat a lot of awesome food together. We're having our first club dinner at Pho Sure next weekend."

Great. The place Oryon took Audrey on their—*our*—first date. God, the world's small. And getting smaller and smaller, it seems, every day. "Nah, I don't think so," I say, trying not to sound like the complete and utter downer I am.

"Why not? It's always a hot time!" she returns, purposely goofy.

"Maybe the next one," I try, not really meaning it. I just want to get my bearings, you know? Don't want to hop on any identity bandwagon just yet.

"I get it," Michelle says, ever upbeat. But she seems slightly dejected nonetheless. "Well, if you want more info on any other clubs here—"

"I think my extracurricular abilities are pretty much tied exclusively to the food realm," I interrupt, before realizing it sounds like I'm making a fat joke at my own expense. Mercifully, neither Michelle nor Kris bothers to comment, though I can sense they noticed. I guess they were tacitly agreeing not to reinforce my self-hatred, which is kind of a departure among girlfriends at this age. So, two for the plus column.

***

The rest of the day was what I'm finding to be typical for Kim Cruz. Waddling through the halls, head down, trying not to trip or bump into people. Other students either passing me wordlessly or sniggering just a touch, in case it managed to slip my mind for a millisecond that I am *less than* they are. Because I'm so much *more than* they are.

At one point between classes, Jason brushed by me, and I felt the heat of his body against mine, before he pressed forward into the masses, many WHOOT-ing and giving him the thumbs-up before today's game. I wondered if he sensed any familiarity at all. If a single cell in his skin registered that I was the girl he once tried to force himself on; that I was the boy he smeared across the football field. I know my skin did. It froze cold the second we touched, as if I'd passed by the devil himself.

"Tell me more about *that*," Tracy says when I mention Jason, as she aggressively suctions a thick strawberry shake through a red-striped straw at the Freezo, where we went to celebrate my surviving a whole week as Kim.

"It was just a vibe. A demon vibe," I say.

"Oh, so the usual then," she says, picking at a rogue strawberry seed between her two front teeth. "Was it helpful to have my boo in your corner?"

"No you didn't."

"What? Is that wrong usage?"

I laugh. If nothing else, at least Tracy is always good for that. *"Boo* works. Only, I'm not sure I want to think of Mr. Crowell as *your* . . . anything," I explain. Then I take a bite of my fat-free frozen yogurt sundae. As I do, I catch a couple of tween-age girls snickering in my direction. "It's fat-free, you jerks!" I yell, before hurling the entire container at their smug faces.

No, I don't do that. In fact, I don't do anything except eyeball my treat like it's nuclear waste, the joy of eating it well and truly gone. Kim Cruz lesson number 53: *When heavyset people eat in public they get food-shamed. Even if it's a salad.*

"You know, the first Changers Mixer is in three weeks. I think it will be very healing for you to go back now, after this time away."

"Time away? I feel like I just left," I shoot back, contemplating what excuse might be good enough to get me out of attending the mixer at all, though with Dad taking up semipermanent residence inside the Council's collective butt, avoiding the mixer seems improbable.

"Well, either way, it's mandatory, so . . ." Tracy takes another deep gulp of her shake.

Mandatory why? I wonder.

"I know you weren't pleased when you received this iteration of your selves," she goes on, easily downshifting into Touchstone-speak. "But I think you're going to fall in love with Kim. And I'd venture once you do, other people will too."

"If you say so." I push my maraschino cherry into its whipped cream dome.

"It's what's inside that counts," Tracy adds.

I make a fake vomit noise. "I don't see you occupying a V that is marginalized and shunned by 99 percent of the population," I challenge.

"Because I knew Tracy was my best me! The outside that matched the inside. I mean, can you really see this personality in a six-foot-two Ukrainian-looking basketball player? Or a petite Latina?"

She has a point.

"Were you a six-two Ukrainian? Please say yes," I ask hopefully.

"No. But I was many other things that felt . . . wrong. And this felt right. Even more right than the me I was born with. And when your insides line up with your outsides, there is no better feeling in the world."

As I let that sink in, my eyes drift around the Freezo. I land on the booth I was in that day with Chase, as Drew, remembering how we were arguing even then. And I think, maybe for the first time, that I'm starting to maybe know what Tracy is talking about.

CHANGE 3-DAY 7

You know what feels worse than being a person of size and innate klutziness wandering alone through the world? Being a person of size and innate klutziness wandering through the world next to the most desirable girl in the universe. As I learned today when I went from Kim Cruz, loser loner, to Kim Cruz the DUFF.

Yep, I was that girl. The Designated Ugly Fat Friend. Not that it was Destiny's fault. (*Desteeni's* . . . maybe). She did what she could to integrate me into her glamorous orbit of unbridled, unearned praise and attention, but as Michelle Hu might helpfully point out in this particular situation, there is no getting around physics. Not even at Ground Hero, a new fair trade coffee shop in Genesis with its clientele of bored hipsters and alternagirls, all of whom took particular notice of Destiny (and me) when we dropped in for lattes. It was like I was traveling with the pope. A pope everybody wanted to . . . *date*.

The usually sleepy joint went from zero to manic frenetic energy in under five seconds, just because Destiny deigned to walk in. She was magnetic, magical, captivating without having to try, her beauty so complete and unabashed that people didn't even pretend they weren't staring.

I would have wanted to kill myself if it weren't so fascinating.

"Can you believe this cray-cray?" Destiny whispered as we waited for our order, the barista hardly able to keep his eyes off her, burning his finger on the milk steamer for his trouble.

"Is this, like, your life now?" I marveled, slack-jawed.

"Pretty much."

"Dang," I sighed. Though I kind of understood what she meant before, about the downside. All that unsolicited attention, 24-7. It had to be exhausting. And numbing too. When everyone loves you because of something that has nothing to do with you, that must mess with your psyche quite a bit. And I knew Destiny wasn't the sort of person to let that wave of adulation corrupt her. At least, I hoped she wasn't.

"Here you go, extra shot free, just for you," the barista cooed, handing Destiny her latte, with, no joke, a heart in the foam.

"Is mine ready?" I asked, standing on my tippy toes, trying to see over the counter.

"Sorry?" he said, eyes still on Destiny.

"Medium soy latte?"

"Oh yeah, in a sec."

"My friend would love an extra shot too," Destiny suggested, not even having to tilt her head or uptalk or anything. Flirting for her would have been gilding the lily. Hell, for her, breathing was gilding the lily.

"Of course, *totally*," the barista swooned back, flexing his old-school tattooed bicep as he expertly ground the beans.

When we sat down at a sofa in the rear of the café—Destiny facing inward the way celebrities do, so they won't get eyeballed—I asked how she was handling being the North Star for every human who crossed her path.

"It's taking some getting used to," she chirped. "But. Not that much." An impish smile spread across her face, and for a minute I saw only Elyse, my cynical, genius, brave compatriot from the Tribulations.

"This is messed up, right?" I said.

"I know," she replied, not quite catching on.

"No," I leaned in, whispering, "I mean being a Changer—"

"Word," she interrupted, softly so only I could hear. "It's twisted, how easily people are manipulated by outside appearances."

"Yeah, people are basically awful," I said, just as the barista strolled by, jingling his keys in a likely attempt to get Destiny to turn around and look at him.

"Most people are massive disappointments," she agreed.

But then, I wasn't acting much better. "I know we're supposed to be learning empathy, but what I feel is mostly rage," I said. "I imagine shoving everyone I see down the stairs. I'm a monster."

"Don't be a dope. What you are dealing with is the weight, ha, of other people's judgment," Destiny chided.

"So are you," I pushed.

"Maybe. But with me, people are giving me the benefit of every doubt. It's like I'm speaking with an English accent and everyone is assuming I'm oh-so-clever. Only what they're assuming is that I'm worthy of special treatment. Because of genetics. They're drawn to me the way humans are drawn to a glittering tranquil pond—to see how gorgeous they might look in the reflection."

"It's the inverse of why they are repelled by me. Any association with someone like me is like tar they can't get off."

"Can't really deny the Changers Council is on to something . . ."

I knew what Destiny meant. Maybe this mission wasn't

so worthless after all. I mean, look around. Empathy isn't exactly growing on trees these days. Maybe we did need to infiltrate the human race with all versions of our otherness and teach these fools what it really means to love and be loved for the right reasons.

After a bit of silence, I asked, "Do you miss Elyse?"

"I do," she said, thinking for a few seconds. "But I suspect that wasn't the last we'll be seeing of her."

"Really? You'd give up your throne? I'm not sure I'd be that strong."

Destiny shook her head. "I know who I am already. And you? You're way stronger than you realize."

But I'm not so sure I believe her. On either count.

CHANGE 3-DAY 11

Today was Drama Club audition day. Also known as "the best day in Kris's public school life." He showed up at homeroom dressed in a crimson muumuu with tropical flowers printed on the fabric, tight jeans underneath, and black-and-red-checked high tops. He said he also wanted to wear a head scarf and mules, but ultimately decided less was more. (And that he didn't want to get bashed and thrown into a Dumpster before call-time.)

The Central High Drama Club had picked *Into the Woods* for this year's musical, and Kris was certain he was going to play the baker—though he added, "I'd consider the witch if needed, because I love me some drama in a wig."

"Pleeeeeeeeeeeeeze," Kris whined across the lunch table. "Pleeeeze come with."

"Fine!" I said, just to shut him up.

"Yayzers," he said, rapid-clapping his palms in front of his nose. "So you'll audition?"

"Hell to the no," I screeched, nudging a limp crinkle-cut french fry to the other side of the tray with my spork. "I'll tag along for moral support, but there is NO way I'm singing and dancing in front of the whole school looking like . . . like . . . *this*."

Kris eyed me funny, bent his head to one side, then the other. I know this is crazy, but it was almost as though he sensed something from the way I said what I said . . . sensed that who and what I am is not immutable. That somewhere

I knew I wouldn't always be "this way," and that that was a possibility for him too.

"Well, that's a mistake," he said after a beat. "You obviously need a serious Broadway education, stat, because big girls rule the stage."

I grunted.

"How glamorous does my hair look?" he asked. "Does it scream Tony nomination?"

The actual tryouts for *Into the Woods* were held after school in the main auditorium. The instant we walked in, I clocked Chloe down in the front row, doing some sort of annoying, unnecessarily loud vocal exercises with her eyes closed. You know, like she was really getting into it: *"Me me me me me me meeeeeee. Me me me me me me meeeeeee!"*

(That sounds about right.)

A few rows behind her, I was kind of startled to see DJ, though I guess I shouldn't have been. Before I processed it, my hand shot up to wave at him, but I covered by transitioning the wave into a stretch and quickly collapsing into the nearest seat.

"You go on, I'll be here," I whispered to Kris.

I'm sure I looked like a spaz, but I don't think anyone noticed, not even DJ. It's a running theme in my life now. I was grateful for all the budding thespians flitting about, too nervous to take note of anything but themselves, pacing around the stage, the rows of seating, behind the curtains, murmuring lines or humming, and curling and arching their backs in and out like cats on crack.

Kris climbed the stairs, found a spot stage left, bent at the waist, and shook his arms loose like a waterfall of noodles. He breathed in and out, master yogi style. After a few more minutes of all of this pre-drama, the theater teacher burst in, and all the kids shot up stock-straight like they were in the military and he was fixing to inspect their bunks.

"Good afternoon, pets," he announced in a voice that both filled the room and sounded like someone's ninety-year-old granny, if she smoked five packs a day. "Some of you may know me from Drama Club, but for those who don't, I'm Mr. Wood, your DIE-rector for this musical, and the person upon whom your dramatic fates rest. For many of you, this may be just another tick on your college application extracurriculars, but I assure you that while this is amateur theater, it is *not* a theater for amateurs. Cast, you will be committed to this production, to your fellow cast mates, and to your performance. Tardiness, absences, and general flakiness or lack of professionalism will not be tolerated. Nor will any ego that deigns itself larger than mine. You have to take the journey into the woods and down the dell in vain, perhaps, but who can tell? Are we clear?"

A collective, anxious, "Yes, Mr. Wood," arose from the seats and stage.

"Lovely. Now pets, let's all line up onstage so I can get a good look at you."

Kris hopped to, finding his place center stage. He squinted into the lights and clocked me, mouthing, *I'm in love!* as about twenty-five other students in various levels of flop sweat lined up on either side of him. It was only then that I spied Audrey, who was nervously shifting her weight from foot to foot stage right, while Chloe stood beside her, fingers S-locked together in front of her belly button and teeth bared in an aggressive pageant grin.

Audrey? Since when did she have thespian aspirations? Oh right, since she became Chloe's born-again toady.

"Nobody else?" Mr. Wood asked, surveying the few of us scattered in the seats behind him. I slouched down in my chair even further, while one other kid hesitantly side-stepped out of his row and padded up to the stage.

Mr. Wood continued: "You should all have your songbooks in front of you, and you should all, since you are here, have deep familiarity with the actual compositions of Mr. Lapine and Mr. Sondheim. Page 104, let's begin. And one, two . . ."

Everybody started singing: *"Into the woods, where nothing's clear. Where witches, ghosts, and wolves appear. Into the woods and through the fear. You have to take the journey . . ."*

(Did the Changers Council write this stuff?)

I strained to try to hear Audrey's voice amidst the chorus, but I couldn't. I did hear Kris, who didn't even need his songbook and was leaning into the number as if his dog's life depended on it. DJ was also killing it from the rear, his voice deep and smooth with that emcee cadence that made the lyrics even more powerful somehow. Not that they needed the assist. The words and music were kind of devastating, once I let them seep in. I can't believe I ever teared up listening to Katy Perry. (Well, just that once.)

"Okay, let's stop there!" Mr. Wood hollered, signaling the accompanist on piano and clapping his hands as everybody quieted. "Promising, promising. Yes, yes. Now, let's hear some solos, please. You in the red, you first. Name?"

"Me? I'm Kris. Kris Arnold. I'll be singing the scene four witch's solo to her daughter Rapunzel."

"Let's hear it," Mr. Wood said.

Kris cleared his throat, and several of the other students gave him some space. Chloe looked positively destroyed that she wasn't selected to sing first, while Audrey sucked at her cheek and gave Kris her full attention center stage. As Kris gazed up into the lights and inhaled, I was seized with nerves on his behalf. *You can do this*, I whispered under my breath. He let it out, coughed again, took another deep breath, and then started, slowly ...

"Don't you know what's out there in the world? Someone has to shield you from the world. Stay with me."

His voice was imploring, tinged with desperation. He wasn't just singing, he was defining the moment.

"Princes wait there in the world, it's true. Princes yes, but wolves and humans too."

He was standing on a dingy high school stage in an absurd muumuu surrounded by strangers, many of whom didn't understand him and thus were afraid of him or of what he might mean in this life, and he was somehow, miraculously managing not only to tune that out but also to break through all of that noise and fear and disdain and insecurity and sing with such clarity and purpose that he exposed the humanity not only in himself, but in anyone who was listening. Mr. Wood inched closer to the stage, his chin raised, head moving slightly with the lyrics.

Kris's voice hitched a notch, but stayed intimate, heartbreaking. Mr. Wood placed a hand on his own chest. When Kris wrapped up, Mr. Wood literally rushed the stage and embraced him, likely thinking, *This kid is a ringer, and we are going to blow the roof off this auditorium come opening night.*

Kris was panting and his cheeks were afire, bookending a wide-open grin. It was clear he had any part in the play he wanted. I was thrilled for him. But as he basked in the glory of his undeniable talent, I couldn't help it. My eyes wandered down the row of hopefuls and landed on Audrey. And I saw immediately that she was crying, but trying to hide it.

God, I wanted so much to run to her.

To confess who I was, what I was.

To tell her I was *home*. Home for her. Or I could be again.

But I could do nothing.

So I did nothing.

I just sat in the dark and watched the girl I loved cry. I had to take the journey.

CHANGE 3-DAY 13

I'm walking on sunshine. And no, not because Audrey finally did the Changer math and figured out who I am and stood below my bedroom window with a boom box hoisted above her head playing our favorite song. I'm proud (and surprised) to admit my joy has nothing to do with a certain unknown/unrequited love, and everything to do with spending the day in the company of people who I guess, for lack of a better assessment, really like themselves.

You'd think this wouldn't be such a revolutionary concept. I mean, we're all indoctrinated into the self-esteem club hella early in America. Ribbons for participation, anybody? But for all the talk about self-love (that particular term never *won't* sound gross) and self-acceptance, I have to say I haven't met that many folks who succeed on either front. I sure don't. We all just stumble around in the same old clouds of insecurity and fear, which, if you think about it, means that all the hoopla about self-esteem is just another thing we all fail at when we realize we don't have any. (Which is why I'm starting to be in favor of going back to the days of unabashed, unedited self-hatred if you feel it—but that wasn't on the agenda today, so perhaps I'll have to take it up another time. I'm sure there'll be plenty of occasions during this year as Kim Cruz, so stay tuned, Chronicles.)

On those rare occasions when you do find yourself in the presence of people who accept themselves and aren't trying with every fiber of their inchoate beings to improve or edit or deny something essential about their makeup, the vibe is flat-out righteous. As it was this afternoon at Michelle Hu's parents' barbecue.

First off, because Michelle has two mommies, the crowd at the party was heavy on the estrogen tip, with women of all shapes and sizes and colors—and very, very little hairspray. (Or bras, for that matter. Something I noticed, then tried not to notice, then couldn't help but notice.) Floppy boobs aside, it was the first time since changing into this V that I didn't feel like an outsider. In fact, nobody seemed to even register that I was heavy or Asian or short or even that I was dressed like an angry pilgrim. Nor did anybody whip their head around and stare when Kris let loose one of his "stereotypically queeny" laughs (his words, not mine—but an accurate descriptor nonetheless).

Amy and Carrie, Michelle's parents, were hosting the shindig, but not in the way I'd seen my mom do it, where she is tense and constantly flitting about, making sure every drink is filled and every spent wooden satay skewer thrown in the trash a.s.a.p., lest someone have a tragic skewer-impaling incident and ruin the entire fiesta. Instead, Carrie and Amy basically kicked back in canvas lawn chairs, barefooted in the grass, and pointed at coolers when people wanted drinks or toward the house when guests needed to pee. They actually seemed to be having fun alongside their guests! I know, crazy concept.

Manning the smoking grill was this hunky Latino dude, who had thighs thick as tractor tires and a beefy chest, the kind where the muscles make a valley between them. In the valley he wore several gold chains strung with medallions, which flipped between his pecs like fish every time he leaned forward to turn a veggie burger or a tofu dog. He was dressed in denim cutoffs and a denim shirt with the sleeves ripped off to accommodate his canned-ham shoulders, a bandanna tied around his head to keep the sweat from dripping into the food. When he noticed me staring—*busted!* I don't know, something about him reminded me of Chase in Y-2—he grinned and waved me over with the greasy spatula.

Kris, who was my ride to the party, practically bolted toward the grill, of course assuming it was he whom Mr. Latin Hotness was summoning. So I followed with less urgency.

"Welcome to the party! You want a burger or a dog?" the guy asked, with the most genuine smile in all of the land. So genuine, I thought, it must be fake.

"I'm always up for a wiener," Kris answered. I shot him a side eye. Why did he have to flirt with every dude within a five-mile radius? I mean, I'm fine with that, I guess, but at least get a few benign sentences in before you go for the wiener-shot.

"What about you, gorgeous thing?"

. . .

Kris nudged me. Oh man. Was I the "gorgeous thing"?

"Uh, burger sounds good. I guess."

Grill Guy grinned again, "Vegan or turkey?"

"Turkey?" I said, so thrown by the welcoming attitude that I reflexively uptalked like I couldn't even have confidence about what I felt like eating.

"Okay, five more minutes on those," Grill Guy said, flipping a turkey burger with my name on it—even though he didn't know it yet.

"I'm Kris," my friend interjected then, extending a hand and (sigh) winking. "And you are?"

"Paulo. Nice to make your acquaintance, Kris."

"Likewise. Charmed."

Oh boy. Two minutes in and I was already the third wheel. I kicked at the tufts of grass beneath the grill with the toe of my Doc Martens.

"And who's your lovely lady friend?" Paulo asked, waving away the smoke billowing between us.

"Oh her? Her name is Kim. She has problems."

I shot him another death glare, but Paulo just chuckled. "Who ain't got those, right, bro?" He held up his free hand to fist-bump with Kris, a maneuver Kris responded to as if he were being attacked by a coiled, angry pit viper.

"Suuure," Kris said, limply meeting Paulo's knuckles. "I'm gonna go score some lemonade. Want one?"

Paulo declined, while I nodded yes, and Kris skipped away (literally—he's big on skipping), leaving me and Paulo alone, which for some reason made me feel even more anxious than usual.

"So, you're friends with Michelle then?" he asked, trying.

"Yes. Michelle is great. I mean, I only just met her, but she seems great, if first impressions are to be trusted, which in my experience hasn't proven such a good litmus test, but, ah, she seems awesome and real, so . . ." *God*. I did have problems. What was wrong with me? What was it about this guy that had me all . . . girly?

"Real is good," Paulo commented generously. "We like real."

Yes. We like real, I thought. But what was real, really? I sure as shinola wasn't. Or maybe I was. Maybe Kim Cruz was finally letting me express what I really was inside. Bitter, angry, scared, lonely . . .

"I should go check on my f-friends," I stammered.

Paulo nodded, saluted with his spatula, and returned his attention to the hot coals. "Swing back in five for the burger," he called as I power walked toward Kris and Michelle, who were sitting hip-to-hip on a giant cooler, drinking organic lemonade out of recyclable boxes.

"Hey, girl," Michelle greeted warmly. "I see you met Paulo."

"He's nice."

"He's awesome!" Michelle nearly shouted. "He went through a really rough time a few years back, but he's on track now and it makes me so happy to see."

"Rough time, how?" Kris pressed, never one to miss out on a potentially dramatic narrative.

"Well, it isn't really my story to tell, but . . ."

I could see Michelle calculating in her head, weighing the pros and cons of trusting us with whatever secret she was considering sharing. She waved her fingers to draw us closer. Kris and I leaned in, our heads almost touching, like I was back in a football huddle.

"He's cool with anybody knowing," she started. "So, Paulo's government name was Paulina."

"Government name?" I asked, while a smile broke over Kris's face.

"The one he was given at birth," Michelle said.

"He's *trans*," Kris interjected, like I was in kindergarten. "He's a trans-man."

A what?

Okay. So I knew what transgender was. The basics anyhow. But to my knowledge, I'd never met anyone who had actually transitioned. (Besides every Changer ever. But that's different. Right?)

"He was designated female at birth, but he transitioned into a male," Kris droned into my ear, gloating slightly. "Sometimes trans people feel they are born in the wrong body, so to speak. Other times they just evolve naturally from one thing to another." Kris had certainly done his transgender research. "Everyone is on a spectrum, you see, and where you slide back and forth in terms of gender and/or sexuality is entirely up to you."

(Thanks, Kris. But I really don't need a primer on gender and sexual fluidity from you, or from any other Static for that matter. Changers pretty much have the market cornered on that, yo.)

"So, Paulo, before he transitioned, was into . . ." Kris turned to Michelle pointedly. "Girls? He used to be a lesbian?"

Michelle looked over at Paulo.

"Or—" Kris prodded her.

"I don't really know what he's into. I think girls, yeah," Michelle said curiously, as though it wasn't really important and had never occurred to her to ask such a thing.

"Ah, the outfit threw me," Kris said, his Trans 101 lecture complete for the moment, an explanation having been provided as to why Paulo seemed more interested in me than him.

"Maybe don't say anything to Paulo unless he chooses to tell you," Michelle added then. "I don't want him to think I was putting him on blast." She stood up and peered at me and Kris, seeming to doubt her decision to trust us a little bit.

"Got it," I said, like I understood completely.

"I filled you in only because it seems like you're kind of in the family yourselves." Then she spotted somebody with purple hair across the yard. "Oh, Logan! Excuse me," Michelle said, and ran off.

At which point Kris turned to me: "I think she thinks you're like her two mommies."

I shrugged. He smiled smugly. But what did he think he knew?

I had long since given up trying to figure out which label fit me. What I AM. As a girl who used to be a boy, I'd loved Audrey, and then I'd loved her again as a boy who'd been a girl (who used to be a boy). And not for nothing, she'd loved both sides of Kris's so-called spectrum. She'd loved Drew, and she'd loved Oryon, and so maybe Destiny was right when she said this Changer mission mattered and could make a difference in breaking down all these identity barriers to real intimacy and trust and acceptance between humans—though really, who was changing whom?

"Well?" Kris pressed. "Are you?" He batted his lashes comically, brows raised in anticipation.

I surveyed the party. There were women sitting in other women's laps. Men wearing lipstick and jewelry. Asian folks, black folks, Latinos, whites. Older women with younger girls who looked like boys. Boys who looked like brothers holding hands. Everyone was chill and happy. Everyone was inhabiting the space that made them feel alive and right. No one was apologizing for anything, or trying to cram themselves into a form that curried favor in the eyes of others. These were people at home in the world, in this backyard, at this barbecue, at least for this moment in their intersecting lifetimes.

And that counts for something, it has to. Like maybe in life you tried to string together as many moments like this that you possibly could, and if in the end you managed to enjoy more of the good ones like these than the dark ones, then lucky you: you had a good life . . .

In that moment when Kris asked me "what I was," I realized I'd never seen anything like the scene at Michelle's family barbecue. It was the polar opposite of high school, where everyone feels uneasy and off-kilter and threatened by exposure at any given moment. Even the most well-adjusted Changers I knew (Elyse, Chase) were in a constant state of flux and questioning. It wasn't lost on me as I strolled through the party and soaked in the scene that I was the least transparent person there. The only one still in hiding.

I decided in that moment to come clean.

"Honestly, I don't know what I am," I confessed to Kris, feeling a small weight lift as I said the words.

Kris, to his credit, stayed quiet, making soft, accepting eyes at me. He gave a small nod, took a pull of lemonade from his straw.

"Some days I feel like I'll never know," I said, a heavy calm settling over me.

Kris poked my thigh, flipped his hair back, and smiled. "Plenty of time to decide, Kimmycakes. Plenty of time."

And it was because of that exchange, because of Paulo and the party and Michelle Hu and all the other "real" people I met and watched and envied today, that when I got home I did two things:

1. I took the friendship bracelet Audrey had given me (as Drew) off my desk and dropped it into the memento box I've had forever, and tucked the box in the back of my closet. And . . .

2. I took Dad's razor and shaved my bobbed hair into a righteous Mohawk.

I don't know if it looks good. But I know it looks like me.

CHANGE 3-DAY 15

Soooooo. Maybe the shaved-head Mohawk wasn't the best decision I've ever made in my lives.

I hate admitting that.

I hate that I care about what other people think of my stupid freaking *hair*, and my relative coolness in the ever-shifting sands of the high school hierarchy. Changers aren't meant to care about trivial things. We're meant to show others the *futility* of caring about trivial things. We're the cure for the disease, not the disease itself, and that's all fine and dandy until you're walking down the hall and you hear yourself called *dyke* 8,517 times before the lunch bell.

To be fair, not everyone said the word *dyke*. But the lesbionic alert patrol was out in full force, whispering and pointing and laughing cruelly at every turn. Because. Hair. Hair is so much more important than you'd ever think. (Find me a more depressing sentence than that.)

And the worst part was, it wasn't really even about being tagged as a lesbian. Lesbians—at least the ones with shiny, long, My Little Pony hair, and sparkly lips, and Victoria's Secret bra and panty twin sets—are considered "hot" these days. I mean, I've seen plenty of girls kiss at school parties where everyone watching just hooted like they were ringside at the Sapphic Olympic Games. Nobody was being a phobic a-hole on those occasions. (Except Jason, of course, who is threatened when girls hug, or play sports, or drive, or, you know, talk.)

But my give-no-effs Mohawk triggered some sort of mass does-not-compute hysteria. I wasn't a sexy lesbian on display for the entertainment of others. I wasn't even a sporty, Ellen-style lesbian who could hang with the dudes and crack jokes and wear a mannish-but-still-made-for-women blazer. No, my haircut seemed to communicate to the entire student body that I'd become, essentially overnight, a girl who didn't care about anybody's opinions anymore. And as I quickly learned, a high school girl who doesn't care about your opinions is like a nuclear weapon that must be dismantled immediately, lest it detonate and blow the whole joint and everyone in it to smithereens.

"Why would she do *that*?" I heard Chloe whisper to a Chloette when I walked by. "I mean, with so much already working against her?"

"Excuse me?" I said, stopping short at her locker.

(Yes, I should have kept on walking. Yes, I should not have taken the bait. But I'd already endured so many smirks and snorts and gasps that I'd reached my limit, and it just happened to coincide with my intersection with Chloe.)

"Excuse you how?" she snorted back.

"I'm sorry," I said, "but I thought maybe you had something to say to me." I glared right into Chloe's reality-TV close-up-ready face. It was there in her stunned silence that I noticed something new. Chloe was scared of me. I think I even saw her flinch. And I know I shouldn't say so, but it felt kind of good to frighten her. To have any power over her, really.

Chloe looked at the rest of her RBF crew, now flanking her sides, the flicker of fear extinguished.

"What could I possibly have to say to you?" she snarled, thrusting her lips forward like an angry duck.

I took a deep breath. "Well, correct me if I'm wrong, but it sounded like you might have an issue with the way I look."

The whole posse burst into laughter, Chloe swiveling side to side to bask in their shared derision. "Who *are* you anyway?" she asked louder than needed, as the giggling subsided. "Or maybe I should ask, *what* are you?"

"What do you mean by *what?*" I could feel my skin growing hot.

"I don't know. Seems like someone might have an identity crisis in the haps," she said slowly, shrugging at the end for emphasis.

And here is the real paradox. Of all the V's I've had, of all the crappy moments when I have indeed not known who I was, or what I should be, this particular second was not one of them. In this particular second I knew EXACTLY who I was. I was Kim Cruz, a girl with a shaved head and a new attitude. And I had given my last shit.

I lunged at Chloe, threaded my short but dexterous fingers through her hair, and yanked. It wasn't a premeditated action. I hadn't planned it. But once my arm launched itself in the general direction of her $300 extensions, there was no stopping the inevitable.

Her scream was bloodcurdling. Like a fox in a trap, I imagine. (If that fox had its $300 hair extensions snatched from its furry little head.) Chloe's palm instantly shot up to the bald spot where I'd done the damage, her mouth simultaneously yawning open in horror.

"You! Fat! BITCH!" she shrieked.

I didn't know what to do next. I stood there in shock, three ropes of "hair" threaded through my fingers like sea kelp. The Chloettes also stood dumbstruck, uncertain of what horror would follow.

"You're going to pay for this," Chloe seethed, her hand still covering the wound.

"I don't know what fake-ass hair costs," I shot back cheekily, and then pointed to my own head. "I mean, obviously." One of the Chloettes couldn't help but laugh. "But feel free to send me the bill."

Chloe's eyes collapsed to slits, her chest heaving up and down with untempered rage. "You think you're a miserable loser *now?*" she asked, not really asking. "Wait until I'm done with you."

"Yeah," another Chloette chimed in, "just wait!"

As they stomped down the hall toward Principal Redwine's office to report my "violent assault," I realized that a small crowd had gathered around me. No one said a word. You could have heard a weave drop. Or you would have, if I'd dropped it. But I didn't. Instead I stuffed Chloe's hair into my pocket like some sort of voodoo queen, something I'm sure would make the gossip rounds along with my propensity to rip hair off other girls' heads. You know, my secret collection of random girls' weaves hanging in a framed case in my room.

Long story short, my parents were called to the office. They couldn't go, of course, per Changers Council rules, but they did speak on the phone with Principal Redwine (saying they were out of town visiting a sick family member), who apprised them of my misdeeds and erratic behavior. "Not the sort of thing we tolerate here at Central." There was speculation that perhaps Kim Cruz wasn't quite making a seamless transition from her intimate, small-town Quaker school to a large public school, and that even though her grades were okay, "they weren't nearly as high as expected." (Which was racist, but I wasn't really in a position to point it out when my parents confronted me about the incident.)

So, I'm suspended for two days and sentenced to trash pickup after Friday night's football game.

Mom just left my room, where she perched on the side of my bed as I was curled into the proverbial fetal position, trying yet again to block out the rest of the world.

"Not your best day, huh?" she had said, stroking the side of my newly shorn head.

I stayed quiet.

"Your dad is worried about you."

"If by *worried about*, you mean *pissed at*, okay. Anyway, how can he be? He's never around," I argued.

"Worry isn't geographically constrained, my love," she said, her fingers soft and gentle on my head. Her touch felt kind of cool and tingly on the shaved parts. "I know this year is going to be a struggle, for so many reasons. I know you miss Chase. And your relationship with Audrey. And you wish so much of your life were different."

I started to cry, the tears rolling onto my sheets.

"But I also know you can handle whatever happens," she went on. "You have already made me so proud."

Now Mom was crying too. She blotted her eyes with her sleeve, then leaned to hug me. I couldn't really say anything—there was nothing to say—so we stayed like that for a while, both of us weeping and squeezing each other like we were each other's rafts at sea. Outside the sun dipped, and the room grew blue with the dusk.

After what felt like an hour, Mom let me go, and took a deep, hard breath. "Okay then," she said, standing up. "Now, let's talk about the hair."

I laughed weakly, tried to explain about Michelle Hu's party, how I was inspired by the people there, all embracing their oddity. No one hiding. No one afraid.

"Was there any one person there who inspired it or something?" she asked, clearly at a loss.

"No," I insisted. Because there wasn't. "I don't know why I did it," I confessed, feeling stupid.

"It's okay not to know."

"I guess I just wanted to feel brave for a minute," I went on. "Like shaving off hair is some brave gesture, anyway."

Mom sat back, gave me a long once-over. "Well, I like the sentiment. And owning who you are *is* brave."

"Maybe. But all it did was make even more kids hate me."

"Those kids don't even know you."

The words made me start crying again. Because she was right. They don't know me. And they can't. "Maybe not. But what I am, whatever this is," I replied, nodding at myself, "isn't something they seem to want to know."

"That's the thing, sweetpea," Mom said then, bending to give me one last kiss before leaving the room. "Growing up means showing your truth, even when it hurts."

CHANGE 3-DAY 17

I've seen *High School Musical*. I'm not ashamed to admit it. When I was Ethan, I watched the whole cheese-fest trilogy on television one weekend with my babysitter, Deb. She was obsessed with Zac Efron at the time. He was weirdly shirtless and sweaty in a lot of the scenes, which made her clap her hands and say, "Mmmmm," at the screen over and over. I thought he was gross then, but whatever. Things change. (Boy did they.)

Anyhow, I don't remember much about the musical part of *High School Musical*, knowledge I wish I had now that I am officially part of one. I decided after the auditions that I would join the support crew. I mean, why not? Kris had begged desperately to get me to try out for the band, but I wasn't sure how I felt about auditioning for the drum slot. I miss playing music, especially playing music with other people. But the theater band performs only a handful of pieces, and drumming is a huge responsibility. Besides, who even knows if Kim Cruz can jam? I wasn't really in a headspace to find out, which is what I told Tracy when she needled me about "getting back out there," like I was a forty-something divorcée wading into the dating pool for a second chance at finding fulfillment in life.

"At least let Mr. Wood know you can play," Tracy implored at our weekly check-in (bumped up in priority because of my sudden outburst of violence against Chloe's weave), this time at Starbucks, where I let her buy me a soy vanilla Frappuccino while she milked me (get it?) for information about my state of mind.

I told her I'd consider it. I mean, I know Audrey was totally attracted to Drew when she played in the Bickersons, and she also grooved on Oryon when he was part of the drumline. So it would seem a logical, Spockian conclusion that if Kim Cruz knew her way around a cymbal, Audrey would at the very least notice her.

"If the right time presents itself, I'll mention it," I told Tracy, who let out a yelp of glee that seemed disproportionate to the promise.

The "right time" turned out not to be the first rehearsal, which, to be completely honest, was a hot mess. No one besides Kris, DJ, and this girl Mia had memorized their lines, and Mr. Wood seemed put out by everything. He stomped around the stage maneuvering the cast here and there like chess pieces, ranting all the while about "losing yourself in the music and the moment," which made me think about Eminem—*"You only get one shot, do not miss your chance to blow. This opportunity comes once in a lifetime, yo"*—something I could tell DJ was also thinking because he started bobbing his head and mindlessly mouthing the lyrics under his breath.

Man, I miss DJ. He was easily the coolest friend I ever had. I don't even know why he wanted to be friends with me. But I was so grateful he did. DJ is the kind of Static who doesn't even need a Changer hanging around teaching him crap about how to be a good human. If anything, he taught *me* stuff.

He must have clocked me staring at him because soon enough DJ is flashing me a smile and waving. I wave back, tentatively, trying not to rattle him, the way respectful fans wave to celebrities when the stars are working a rope line.

"Places, pets!" Mr. Wood shouts, and DJ snaps to attention. "Remember, you are in a relationship with everyone here. This is not just about you. Connect! Connect!"

In a back corner, Audrey and Chloe whisper about something. It still shocks me to see Audrey so tight with a girl we used to call Chlo-zilla. The old Audrey saw Chloe for who she was . . . and, oh geez, Chloe's pointing at her scalp . . . and now she's . . . POINTING AT ME.

Awesome.

Wow.

I see Audrey's brow knit when she leans forward, trying to get a better look at me in the dark. She shakes her head as Chloe seethes in my direction. Thankfully, Mr. Wood yanks Audrey by the shoulders and marches her away from Chloe, stepping back to survey the blocking and giving me a short reprieve from whatever revenge the bitch squad is cooking up.

"Are you in love with her or something?" Kris asks me after rehearsal, apropos of nothing, as we're walking out of the auditorium toward the parking lot. "You go all single white female around her."

"I'm Asian," I joke, like I don't care what he thinks.

"Well, get over it. Audrey is straight as a church pew."

"How do you know?" I push, now kind of annoyed.

Kris smirks. "How do I know no one looks sexy golfing? Some things are freakin' obvious, Kimmycakes."

"Yeah, well, I heard she had a girlfriend freshmen year," I say. *Dying to tell him.*

"Yeah? Well, I heard her family is in a fundamentalist cult that likes to drag people like you and me behind four-wheel camouflage ATVs for sport. So maybe find another Betty to crush on."

I bite my lip, chewing it on the inside.

"For rizzle, Kimbo. She's a cheerleader! A boner-fied member of the bitch squad. And if she *is* a lesbian, which she's not, but let's say she is . . . she is not in the closet, she's deep inside a freakin' Stephen Hawking black hole! And besides, after that weave-ripping incident with her bestie, she's probably not exactly seeing you as girlfriend material."

"She's not like Chloe," I mutter.

"Mmmmm. Okay."

"She's not!"

"Wow girl, you got it bad. But far be it for me to try to talk you out of an obsession that will only lead to pain and stress-plucked brows."

I don't answer. I don't know how. Because maybe he's right. I don't know Audrey anymore. Maybe I never did. My walk slows to a shuffle. I feel all my breath trapped beneath my (giant, still annoying) chest.

"And now you have the sads," Kris says, frowning conspicuously. "Well, ex-squeeze me, but that's not going to fly. I'm just being real, which, I'm sure you agree, everybody could use a little more of around here."

"Whatever."

"No, no, no, no, this will not do," Kris says, shaking his head wildly as he *beep-beeps* his car to unlock it for us. "I'm going to take you someplace special this weekend. Guaranteed cure for the sads and the hopeless pursuit of lost kitties. Strap on your wig and cancel your Saturday plans, 'cause we're going out, baby!"

"I don't have anything planned on Saturday," I sigh, lowering myself into the front seat.

"No way, really? I thought you had, like, three dates lined up."

"Suck it."

"You suck it," he says. "Actually, no, I'll suck it."

We laugh, and Kris drives me to the bus stop a few blocks away from my house, where I always insist he drop me. I don't start walking toward my place until I see his little yellow car disappear around the corner.

CHANGE 3-DAY 18

I had to lie to my folks. ("Better than lying to yourself," Kris pointed out—not very helpfully, I might add, since it always feels terrible lying to my parents, particularly after seeing how Mom especially was devastated by the Tribulations.)

"Uh, I'm going to a late movie with Destiny?" I said, tentatively upticking as I do when I'm nervous.

"A date with Destiny," Dad joked from the kitchen table, where he was busy cross-referencing some Abiders-related data for the Council.

"Something like that," I said, trying to sound innocent. I could hear Destiny pulling up out front. "Gotta go!" I yelled, then grabbed a hoodie and ran out the door before Dad could reply.

Mom came out of her bedroom and followed me to the front porch. "Whoa, wait one minute."

"Sorry," I said, backtracking. I hugged her impatiently.

"Please be careful," she implored.

"Hi, Mrs. Miller!" Destiny yelled through the car window.

"Nice to see you again, Destiny. You want to come inside for a juice?" Mom hollered, as I hustled out to Destiny as quickly as possible.

"No thank you," Destiny answered while I rounded the front of her car. "We'll be home after the movie. Don't wait up!"

"You girls have fun!" Mom chimed back, face beaming. Even she was not immune to Destiny's charms.

As we pulled away, I finally had a second free from worrying about lying to take in Destiny behind the wheel. "Oh my."

"What? Oh ..." She giggled. "My ensemble."

"If by *ensemble* you mean *slutty onesie*, then sure, let's call it your ensemble."

"I didn't take you for a slut shamer," Destiny teased.

"I didn't take you for a slut," I teased back.

"What? It's cute."

"It's made entirely of red sequins. And by entirely, I mean the pocket-square portion of fabric that you have somehow managed to stretch over your naughty bits. It looks like an outfit Liberace would dress his baby in, if he had a baby."

"Amazing, right? Did you check out the heels? Five-inchers!" She took her foot off the accelerator to show me.

I could only laugh.

Destiny plugged in her iPhone and cranked up the music. "Throw-back time!" she bellowed over the sound of Cyndi Lauper's breathy, childlike voice. "Girls just want to have fun! Am I right?"

"Woo hoo," I deadpanned.

Forty-five minutes later, we pulled up to the address Kris had given us. The streets were dark, with mostly unlit, cavernous buildings flanking both sides. Destiny parked, double-checked she locked the doors, and we stepped out onto the dark block beside a mountain of about twenty black garbage bags piled chest-high.

"It's supposed to be called the Carousel," I said, scanning for a sign that we were in the right location. Hell, scanning for a sign of *life*.

"More like Scare-ousel," Destiny said, shivering in her ensemble and teetery heels.

"Maybe we should bail," I suggested, seized with fresh nervousness. I mean, this was feeling kind of crazy. Like we were "borrowing trouble," as Mom frequently says.

Just then a door opened to what seemed like an abandoned factory and a bunch of men toppled out, laughing. A closer look revealed one of them was wearing a tutu.

"I'm going to go out on a limb and guess that's the place," Destiny said, cheerfully tucking her wallet and phone into her bra and clacking on her heels over toward the men. "Is this the Carousel?" she asked.

"Well, if it isn't Diana Ross circa 1971!" an older guy in a dress shirt swooned. "You are the most gorgeous thing I've seen in centuries!"

"Centuries is right," another dude chimed in, making everyone else laugh.

"Careful, Randall," the first guy said. "You'll be old too one day."

"Yeah, but unlike you, I won't look it!"

The men all laughed again, not really paying much attention to the question. Destiny decided to take their indifference as a yes, and flagged me to join her. I walked over slowly, a little nervous but not really knowing why.

"Excuse me, pardon me," I said, squeezing my way through the clot of bodies blocking the door.

As I passed the guy in the tutu, he grinned broadly at me. "Now *those* are some tee-tahs!" he remarked.

I was instantly, completely, and utterly embarrassed.

"Girl, you got a body to die for," he added.

For some reason it didn't feel like smarmy sexual harassment, but rather genuine appreciation. A first for Kim Cruz.

I smiled at the guy and popped through the door, nearly tripping as I emerged into the club. Destiny was already stepping to the dance floor, her head jerking to and fro, absorbing the spectacle. The place was packed like an airport at Christmas. The population was overwhelmingly male, with a few women here and there, most hanging off the shoulders of their guy friends or dancing beside them, twirling in a frenzy. The music was all about that bass, no treble, and when you gazed across the dance floor it was like observing the movement of tall grass on the African plains. Everyone swaying in unison, becoming one giant, undeniably striking, undulating mass.

"Let's go!" Destiny squealed, coming back to grab my hand and tug me toward the floor.

"I need to find Kris first!" I yelled, as she shrugged and merged into the swarm of bodies, a giant toothy grin on her face.

I did a slow turn, searching everywhere for Kris, but I couldn't see him, or much of anything, with all the smoke from what smelled like a hundred thousand cigarettes. In one corner I saw a long bar, men standing on top of it at either end, dressed in tight red bikini underwear and what looked like neon-green paint circles on their nipples. They alternated thrusting each hip forward, taking care not to smile, though they did squint their eyes in some approximation of resentment.

In another corner was the deejay booth, which was manned by a very fit, shirtless black dude who had a microphone in front of his turntable. Every few minutes he'd lean into it and say in a sexy voice, "You are all beautiful people. I am drunk on so much gorgeousness. Dance, queens, dance!" After which, the whole crowd would let loose a loud

"Whooooo," before resuming their synchronized undulations, even more feverishly, per his instructions.

"Why aren't you out there?" a familiar voice yelled in my ear.

"Kris!" I threw my arms around his neck, filled with a relief I hadn't anticipated.

"What, are we dating now?"

I let go, took a step back, and noticed that he was dressed like he was performing in *The Arabian Nights*—diaphanous turquoise pants and matching halter, a chintzy gold turban wrapped around his head.

"Where do you even buy something like that?" I asked.

"Barbara Eden's garage sale," he quipped. "Don't I look divine?"

I nodded, because he really did. His eyes were rimmed with liner and covered in deep blue shadow, his lips stained bold red. On anyone else it would have been clownish, but on Kris, the look was pure glamour. "You're actually really pretty," I said, and noticed that the honesty threw him off a little.

"Don't start making me cry with your sweetness," he replied, shaking off his feelings. Not the time or the place for those. "Can't have this perfection running down my face and into my chiffon." He wriggled his shoulders in a quick shimmy. "Let's you and me go dance our fat asses off!"

I didn't have a choice. In seconds I was dragged onto the floor, into the masses, where we joined Destiny and her circle of admirers (already, even here), and fell right into the ebb and flow of my first real club dance party.

Initially, I was panicked. I worried about my body, being uncoordinated, looking like a fool. But soon enough I realized 1) no one was even looking at me, and 2) if there were ever a place to dance like no one was watching, it was at a dodgy gay club in a smoke-filled warehouse on a nameless street in downtown Nashville.

"I wanna see you *slay*, queens!" the deejay commanded, and sure enough, I gradually did. My hands floated into the air as though tied to helium balloons. I pumped my shoulders up and down, I did the bump with strangers, dropped it like it was hot, even gyrated my thick hips like a video vixen on the prowl.

If anyone had been watching me, they'd have suspected I was drunk—or high, and I guess in some ways I was. Not on anything illicit, but on the energy and the freedom in the room, the complete, intoxicating abandon of being literally in the center of a crowd that has zero designs on you, passes zero judgment, and gives zero fracks about whatever superfreakiness you choose to inhabit.

"I need some water," Destiny leans and shouts into my damp face. I nod, and we dance our way off the floor and over to the bar.

Kris follows, whipping out a collapsing fan from God knows where and waving it in front of his face like a professional geisha. "Sick moves, Kimmycakes," he says, propping an elbow on the bar dramatically, then ordering a rum and Coke.

"Water, please," Destiny tells the bartender, who gives her a wink.

"Anything for you, sugar?" he asks me.

"Uh, water?" I say. Then out of nowhere, "And . . . a rum and Coke too. Please. Sugar."

I brace myself for rejection, but the bartender is already busy shooting soda from a grimy nozzle into two clear plastic cups, clearly not too concerned about the legalities of serving alcohol to minors. Kris slides a twenty-dollar bill across the bar ("Keep the change"), and we get our drinks.

"To us!" Kris yells, hoisting his cup.

"To my second arrest in as many years!" I say, still worried about the underage drink.

"To the best year ever!" Destiny adds, as we tap the lips of our three cups together, the syrupy soda sloshing onto our fingers like an alcoholic sorority blood-bond ritual or something.

"Maybe for you," I murmur out of Kris's earshot, as the first sip of liquor burns my throat. I shake my head wildly, and Destiny gives my ear a flick. Over the speakers we hear "Raspberry Beret" come on.

"All you sexy things, get out on the dance-floor!" the deejay growls into the mic.

"That's my cue!" Destiny announces, strutting back out to the masses, her red sequins catching the light.

"That girl," Kris says, shaking his head.

"Right?"

He signals the bartender for another round. "I don't know if I'm jealous of her," he says, pounding his second rum as soon as the bartender sets it in front of him, "or if I want to *be* her." Kris turns his eyes toward the bar, avoiding my gaze.

Prince thumps in our ears, the sound rattling the liquid in my cup as I stand there, saying nothing, not sure if there is anything to be said. I take a gulp, the rum searing a bit less this time.

"I know what you mean," I offer, finally.

"Pshhht," Kris snorts. "Unlikely."

"No. I'm serious."

"*You* know what it's like maybe wanting to be another

gender than the one they tell you you are at birth?" Kris asks. "Bullshit."

I let his question hang in the smoky air. Part of me wants to tell him that I more than know what that feels like; I LIVE what that feels like. That my whole high school life is one giant gender wheel of fortune. That in some ways he's lucky to have the liberty to be able to choose who he does or doesn't become, and when and how.

"I don't know what it's like wanting to be a different gender than the one I was born into," I start, carefully selecting my words from the thicket of them cluttering my brain, "but I do know what it's like feeling like you're walking around in the wrong body."

"I hate that oversimplified narrative," Kris snaps.

"Oh, there's nothing simple about it," I snap right back.

We stand there, the unexpected hostility between us killing the joy of the music. Soon the song bleeds into a slow jam, and Destiny skips over to us, quickly sniffing out drama.

"What damage is happening here?" she asks, sucking in her cheeks and shaming us with her eyes.

"I'm being a jerk," Kris says flatly. "Just something I don't have figured out, so I'm taking it out on her." Which softens me in an instant. I hook an arm around his neck, plant a wet kiss on his cheek. "Oh, and Kimmy wants to be a boy," he adds suddenly, winking.

Destiny shoots me a look. "And what exactly would Kim know about being a boy?" she asks slyly.

"Girl, what would *any* of us?" Kris laughs.

CHANGE 3-DAY 19

This morning Dad woke me up with a big bucket of guilt dumped on my head. Apparently the stench of the Carousel had permeated my room, and when he came in to rouse me for breakfast, he smelled the smoke and sticky alcohol residue, and decided I needed a stern scared-straight talking to.

He was deep into addiction stats when I tried to interject that I'd had only one drink and zero cigarettes, but Dad wasn't in a place to listen to reason. I'd lied, I'd let him down. What else was I lying about?

"Dad, I just wanted to blow off some steam," I explained. "I knew you'd never let me go to a dance club."

"Damn *right* I wouldn't . . ."

"It's harmless. Every kid does it."

"I'm not every kid's parent. I'm yours."

"I'm not a chronic liar face. I'm not a raging drug addict."

"Not yet."

And so it went. Cuckoo lecturing. Zero listening.

Okay, okay, so I probably shouldn't have lied. But there was no other way I would have gotten to go, and I guess that mattered more to me. I mean, what the hell? I've been entrusted with helping to evolve the human race, but I'm not allowed to go to a gay bar and dance with my friends?

"Nothing bad happened," I insisted. "In fact, being there made me feel good in a way I never have before."

"Well, booze will do that," Dad said.

"It wasn't because of the alcohol."

"How would you know?" he asked. "Is this a frequent thing?"

"I could've lied about that," I said, "but I'm telling you the truth. I had a drink. Destiny was completely sober because she was driving. If I was abusing or using, do you think I'd be admitting I had a freaking drink?"

He just shook his head at me. Seemingly seeing me in a completely unfamiliar, unflattering light.

"I'm serious. I felt at home there. Less alone. There wasn't any pressure to be anything I didn't want to be. Surely you remember feeling something like that during your Cycle," I said. "For once, nobody was looking at me like I was the weird fat girl."

I could see my father wince. "You aren't either of those things."

"Yes I am, actually. In the world where I spend the most time, I am the person no one wants to be. I am the short straw on every front, and if I'm not being teased or ridiculed, I'm being ignored. That's how little who I am matters."

"Kim, everything you're saying is about the exterior," he tried pointing out.

"What do you think counts in high school, Dad? Or the world, for that matter?"

He let out a labored sigh. "I think you're beautiful," he said, his eyes welling slightly.

"Great. You can be my escort to the prom."

He laughed, and so did I.

"I'm sorry I lied," I said, and I meant it. "But it really felt good being me last night."

"Just don't pull that crap again."

"Promise."

"Well, breakfast is ready. Maybe shower before you come to the kitchen. You smell like a truck stop." Dad got up, paused at my door. "Oh, I forgot. At the mixer next week, the Council wants you to talk about what happened to you."

"Sorry?"

"You know, as a cautionary tale to all the Y-1 Changers. What to avoid, how to keep yourself off Abiders radar, et cetera."

It felt like I'd just been slapped in the face. Twice.

"What happened to me wasn't my fault," I whispered, my voice thick with spite.

"Your experiences can help other Changers. Don't you want to be of service?"

"It wasn't my *fault*, Dad," I tried again, dead serious. "I need to know you know that."

But he didn't answer. We sat like that for what felt like a full minute. Which doesn't sound long, but when you're in an eye-lock throw-down with your angry father, it's an eternity.

"I'll see you downstairs," he announced finally, yanking the door shut behind him.

CHANGE 3-DAY 28

The curtain billowed and then delicately slipped off the statue beneath it, uncloaking an odd Mr. Olympia–meets–G.I. Joe figure, cupping the world in his hands.

Hmm, I wonder what the sculptor was trying to convey with this particular imagery?

Needless to say, the "tribute" statue to the fallen Chase looked NOTHING like Chase, neither Chase V-1 nor Chase V-2. (Was it supposed to be an amalgamation of the two? Or was the artist the Council hired to memorialize Chase just entirely ungifted?) Nevertheless, there we all were at the mixer this afternoon, clapping away at the big reveal, as though it were actually "breathtaking" and "uncanny how it captures his spirit," as many fellow Changers uttered around me, loud enough to be certain Chase's mom and dad could hear, and what, feel better? Like the paltry gesture to honor Chase's "ultimate sacrifice" did anything to make it okay that he's gone, or did anything to even remotely replace his energy and larger contributions to this world? Did anything, period, besides become a clunky, embarrassing reminder of loss?

While all this was going down, Destiny and I basically just stood there next to our respective parents, lazily clapping along, catching each other's eye, realizing we were thinking the exact same thing at the exact same time. Which was: it's basically our fault Chase is gone, and almost everybody here knows it, and if Chase didn't risk his life to find us, we would be the ones replicated in the cheesy statues right now (probably in some stupid cross-legged position facing each other and tossing a ball of the world between us) and he'd be standing here being forced to clap for us. (Though he never would; he was less of a suck-up than we are.)

After the big reveal, my back started aching from standing for the three-minute ovation. During the applause, Chase's parents kept looking my way. And I kept looking away. It was too much to bear, his mother an absolute mess, his father trying to hold her together beside him.

I couldn't take it anymore and excused myself before anybody could stop me, and ran to the bathroom, where—thank God—Destiny soon joined me. She threw the bolt on the door behind her, and hopped up on the sink, swinging her legs below. I kicked the seat down and sat on the toilet.

"This is absurd," Destiny said, whipping out an e-cig and pushing the button a couple times until it turned on.

"You *vape*?" I asked, completely off-guard after initially thinking the doohickey was a G.D. Changers emblem brand, but then recognizing what it really was from the few kids who blatantly vape on the steps before and after school.

"Just started," she said, sucking on the little stick and then blowing a giant cloud of vapor out her nose, then mouth.

"You look ridiculous," I said.

"I don't care. And, I don't."

"Yes you do," I said. "Let me try."

"You sure?" When I nodded, she handed it over.

"How do you do it?" I asked, feeling the weight of the thing and trying to figure out which end to suck.

"Just put your lips around it and sort of inhale with your mouth, not your lungs."

"What do you mean?"

"Like, bring it in enough to puff out your cheeks, but not down in your chest."

I did just as she said. It tasted bitter. Burnt. And strawberry-y. My tongue immediately felt hairy and swollen, as if wrapped in a fruit roll-up. I coughed out the vapor, and Destiny laughed.

"What?"

"I don't think you did it right," she chuckled, reaching for it and taking another deep inhale, all the way into her lungs the way she told me not to.

"It's gross."

"And?" she said, exhaling with her eyes half-closed.

"Anyway," I said.

"Anyway," she repeated, then fell silent for a beat. "Chase was a good dude, huh?"

"He was a self-righteous prick. I loved him so much."

"This feels wrong. Let's bail."

"We can't. Well, I can't. My dad is on a mission to impress the board," I said, "so I have to talk, or he'll basically disown me."

"Yeah, I can't drop out either," she said. "I promised my parents I'd honor my commitment."

"What's worse than commitments?"

"That statue out there."

We both laughed, vapor leaking out of Destiny's mouth.

Luckily, Turner's sermon on the mount about Chase was just wrapping up by the time Destiny and I inconspicuously rejoined the huddle. ". . . And that is why this beautiful and powerful figure is meant to honor not only Chase, but *all* of our fellow fallen Changers across the world—and the millennia. In the many we are one."

"In the many we are one," repeated the crowd solemnly, as Destiny and I shook our heads at each other. I didn't care who saw.

"Please, everybody, enjoy some fresh apple cider and Stevia cookies, and then join us in the main auditorium in thirty minutes," Turner added, "for a special multiformat presentation about the State of the Changers Nation."

Great. Showtime. The moment when Destiny and I got to testify, to play our part as Abiders witnesses, the walking, talking, surviving cautionary tales. I took a few steps backward, fought yet another instinct to run, and it was then that I heard murmuring as a rift in the crowd widened, and I spotted Benedict and a few raggedy compatriots whom I assumed were also RaChas making their way from the rear of the group. They were actually *inside* Changers Central (as opposed to being relegated to their usual spot outside the fence protesting). I guess it would've been a bad look to lock out the RaChas when Chase (as a card-carrying RaCha himself) was the reason three Changers were alive, and a potential Abiders nest was exposed and neutralized.

"Well, what do you know?" Destiny whispered. "Evolution."

"More like PR," I snapped back. There's no way Turner voluntarily chose this joining of forces. "The enemy of my enemy is my friend," I theorized. "He had to let them into the tent."

"Whatever works," Destiny smirked, pushing on toward the auditorium.

I was about to head over to introduce myself to Benedict for the first time as Kim, when I felt a hand on the inside of my elbow, tugging me in the opposite direction. I knew instantly from the girly perfume that it was Tracy yanking me toward a quiet corner, eager to run down one last time what to say, what *not* to say, how to say, how *not* to say, et cetera et cetera, about my experiences during the Tribulations.

"You got this," Tracy pronounced for the fiftieth time, squeezing my hands between hers.

"I-I," I stuttered.

"Do you want some ice water?" Tracy asked, and when I shook my head, she quietly minced over to the curtains that opened onto the stage and pulled them aside to check on things. One of Turner's minions was adjusting three chairs on a plush Persian rug just so. All the new Y-1 Changers and their Touchstones, in addition to a few older Changers, were milling about the auditorium, nervously high talking, finding seats.

Over Tracy's shoulder, I spotted Dad on the other side of the stage speaking with some Changer parents, all of their brows stitched into an expression of general severity and concern. When Dad saw Tracy peeking through the curtains, he looked past her for me, made eye contact, and gave an inordinately energetic DOUBLE THUMBS-UP in my direction.

To which all I could think was: 1) *I'm going to puke*, and 2) *Why does everybody keep telling me I "got" this?*

The only thing I "got" was my best friend/old bandmate killed. How about I go up there and tell all the baby Changers THAT when I get onstage? I was seriously considering doing just such a thing when I felt a tap on my shoulder, kind of hard.

"Hey, man."

I turned around to see a compact, yet ridiculously good-looking white dude with dark hair and a cool haircut.

"Hey?" I said, a little nervous because he was the kind of handsome that freaks you out a little, regardless of attraction or sexuality or whatever.

"It's Alex!" he announced enthusiastically, pointing at his face and laughing in an insecure way that didn't match what his new looks were projecting. "Well, Theo now."

"Alex. *Alex*?" Alex, as in Alex with whom Elyse/Destiny and I endured the Tribulations? Alex the terrified little nerd who used to be a girl who liked freaking PONIES? Alex who pissed his pants a little every time the goons would come into the basement and throw us sandwiches and water? Alex who somehow ended up in a coma after we got sprung, but who has now, obviously, settled nicely into his brand-new, perfectly healthy V and (not unlike Destiny) won the freaking Changers lottery?

"You're on!" I heard Tracy call over my shoulder, as Destiny blew in at the very last second with a can of Coke in one hand while stuffing her e-cig into her back pocket with the other.

"This is Alex," I spat out, trying to contain my stupefaction, as the three of us were ushered onto the stage to raucous, overly supportive applause, led by Turner in his stupid robes and beads, as he pressed his hands together and bowed theatrically to each one of us while we found our seats: Alex-now-Theo stage left, me dead center, and then Destiny stage right.

It had to be some sort of sad, sad joke (on me): my wide, resentful, Mohawked butt flanked by these two perfect specimens. Really, Changers Council? You put all three of us through the same Tribulations, and these two get rewarded with modeling contracts, while I get . . . Wait, what do I get? Oh yeah, lower back pain and rashes on my inner thighs.

FRACK THAT CRAP, I decided right then and there.

Since it was video-recorded like all events at Changers Central, I suppose I don't need to go into too much detail about my monosyllabic "share" re: being kidnapped by Abiders. Some shiny-forehead dude came up first and introduced the three of us, telling the crowd that the Council believes the incident was the first phyiscal Abiders-related (or "possibly Abiders-related") attack on Changers in the region, and that they are working their hardest, having formed a special Abiders Task Force (of which my father is the chair) to fully investigate the situation and take appropriate action. Like, whether Static law enforcement will be brought in, how the RaChas and the Council might work together (that sure was a change of tune from our Y-1 experience of "ignore those crazy hooligans you saw protesting on your way in here today"), and how to anticipate and deter more attacks in the future.

Then he went on to the audio/visual portion of the intro, briefly delineating new, tighter rules for Changers, which honestly just sounded like the old rules, but written in **BOLD TYPE** instead of the usual *italics* you'd find in *The Changers Bible*.

Don't reveal yourself as a Changer to Statics; don't bring Statics home; don't hook up with other Changers, blah blah blah.

When it came time for me to share, I detached as much as possible, almost going into a trance, keeping to the facts: I was out walking my dog, I got hit on the head, thrown in the back of a truck, woke up in a dark basement. Didn't know how long I was in there. They threw my friend (the now-statue) Chase in with us, he croaked, or was about to, and then there was a bunch of smoke and noise and the next thing I knew, I woke up in the Changer clinic with my horrified parents staring at me.

I honestly don't remember much from my talk besides

barely managing to eke out those bullet points, and the complete and utter stillness in the audience while I was talking. (Needless to say, this latter aspect was the most unnerving part. I mean, *crickets*.) I recall Destiny getting a few laughs when it was her turn—and her seeming to really try to communicate in a way I couldn't muster. Alex-now-Theo got no laughs when it was his turn, but he wasn't trying to. I could see the baby Changers struggling to do the math of the pitiful boy he described in the basement versus the hot stud-muffin sitting before them now. They were probably thinking about who they were a mere month ago, trying to determine if they got an upgrade or a downgrade. As you do.

To be frank, I mostly just spaced out and shut down while my fellow Tribulations-survivors took their turns. It was like my brain made me, to keep the rest of my body from exploding all over the Persian rug. I distracted myself by considering how in our new V's, I could still see the same core in the three of us onstage, only I could also see how each of us had already adapted to living in our new forms after just a month. We were changing inside whether we wanted to or not. My adaptation being confrontational and pissed off 90 percent of the time. Whereas the two perfect Changers on either side of me (*What the hell, Destiny?*) seemed more than happy to accommodate and answer the many ridiculous questions from the Y-1s in the audience who were all now sufficiently paranoid and terrified into following the Council's rules to the letter, so as to avoid an Abiders encounter like ours.

"Were you scared?"

Of course, moron.

"What did you do to pass the time?"

Oh, you know, played Connect Four *and* Apples to Apples.

"Where did you go to the bathroom?"

There was a heated, gold-plated toilet behind a privacy screen in the corner of the basement . . . IN A GODDAMN BUCKET, WHERE DO YOU THINK??

"Did you ever think about telling them you weren't a Changer so they would let you go?"

They knew. Somehow they knew.

"What did it feel like thinking you were going to die?"

. . .

"Okay, okay," I heard Tracy breaking in at the podium after this last one, interrupting the Q&A period, and also my zone-out. Alex-now-Theo looked like he was about to burst into tears at this point. Even Destiny seemed rattled. "I think that's about all the time we have for Q&A," Tracy said into the mic. "Why don't we give these brave heroes a nice round of applause, and then y'all can move on to the breakout sessions."

There was an awkward silence as that final question hung in the air before people gradually started to take Tracy's suggestion by tentatively starting to clap for the three of us. Tracy took the other mic from Destiny, shut it off, crossed directly to me, and whispered, "You okay?"

"No," I heard myself speaking the truth. "This is not okay at all. It's actually quite effed up when you think about it."

Dad came up then, put an arm half around me, and tried to pull me into a hug. Like he was performing the gesture for the sake of the audience. "Proud of you," he said stiffly. "It's difficult but important work you're doing."

I didn't know how to deal with him. Mom came up then too, while people were talking to Destiny and Theo on the side, asking private questions. I stood there looking at them, looking at Mom, Dad, Tracy, and just thought to myself, *What is wrong with me?*

"Are you okay, petunia?" Mom asked, sensing trouble.

"I just want to leave," I said.

"No," Dad muttered tight through his teeth, clearly hoping only I could hear. "You need to stay right here, to make yourself available for others who might need you in this moment."

"What about what *I* need in this moment?" I screamed, loud enough so that the single mic that was still live broadcast my outburst to every lingering Changer in the room. They all whipped around and eyeballed me. Destiny and Theo too, and their Touchstones. Even Turner, who was way, way in the back of the auditorium, chatting up some new Y-1 parents with that phony, placid expression he's always working. Clearly, I had projected to the back of the house. Mr. Wood would have been proud.

"Shut up," Dad hissed in my ear, grabbing my arm and pulling me toward the backstage curtains.

"William," Mom stepped between us, "what the hell are you doing?"

He let go of my arm, and I beelined backstage, Tracy, Mom, and Dad in hot pursuit. I could hear Destiny trying to excuse herself from an audience member who wanted to meet her.

"I need to be alone," I said, pushing through the curtains into the muffled quiet of the side stage.

For a second it was just me, but then Dad poked through, followed by Mom, whom I could hear telling Tracy and Destiny (I'm assuming), "It's fine, let us handle this."

Then it was the three of us, the happy nuclear family in the quiet room, them studying me for a clue as to what my damage was. As if it weren't obvious.

Mom hugged me. "I know that had to be excruciating, honey." My tears started. "Maybe this is just all too soon."

"Too soon?" Dad bellowed, almost mocking what Mom was saying. Mocking my feelings. Mocking me.

"*Later*, Will," Mom shushed him fiercely.

"No. This is happening now. We're here today, she has something to offer others that might actually help them, might actually help all of us, mind you, and she's acting like a whiny baby. It's embarrassing."

I could feel Mom starting to shake as she held me. So I started actually holding onto her. But after a few seconds of this, she let go, and slowly pivoted toward Dad, keeping her distance from him like she was trying not to launch over and wrap her hands around his neck. I don't think I'd ever seen her so angry at him. So angry at anybody.

"You have lost your damn mind," she said.

Dad just shrugged, like he wasn't getting it.

"Don't you pull that nonsense with me," Mom went on. "You know exactly what you're doing, and I'm not going to stand here and watch you do it."

"Individual feelings are not more important than the collective mission," he said calmly. "This is a battle, and there will be casualties. She's a big girl."

Mom inhaled deeply. Exhaled slowly. Her jaw set. Inhaled/exhaled again, and then: "Perhaps, but abandoning your actual family for the larger Changer one—"

"Honey," he interrupted, "there is only one—"

"Let. Me. Finish," Mom shut him down.

He shifted his gaze from one set of curtains to the other, then looked directly at Mom. But she didn't continue. "*What?*" he asked curtly after a few seconds.

"Be careful what you choose," Mom said, "because you're in danger of losing what matters the most."

Needless to say, it was a silent ride home.

It's three hours after we got back from the mixer. I've been holed up in my room, binge-watching old *Twilight Zone* episodes, which always make me feel better. Mom and Dad haven't spoken since we were backstage. Over dinner they would talk to me, but not to each another. It was freaking strange. *Twilight Zone*-y, in fact.

Like Chase. His absence. The negative space of Chase. How different things would be if he were still around. How different that mixer would've been. How different I would be.

Chase saved me. More than once. And now I'm supposed to help (and save?) others. But what about people who don't need saving? Or, more to the point, who don't *deserve* saving? Maybe there are just a few individuals out there in the world who warrant rescue, and the rest should be left on their own, to their own devices. Women and children first. The lifeboats can't float everybody. Choices have to be made. Who's putting—for instance—Jason in the raft? Not me. I'm not even sure I'd put Chloe in.

I guess that makes me an a-hole.

The Changers Bible tells me: *Those most resistant to change are the very individuals who most need to change. Those who fight hardest to win have the most to gain by losing.* (Don't see that one on many T-shirts.)

I Skyped briefly with Destiny when she got home. She wanted to check in, see how I was doing after my anxiety meltdown at the mixer. She listened, completely understood why I had to get out of Dodge. But she also described how this feeling had come over her earlier when she was onstage. This thing she couldn't quite name. It was a complete transfer of focus off herself and onto the others in the room who were looking up at her. And she said all her cynicism and skepticism and annoyance at having to be there essentially evaporated. How the minute she started sharing, she was overcome with this enormous urge to *help*. Even if it was just one person in that room. Could have been the vaping, maybe.

I don't know. I suck, I guess. Clearly I had no such spiritual epiphany. *#Changerfail*. More like *#Changerfailing*, because I still don't care. Not really. Dad was right to be disappointed in me. It's just, I don't know how I'm supposed to save anybody else when it's beyond evident I can't even save myself.

WINTER

CHANGE 3–DAY 73

"What a lovely little lady you are," Nana says to me as I roll her into the living room and set the brake on the gray rubber wheel of her chair. From her tone, I'm 98 percent certain she doesn't know exactly who I am.

"That's Kim, Ma!" Dad yells in from behind us, where he's schlepping Nana's overstuffed suitcases, a hat box clamped under one arm, a bronze and glass antique lamp under the other. "Ethan, Drew, Oryon? Remember?"

"I know who she is!" Nana scolds him. "I may be an old woman but I'm not brain dead."

"Just reminding you," Dad says, wounded, almost like a teenager, as he shoots me a look like, *She probably doesn't actually know, but just roll with it*, as he disappears into the garage to store Nana's belongings. Ever since her accident in the shower, Dad's wanted to move Nana in with us, and now, silver-lining alert, thanks to us having to relocate to a new house after the Tribulations, we finally have the space. I for one am glad. Someone else for my folks to focus their concern and anxiety on (especially during the holidays, which is the super-plus-ultra of anxiety for pretty much every family I know). Plus, I just feel better when Nana's around.

"Kimberly, you sit down here and tell me what you've been up to," Nana says, her tone kind again as she pats the couch cushion beside her wheelchair. "Such a beauty. You remind me of someone I used to know."

"I'm . . ." I start, taking a seat.

"What?" she yells.

I raise my voice a notch, trying not to sound condescending: "I *said*, school is on a break, so I haven't really been doing much."

"Everybody's always up to something," Nana replies with a wink. "You've lived *what?* Three, three and a half lives at this point? That's not nothing." Maybe she remembers more than we think. "Tell me about your friends."

"Well, there's Destiny, but I'm not in school with her, so I don't see her as much as I want to. She's probably my best friend."

"Destiny. That's a pretty name. Fraught, but pretty."

"Yeah, you should see the face and body that goes with the name." I can scarcely contain the jealousy in my tone. "She's a Changer. And she's way living it up with this V. Embracing every gift the gods gave her."

"Not the worst notion."

"Yeah. But she's staying nice. The one V where she could really get away with being a grade-A jerk, and she's staying grounded. It's all super unnatural. And annoying. But I love her for it."

"Destiny sounds like a keeper," Nana says. "What about friends at school?"

"Well, there is this one guy, Kris."

"Boyfriend?"

I snort, shake my head vigorously. "Ah. No."

"Pretty girl like you . . ."

"That's just it. Kris thinks *he* might want to be a girl."

"So he's one of us?" Nana leans in. "Tell me the name again."

"Kris. Kris Arnold. And not exactly."

Nana furrows her brow. "Either he is or he isn't."

"He's like, you know, exploring the limits of what it means to be a boy, what it means to be a girl. You know, sometimes he's comfortable with people treating him like a guy, whatever that means, but some days it makes him feel really wrong when people call him *he,* and he prefers *she* and it gets a little muddy and all, so I guess—"

"Oh, so he's a transgender," Nana interrupts my rambling.

And . . . I about fall off the couch.

"I listen to NPR," she says, as Mom rolls up with a cup of Taster's Choice, Nana's favorite instant coffee.

"It's transgender, Nana. Not *a* transgender," Mom clarifies gently. "Will is setting up your room, and as soon as he gets out of there, I'll make your bed so you can get some rest. I know it's probably been a disorienting day all around."

Nana swallows a frown at the word *disorienting*. "I'm fine," she insists, shooing Mom with a veiny hand. "I don't know why everybody is making such a fuss over me. Now, where were we . . . ?"

"Kim."

"Kim! Of course. Noble. Brave. A leader," she says, smiling and squinting her eyes at me as if I were the most spectacular person in the world. "The other day they were playing a story on the radio about this little girl who was starting at her school as a boy. Such a thing to hear, these parents doing that. Confused the heck out of everyone, and yet it made sense to the child. Which is all that matters in the end, don't you think?"

I nod.

"So much fuss about the bathrooms," Nana says, shrugging. "Still. Different times. Better, I think."

I want to agree. But I don't.

"What about the other one?" she asks.

"The other what?"

"The girl? From last year?"

"Oh. Audrey?" I say, shocked that Nana remembers. "Yeah. She's . . . different this year."

"She is? Or you are?" She begins coughing, quiet and dry at first, but the hacking grows deeper. "Can you pass me my coffee please, cutie pie?"

I do as asked, and Nana takes it, her hand clattering the cup against its saucer loudly, as I'm thinking to myself, *It's surely Audrey who's different. Or maybe she's been that way all along, and I never noticed before. No, can't be . . .*

Nana takes a sip of her coffee, and I watch as a tiny brown drip at the corner of her mouth slides off the side of her wrinkly chin. Something about it makes me want to cry.

Outside, dark clouds skim across a light gray sky. The trees have lost most of their leaves, making them appear skinny, malnourished, half-alive, half-dead. I know there's always life in the core, biding its time even when they're bare and frozen, but looking at them now, all I can sense is loss.

I try to distract myself, to stop from tipping into an unsolicited depression. Kites. Airplanes. Birds. Not working. Uh, Mazda, Toyota, Kia. Shovel, ladder, gutter. Asphalt roof shingles. That's a little better. Oh yay, a fat squirrel is fretting over a nut, manically digging in the dirt where the sidewalk ends. Why are they always so frantic and twitchy? What is their massive hurry anyway? So busy all the damn time. You're a squirrel, you aren't running a Fortune 500 company. You aren't even running a taco truck.

"What about that Chase boy?" Nana asks out of nowhere.

My heart bottoms out. My eyes well up all over again. *Great.* "I thought, I guess I thought you knew," I stutter. "He's, he's—gone."

"Oh, honey, I wouldn't count on it," Nana says, smiling at me knowingly, but then her coughing cranks up again, even more intensely than before. She hands the cup back, which I take, but she drops the saucer before I can completely grab hold of it, and it bounces off the couch, shattering on the wood floor.

"I'm—" *cough-cough* "—sorry," she warbles.

"No, I'm sorry," I say, kneeling to pick up the ceramic shards. "I should have caught it."

Mom rushes in from fixing up Nana's room. "What happened? Are you two okay?"

"I just dropped the saucer," I say, and look up at Nana, who has suddenly fallen silent, her eyes flat, reeled back into one of her spells that seem to last longer and longer these days.

"That's okay," Mom says calmly.

"Nana?" I ask, but there's no answer.

"It's okay, baby," Mom soothes, gently rubbing Nana's shoulder. "It's been a big day. We're going to get Nana to bed. Don't worry about that, I'll clean it up later."

Mom unlocks the brake and nimbly backs Nana up. As she wheels her toward the back bedroom, I think about how Mom handles things like she's pretty much the pro of every situation. I can't imagine ever having my shit together like that. Not even to pretend.

Needless to say, Thanksgiving dinner was low-key. Since Nana wasn't feeling well enough to sit at the table with us, we decided to keep it super simple, and I was more than happy to eat my pain and gobble up slices of Hawaiian pizza while watching *The Wiz* (for the hundredth time) on DVD, with Mom, Dad, and Snoopy on the couch. It was almost like old times. That is, old times before the Tribulations, when Dad was less burdened by the world, and Mom was less burdened by how Dad was handling the burdens. And I was straight-up less of a burden.

As I ate, I ruminated on what Nana said before she mentally checked out today: Chase not really being gone.

Before dinner, I dug my memento box out of the back of my closet and opened it up. There, under a few old snapshots of me and Andy—well, Ethan and Andy—and the bracelet Audrey gave me, was the letter Nana wrote to me when I was Drew. I read it again, her telling me about being a boy in the fifties, working the docks down in Florida, eating boiled shrimp salt-and-peppered right off the boats. I scrutinized the fuzzy black-and-white photograph she included—a faraway shot of a handsome, wiry-muscled boy in overalls, flexing beside the shore, with the inscription on the back: *To Chase, the boy of my dreams . . .*

I wanted to ask Nana what she knows about Chase—hers, mine—but I knew it wasn't the right time. And she might not even remember . . . But still. When I put the box away, I felt an unexpected rush of gratitude.

I feel the same now, feeding Snoopy my leftover crusts, watching *The Wiz* scene in the sweatshop where Evilene is yelling at all of her slaves to WORK! It thrills me every time Dorothy and the gang burst in with the Flying Monkeys, and the fire sprinklers get tripped, and Evilene melts, dying on her giant, bejeweled toilet-throne. As soon as she's gone, all of the sweatshop slaves realize they're finally free, and unzip their heavy brown leather bodysuits, which fall to the floor in hideous clumps and burst into flames, revealing these gorgeous bodies and souls underneath. And then everybody just starts dancing and singing like life is wonderful.

Can you feel the brand-new day?

It makes me believe, at least for a moment, that it can all be so beautiful, what's underneath, if you just get the opportunity to zip yourself out.

CHANGE 3-DAY 79

"*You've changed. You're daring. You're different in the woods. More sure. More sharing . . . If you could see— you're not the man who started . . .*"

At dress rehearsals I was watching Mia, this reedy wisp of a girl, a self-possessed freshman (who barely looks like she should be in early middle school, much less high school). You wouldn't think she had such a voice buried in her, but there she was in her bonnet and giant apron, center stage as the baker's wife, belting out "It Takes Two" like she was in the finals of *American Idol*.

DJ stepped out from behind Mia, him in his floppy baker's hat and puffy white shirt. There was a dramatic pause, and then DJ echoed the lyrics, putting his own spin on the melody as he likewise twirled Mia around twice until they stopped face-to-face, both of them out of breath, palm-to-palm, crackling with (stage) love.

As I sat behind the the action, listening to the duet while putting final flourishes on the hundreds of leaves in the trees of our makeshift stage forest, I tried to shut out the lyrics and just, like, do my job of painting the scenery and bringing the stuff in the background to life. (If that's not a microcosm of my present existence, I don't know what is.) But every time DJ and Mia get to this number in practice, I can't help but stop what I'm doing and let the words penetrate my being(s), and . . . Stephen Sondheim? If that guy's not a Changer, I'll eat these cardboard leaves.

Which reminds me: Tracy recently revealed to me that there's apparently some book of renowned Changers that we get access to once we've completed our Cycles and have chosen our Monos. I don't know whether she was just messing with me to get me to "keep going" despite my obvious ill-adjustment to this V, but nevertheless, note to future self: look up to see whether Sondheim appears in that book. (Same for Dolly Parton and David Bowie.)

As DJ and Mia finished their duet in perfect harmony, Chloe blew by me, achingly mouthing the lyrics in her official role as Mia's understudy/the baker's wife (this in addition to her assigned, considerably smaller role of Florinda). Apparently Mr. Wood doesn't feel the same way about Chloe's talent as Chloe does, and as somebody must be to blame, when she passed me, Chloe's pointy shoe just happened to hook around a leg of my stepladder, making me lose my balance and fall off my perch, my paintbrush streaking green across my chest on the way down. I hit the floor with a thud, a turtle on its paint-smeared back.

Oops, she mouthed insincerely over a shoulder, before returning to holding the last few notes along with DJ and Mia: *"It takes twooooooooo."*

(If I'm Mia, I keep a keen eye out that Chloe doesn't pull a Tonya Harding and have Jason splinter her shin or something, sidelining her before opening night, because that B defines *thirsty*.)

"Okay, okay, okay," Mr. Wood said, halting the scene just as Jack ran onstage chasing an invisible chicken, yelling, "Stop her! Stop that hen!"

The music ceased, and the whole cast turned their full attention to Mr. Wood.

"Everything okay back there, pet?" he hollered from his second-row seat in the audience.

"Yeppers!" I shouted stupidly, my cheeks and neck blazing up at once. "All good!"

"Great," he said, side-eyeing Chloe like he knew she was guilty of something, even if he couldn't prove it. "It's getting late. Now, let's try that abominable opening one more time, and then I'll let you go home for the night. Narrator, Cinderella, Jack. Places!"

As Kris all but floated across stage in his Cinderella frock, I righted myself, wiping at my sweatshirt, inadvertently smudging green paint across the tips of my boobs. *Perfect*.

Audrey, dressed in her red riding hood, must've caught the little do-si-do with Chloe, because out of nowhere she padded over to me while the narrator began, "Once upon a time," and Kris busted out singing, *"I WISH!"* She stooped to pick up the paintbrush, then held it out to me and whispered, "Are you alright?"

Not really. Which is what I wanted to say to her, but I couldn't. I didn't really know *what* to say to Audrey. It wasn't every day—heck, it wasn't *any* day this year—that Audrey willingly talked to me. I've gone over in my head so many imaginary conversations we'll have, but I'm always too afraid to actually open my mouth, for fear that all the familiarity and history might come tumbling out.

"I think it was just an accident," Audrey added then, flimsily.

"Mmm-kay." I took the paintbrush from her. "Thanks."

A wet *"Shhhhhhhhhh"* was spat toward us from the side of the stage, where Chloe was giving me the thousand-deaths-glare before she went back to sweetly trilling,

"*More than life . . . more than anything,*" along with Mia.

So now Audrey was Chloe's official apologizer/denier? Awesome sauce. I think I'd respect her more if she was a flat-out bitch under her own steam. I mean, did she really think Chloe just happened to trip over my ladder? Or did she know it was on purpose, but think that I was stupid enough to believe her when she suggested it could've been an accident? None of the possible scenarios were cool. Not to mention consistent with the Audrey I used to know and love. Okay, maybe the fact that Aud actually noticed that it happened in the first place, but that's it. She was still standing on the side of awfulness. On the side of the shady, sneaky wolf.

Audrey smiled thinly, then went over to rejoin Chloe behind the curtain. The narrator soon ended the scene: "And her father had taken for his new wife a woman with two daughters of her own. All three were beautiful of face, but vile and black of heart."

You said it, sister.

Watching Audrey sewn to Chloe's hip like that, the glow of the stage lights blasting both of their faces into horrific contrasted angles, a vivid memory came rushing back at me: How unabashedly cruel Chloe had been at the start of school last year, when Audrey showed up on the first day with her adorable short haircut. Chloe calling Drew (me!) a retard and Audrey a retard-loving lesbian, claiming Audrey had chopped off her hair because she was mourning her break-up with Drew, suggesting Drew never even loved her, because check it out, yo, that girl was gone without a trace. Audrey looked so defeated. And now? Now she just looked . . . empty.

After the number, Mr. Wood wasn't happy, but he was

"happy enough" with the run-through to let us break for the night. Kris leapt off stage like in *Dirty Dancing*, into the arms of his very new, very cute (older) boyfriend Rooster, whom he met I don't really know where, come to think of it, but whose mere presence in rehearsal seemed to make Kris positively buoyant. Seeing them embrace so passionately, Kris hugging another boy while wearing a dress in front of everybody, made me jolt with concern for them. I instinctually scanned the room, in case anybody was about to jump them or drop a piano from the rafters and leave them in a crushed, phobic splat.

Then I realized this was the theater, not varsity football, where Jason and his douche-jockeys wouldn't waste a second flexing in the mirror before pounding Rooster and Kris into two thin, glittery crepes if they caught even a glimpse of their gay on display. Here, nobody seemed to give a rat's ass. And for a moment, I felt good. Happy that I'd forgone the traditional route and forged into more freak-hospitable territory.

But then I watched as Chloe threw her expensive European backpack over a shoulder and tried to sidestep the boys, making a face like she was smelling broccoli that had gone off. "Get a room," she slurred, before she marched out of the auditorium, pulling her loud, ginormous key ring out of her even more loud and ginormous designer purse. *Size queen*, I thought to myself, just as Kris scooted over, still in his dress.

"Kimmycakes," Kris said, pulling Rooster by the hand, "I told you about Rooster?"

"Not everything about him," I said cheekily.

"You're *flawless*," Rooster gushed to me, taking my hand and kissing it.

"I like what you've done with your boobsicles," Kris snarked, elbowing toward the green paint. "They definitely needed more attention drawn to them."

"You going to take a spin on the Carousel with us this weekend?" Rooster broke in, Kris hanging off his arm like a love-struck macaque.

"Can't," I said. "My father practically sentenced me to seven years on the chain gang for sneaking out there last time."

Kris pulled an exaggerated sad face, his plump red lower lip sticking all the way out. "Come on, boooo."

"If she says she can't, then she can't," Rooster piped in. "Boundaries much?"

"Yeah," I said, "listen to this man. That's healthy."

"What is this word, *boundaries*?" Kris queried in a faux-European accent, and we all giggled just as Audrey walked by, glancing at us the way a single person does when a group of people are cutting up loudly about some seemingly inside joke.

"Good night," I said brightly to her as she passed.

"Yeah, 'night," she mumbled quickly, and sped by.

"Gurrrl, you got it, you got it bad," Kris crooned, loud. So loud that I shushed him, because I was pretty sure Audrey could hear.

"No I don't."

"Oh, you do."

"Not anymore."

Kris studied me like a doctor trying to settle on a diagnosis. "Whatevah," he concluded. "We're off to do bad things to each other."

"Please don't tell me that."

"Too late!" Kris chirped, then skipped away, Rooster

staying behind just long enough to hug me goodbye, green paint be damned.

"I'm glad he has a friend like you," he said as he broke the embrace. "Kids in high school can be so cruel and dumb."

"You think?"

Rooster smiled, then trotted after Kris, who was miming looking at his watch and tapping his foot impatiently. As I turned, I noticed Audrey lingering in the wings. She was staring straight at me.

CHANGE 3-DAY 81

I hate that fracking stuffed chicken.

The stupid, useless, uncooperative chicken that refuses to act even a teeny bit chicken-like. I have one week to make the prop seem like it's running across the stage instead of being dragged like a toddler's blanket. Seems simple enough. But no. It either bounces across the stage comically, or is lifelessly towed, or gets stuck on the floor so that when I reel it from the other side of the stage, it springs ten feet into the air, more often than not hitting one of my carefully painted trees, or knocking over the cardboard Milky-White cow, which is comedy, sure, but not the sort of comic relief Mr. Wood is after.

"No one wants to be upstaged by a chicken, Miss Kim," he told me last chicken-fail.

"Got it, Mr. Wood."

Thank goodness I have Michelle Hu, science goddess (which she jokes is really the only stereotypically "Asian thing" about her), to help me navigate the physics of chicken propulsion.

"I think it's going to be about the friction," she posits when I present the problem to her after school.

"That's what *she* said."

"Har har har," Michelle cracks, as she turns the stuffed chicken every which way in her hands, really considering the conundrum I put to her, like if she solves it, the universe as we know it will become a better place—and for me, it will.

"Gotta figure a way to reduce the drag, or at least control it, so with a continuous tug, its velocity is kept at a more constant rather than variable rate."

"My thoughts exactly," I say.

"I think I can do this. My mom has some stuff in the garage I can use," she goes on, still pondering. "Mind if I take her home? Alter her a bit? Nothing obvious."

"Like Monsanto?"

"Less insidious. But yeah."

"Genetic engineer away."

"Shoot, dinner's in twenty," Michelle says, checking her digital watch and stuffing the chicken into her backpack. "I'm really glad you decided to join the ACC. I think you're going to have fun."

On that front, Michelle was mostly right. I did have fun at the Asian Cultural Club dinner. The spotlight was on South Asia this month, so the venue was Punjab Palace in the mall. It wasn't Fun with a capital F, but it was definitely lowercase material. Lowercase because while Amy, Adelle, Christine, Sarita, and (another) Kim, plus Henry (the only guy brave enough to hang) were all cool and kind and friendly, and we laughed a lot and the food was decent, and nobody was throwing shade at anybody, I couldn't help feeling like the imposter I am.

It was like I was back at the "black kids table" all over again. Oh yes, I'm the great pretender. Tracy would say I'm not pretending anything. That once you inhabit a V, and the world responds to you as that V, you are that V, period. She has a point, I guess. But being Asian, or black, or differently abled, or anything outside the Barbie–Ken doll norm for one year isn't exactly the same as being that way your whole life. As John Legend would say, *I can change*. And my new friends who are feeling me because they see themselves in me, well, they don't know that this is like an outfit I can ultimately take off if I choose to. And if I do choose to? What does that say about them?

There they were accepting and taking me in over veggie samosas and pakoras, but only because of what they *thought* I was. Not anything on the inside, just this general, regional familiarity. In truth, I actually couldn't relate to a lot of the stuff they were saying, not any of the familial or cultural in-jokes. And to front and agree and laugh along would make me feel like a big ol' racist. (I bet Tracy never felt like a racist in her entire life. She probably went way overboard and did accents and crap—all in the name of finding her best self.)

I know I'm not living in some refugee camp in Turkey, or emptying Porta-Potties at seven dollars an hour for a living, but all this circular thinking is making me crazy, like a hamster in a Habitrail. Around me is all clear plastic that makes it look like freedom's right on the other side, but ultimately, part of me knows I'll never escape.

I guess in a lot of ways, I'm still a white boy who grew up outside of New York City and loves to skate. At least, that's my history. I guess that is the million-dollar Changer question: what matters most, the past you've been given or the future you choose?

To which I say a definitive . . .

For now, I guess it's cool to have the Asians of Central High on my side. Because at least for the year I'll have a group I "fit" into. Even if I actually don't fit.

What do I know for sure?

1. I am what I am on the inside.
2. And I am what I am on the outside (for now).
3. I fit with Audrey.

I can say *that* again. I fit with Audrey as Drew. And I fit with her as Oryon.

Do I fit with her as Kim? H. E. double hockey sticks NO. But who can tell? We haven't even hung out. Maybe we will. Somehow. If the core of her could reemerge and connect with the core of me. (That sounds gross. Who am I now, Turner the Lives Coach?)

Why do I still care about her so much?

Because you do, Kris would say. The "why" hardly matters.

Which is good advice for this whole Changer gig.

CHANGE 3-DAY 87

I don't have more than a minute to Chronicle. I'm so weary. It's eleven thirty on a school night, and I just got back home.

Overall: the play's opening night went pretty well, considering.

Kris was amazing, didn't flub a single line, fudge a note, miss a mark.

Everybody else? Not so much.

Even Mia, who seems like she should already have her own show on the Disney Channel, tripped up in scene two: "The cow as white as blood, the cape as red as milk," to which DJ broke character momentarily as he tried to stifle a laugh, which made the audience laugh, and the rest of us backstage laugh ... until we saw Mr. Wood's "disappointment face," which whipped all our butts back into line for the rest of the show.

Michelle's chicken rig worked beautifully in scene three, but I screwed up in the finale, when I didn't have the pillow prop readily available (for Mia to stuff under her dress to look pregnant). We grabbed somebody's down parka and balled it up and used that instead, and nobody was the wiser (even if Mia looked like she was about to give birth to a Patagonia store onstage).

Just two more shows. And then the nightly stress of being the scenic, prop, and costume wrangler with everybody relying on me to make *them* look better will be safely in my rearview ...

I'm so tired, I don't even know what I just Chronicled. I'm going to have a glass of warm milk as white as blood, and then I'm going to pass out in bed and wake up and do it all over again tomorrow. Kim Cruz out.

CHANGE 3–DAY 89

The audience was on their feet, Kris, Mia, and DJ taking their final bows out in front of the rest of the cast. Grocery-store bouquets of roses and baby's breath landed onstage, seemingly being tossed out of a black void in the audience, Kris gathering the bunches up and stacking them in the crook of his elbow like they were all intended for him. (They kind of were.)

Then the entire cast pointed to Mr. Wood, who happened to be standing in front of me stage left. The audience roared even louder, but Mr. Wood was not interested in going out there, despite the unambiguous encouragement. He was waving his hands and making the "cut it off" gesture with a flat hand in front of his neck, but the cast wasn't relenting, the audience wasn't piping down, and so there was nothing left to do but for me to (gently) push him out from behind the curtains and onto the stage.

Which I did.

And which he did not appreciate, judging by the *We're gonna talk about this later* look I got as he shuffled onstage.

Nevertheless, it was kind of a cool moment to see, Mr. Wood surrounded by the whole cast and Kris presenting him the largest, most over-the-top bouquet while the audience stayed on their feet clapping, hooting, hollering, and generally bathing everybody onstage with mad love—until the curtain fell.

Then the whole cast hugged, slapped hands, pumped

fists, acted out all the various personal celebration styles. Other "support" crew members like me were out there too. But something held me back. I didn't feel like joining the congratulatory riot. As has become my routine of late, I stayed on the outskirts of the pack, watching everybody's joy and sense of accomplishment, while trying to figure out my feelings from afar.

I peeked from behind the curtain to see if I could spot Destiny, who promised she'd come to closing night. I couldn't immediately find her, but what I did see in that auditorium kind of bowled me over. Something that, come to think of it, I don't really see very often: a crystalline moment. Before everybody started whipping out their phones to read their e-mails, scan their texts, check their stocks, swipe left or right, scroll through cute "unlikely pals" animal videos, there was a brief, still window, where I saw a group of people who were relaxed and content, no anxiety, distraction, no need to feverishly connect with anything but what just happened in that room. It was as if everybody there felt (just for a flash) that maybe they truly *aren't* alone in this world. Like Kris and DJ (as Cinderella and the baker) had just sung: *No one is alone. Sometimes people leave you halfway through the wood. Others may deceive you. You decide what's good . . . Just remember. Someone is on your side. No one is alone . . .*

It made me realize that that's what good art is capable of. Connection. Making us *feel*. Reminding us that others feel too. Even if its effects seem to last shorter and shorter times. I mean, back in the day—like way back in the day, in the seventeenth century—if the Globe Theatre presented *Hamlet*, everybody in town would see the play. It would be all anyone talked about, thought about, for like a year. The play took over everything, because there was nothing else to take it over.

Nowadays, whole Shakespearean dramas play out across our Twitter feeds and Snapchats in a single instant. How are people supposed to be affected by one amazing thing that's meant to move us, when *everything* is trying to move us every second of every day?

That's what I was wondering as I stood there, hiding behind the curtain, part of neither audience nor cast, observer of both. Luckily, before I sank too deep into the "I don't fit in; what's wrong with me" quicksand, I spotted Destiny by the rear right exit, pointing to the bathroom and gesturing, like, *Meet you out in the lobby post-pee.*

A second later, Kris screeched, "AFTEEERRRRR-PARTY!" behind me, yanking my attention back into the microcosm of our theater world, where nobody seemed to want to let the moment die. One of the sound techs passed around a stack of flyers with the address of the wrap party, which was going to be at somebody's parents' house about fifteen minutes from school.

"Yes, yes, yes. By all means, celebrate a show well done. But let's everybody break it down first," Mr. Wood called out. "Nobody's leaving until all the jobs are completed. You can finish up on Monday after school, but do what you agreed to do before you exit, stage left."

People complied, and as they did a giant smile broke across Mr. Wood's face (something I don't think I'd seen since he first heard Kris's audition months ago). "Good job, everybody. I mean that," he added, and it seemed like he was trying not to cry. "I'm—I'm proud of you. And—" here he was getting really choked up "—thank you pets for making my job so easy."

An hour later, we're all at this kid who played the wolf,

Joey's house. It's a medium-sized, historic-looking house in a cool neighborhood, and his parents are present at the party, though they're giving us space and hanging out in their upstairs bedroom, only checking in downstairs when something crashes (the requisite broken lamp) or to make sure the snack foods are replenished (pigs in a blanket, pizza pockets, hummus, and chips).

It's not wholesale chaos, but it's totally fun. A lot of kids are being loud and performative Broadway babies, but in truth it's kind of awesome. The Cure's *Greatest Hits* album (actually on vinyl) is blasting through two large wood-encased speakers, and sure, a few people are drinking, and a few more are smoking (both tobacco and other stuff) outside, but it's totally chill: nobody is being a douche, nobody is acting rapey, nobody is being bigoted or otherwise hateful. There are, not uncoincidentally, zero football players present. Which is to say, it is hands down the best party I've been to since starting high school at Central.

Soon enough, though, Chloe sidles through the front door with an air of disdain, as if she were stepping into a crack den, with Audrey and a couple of the Chloettes in tow. "Where's the keg?" she loudly asks, and when she is greeted with shrugs and general indifference, she announces, "OVER IT," snaps her fingers, turns on her wedge Skechers, and marches right back out the door they all just came through, having spent a total of twenty seconds at what I can personally guarantee was the best thing going on in town—not to mention way more Audrey's style than any jock throw-down Chloe was about to drag her to.

I could tell Audrey wanted to stay by the way her face lit up when she heard the music, not that Audrey is my responsibility anymore. (Was she ever?) I watch the door shut behind them, and then "The Love Cats" comes on, and it actually makes me feel like dancing. I grab Destiny and we shuffle into the TV room, where most of the cast, including Kris and Rooster, are already jumping around in unison to the jazzy *Ba, ba, ba, ba, ba, ba, ba ba da, baaa, ba bop bop ba ba* chorus.

As we're pogoing beside one another (me noting how I seem to be getting more respect across the board since I've brought the magical, drop-dead-gorgeous stranger with me), Destiny bounces closer and yells, "So what's the Baker's deal?" and juts a thumb toward the corner of the room in DJ's direction.

After a brief, inexplicable jealousy jag that dissipates as soon as it materializes, I yell back, "DJ! Senior! Politicized! King of spoken word! Really good guy!"

Destiny nods her head appraisingly, jokingly pats her hair, smoothes down her eyebrows, and heads in DJ's direction with an exaggerated hitch in her step.

"I want a swing like that on my back porch," Kris jokes, grinding his bony butt against mine as we watch Destiny go. She looks back over her shoulder, and I give an encouraging, jokey wink.

I watch the encounter unfold, the puzzle pieces fitting into place like a really good indie romance: DJ on an easy chair, one leg slung lazily over an armrest, enjoying the music, completely cool and in his own world. Destiny does a pass, sees if he looks up. He does. (Nobody doesn't.) But DJ doesn't lose his cool when it seems like she's paying him attention. Destiny takes another lap, says something that makes him laugh. Then he says something back that makes her laugh, and he sits up straight (to show more respect), offers her his seat, and when she refuses, he clears a place for her on the hearth beside him.

And they're off. Every time I eye-check the two of them, they look like they're having a blast. A real one. Not fake. One of them is always talking, the other either listening closely or laughing. It's easy. Makes sense. At least from the outside. Which, let's be honest here, is all that mattered in the second before either of them opened their mouth.

By this point I am sweaty and exhausted from dancing and decide to take a break.

"Five minutes," Kris yells, "then you're getting your jelly back on this dance floor!"

"It's an area rug," I say, pointing down, but I don't think he hears, because Rooster has pulled him closer, now that "Boys Don't Cry" has started.

I head to the kitchen, grab some water. I look over the hors d'oeuvres, but am too shy to eat anything because I don't feel like being stared at with judgey eyes. I feel this way for precisely five seconds before I say (out loud to nobody in particular), "Screw it," and pop a mini–hot dog into my mouth. It is so oily and salty good. The dough is sweet. I'm contemplating having another when Rapunzel's prince—a sophomore who actually looks like a prince, hard times for him—saunters in, still wearing his Elizabethan shirt and vest, though both are unbuttoned, so he is less Rapunzel prince than bachelorette-party-stripper prince.

"Those are good, huh?" he says, pulling a Coke out of the fridge.

"Yup," I mumble, still chewing.

"I had like a dozen earlier." He cracks the can open and takes a giant swig, tilting his head back and letting the soda barrel down his throat for a few gulps. So much that he exhales, "Aaaahhhh," after swallowing, just like in the commercials.

"Good job tonight!" I yell over the music after a few seconds.

"Thanks," he says, a little taken aback. "You too. Good job with the, uh, chicken."

Great. So that's what people think of me. I'm a proficient fake-chicken wrangler. Who gobbles pigs in a blanket. I'm like the farmer in the freaking dell.

"That probably wasn't easy to pull off," he says, bobbing his head.

"I love this song!" I yell suddenly.

He listens for a bit, then says, "It's not really true, though. Boys *do* cry." He chuckles to himself.

"Not as much as girls," I say.

"I guess."

And at that we're back to silence for a bit. I stand there convinced I have flaky pastry crumbs all over my cheek.

"Well—" he says, at the exact time I say, "So—"

I let him finish: "Well, I'm going to see what my buddy's doing."

"Yeah, totally," I say. "See you around."

And he's off.

I exhale, then pour myself some punch and glance into the various rooms off the kitchen. People are still singing like crazy in the den by the record player: "*I try to laugh about it. Cover it all up with lies. I try and laugh about it. Hiding the tears in my eyes.'Cause, boys don't cry.*"

In the living room, Kris and Rooster are now on the couch, tangled up in one another. I pop my head around the corner and glance over to where I last saw DJ and Destiny, but they're not there. I look to the deck, then the hallway, and suddenly Destiny catches my eye, waves me over.

"Deej, you know Kim, right?" she says, putting an arm around me.

"Yeah, of course," DJ says, ever the gentleman. "We haven't gotten the opportunity to talk a lot, but she's a cool chick, from what I've heard."

"She's *boss*," Destiny gushes, then mock punches DJ on the shoulder.

"You seem like a woman who would know," he says, laughing.

And . . . they are goners. I've never seen either of them like this before. Destiny is usually so chilly with potential suitors. And DJ is usually Mr. Smoove. (Not that DJ would know that I've ever seen him like *anything* before. *Hey, dude, I was there when you won the state slam championship last year. We got arrested for Shopping While Black together, remember? Yeah, that was me!*)

"Uh, I'll leave you two to it, then," I say, feeling acute third-wheel vibes.

DJ gently places a hand on my arm. "No, stay. Hang," he purrs sincerely.

"Yeah, hang," Destiny seconds, also seeming to mean it.

"So what's up?" DJ asks. "Who's the real Kim Cruz?"

"Yeah. No," I stammer, shutting that shizz down.

"Yeah, Kim, tell him who you *really* are," Destiny says with a devilish smile.

We both just start cracking up. At first DJ is confused, but then he joins in, snickering through his nose.

"You guys are too cute," he says, still laughing. "I see how this is gonna go. BFFs for real. PB&J. Can't have one without the other."

My heart double-beats. Not that I have feelings for him or anything. Or that I'm flattered, not *that* way. It's just that

I feel suddenly human somehow. I'm not on the outside peering in. I'm in the room where it happens. I'm part of the party.

ZZZZZZZT—ZZZZZZZT, I'm interrupted. My butt is vibrating.

"Excuse me," I say to the two of them, as I pull out my phone and click on my texts. They go back to giving each other 100 percent, cut-the-right-wire-to-disarm-the-bomb focus as the trance-like beat for "Close to Me" surges behind them. I start reading . . .

Mom: *CALL NOW.*

Mom: *Where are you?*

Dad: *You need to call home right now. Try Mom's cell.*

I head for the screened porch, Destiny shouting after me, "Everything okay?"

I wave her off, slide open the glass door, and am assaulted with smoke as I dial Mom's cell. No answer. I try Dad's.

"Where are you?" he answers.

"At the cast party. Why? What?"

"I need the exact address so Mom can come get you."

"Dad, you're scaring me. What's wrong?"

"It's Nana. She had a stroke."

CHANGE 3-DAY 90

Nana is unconscious. Hooked up to all sorts of beeping contraptions, IV bags, tubes. The machine is breathing for her. We stayed up all night at the hospital, and Mom just dropped me back home so I can walk Snoopy, wash and pack some clothes for Dad, and maybe get a little rest.

But I don't want to rest. How could I? I flip open my laptop, check to see who's on. Destiny's light is green, but as soon as I notice, she's already pinging me.

"Are you okay?" she asks when the video comes on. "I was calling you all night."

"It's my grandma, she had a stroke," I say, my eyes welling.

"Oh my God, I'm so sorry." Pain and concern are visible on her face. "Is she going to be okay?"

"I don't know," I say, trying to hold it together.

"Can I do anything?"

"No. I don't know."

"Can I bring you anything, or drive you anywhere, or . . ." She trails off.

"How was your night?" I ask, wiping my eyes with the back of my hand.

"Really?" she replies. "You don't want to hear that noise right now."

"No, I do. I want to hear," I say. "Anything besides *intubation, intracranial pressure, angiography, comatose* . . . I need a distraction."

"I dunno." But there's clearly something she wants to share.

"TELL ME," I say. "*What?*"

After a respectful pause, giving me ample opportunity to change my mind, she announces: "I kissed him."

"DJ?"

"He's kind of amazing."

"I know. He was one of my best friends last year," I say, feeling the jealousy monster lurking once more. "Was it good?"

"Beyond good."

"I need to know everything."

"Ew," she says. "There was just some kissing and a little moderate-to-heavy groping. And . . ."

"And?"

"I saw it. I had the vision."

"OMG. What was it?"

"This feels weird. Should I be telling you this? Is there any rule about that?" she asks, and my mind searches through what I've retained of *The Changers Bible*. "I never had a Changer friend to share this with before."

"Who cares," I say. "What did you see?"

"Well," she starts, "it's good. He's, like . . . He's going to be a professor or philosopher or something. I saw him speaking about politics in front of a giant crowd of people. There were reporters there, and TV cameras. I think it was at a giant university, or maybe some venue in Washington? I don't know. But a lot of people are going to hear what dude's got to say."

"Did you blank out when it was happening?" I ask. "When I had the visions, well, only the two of them, I like, went somewhere else, and it was really hard to stay present and not have the people I was kissing think I was a total weirdo and not into what we were doing."

"Uh, I have a lot of practice avoiding that."

"Right, of course. What with your being a slut whore," I say, smiling.

"Exactly," she says, smiling back. "This feels wrong to talk about, when your family is in such a bad place."

"It's *okay*," I say. Though nothing ever truly feels okay these days.

"Are you sure I can't help somehow?"

"No. It's just nice to talk."

"You have to dish about DJ from last year," she says. "You know, later, when your grandma's better."

"Will do," I promise, praying there is a later like that.

CHANGE 3-DAY 91

Nana hasn't woken up. Skipped school today.

CHANGE 3-DAY 92

Nana still hasn't woken up. Mom and Dad made me go to school today.

CHANGE 3-DAY 93

The doctor said there was minimal activity in Nana's brain. Somebody even used the word *vegetative*.

Mom was going to let me stay home today, but Dad made me go to school.

CHANGE 3-DAY 95

I don't even want to Chronicle this. Because if I think it, if I actually put it down in words that get locked away somewhere in the mainframe at Changers Central, then it'll become history, it'll be on the record, it'll make it real. But I don't want it to be true, so I just won't think it into being.

Like that matters.

Like anything does.

. . .

Nana's dead. Gone.

This time forever.

Another person I love is dead. *Just like that*. Another person who loved me. Knew me. Another black cloud will follow me around forever, because no matter who I become, they won't be there to see it happen. I am a tree falling in the woods. I am a selfish baby. I am angry and I am alone and I don't care about anything anymore because it all leads to pain.

No matter who I was or how I looked or acted, Nana always saw me as a thing of beauty. She believed I was good. And because she believed, I could too. Her faith in me gave me faith in myself.

Where will I find faith now?

CHANGE 3-DAY 96

When Changers die, we are all supposed to be flooded with peace. That is the official Changers line. That there is no true death. That our energy travels, merrily flitting along from one life or manifestation to another. No purgatory here. No sad times. Just a passing from this form into that form after a full life of serving the world as the person you chose to be.

To which I call everlasting, eternal bullshit.

I am not flooded with peace. I hope Nana is, but I remain suspect about that as well. Who is to say? It's not like her essence is going to show up in the body of a toddler, seek me out at a playground, and say, *See? No harm, no foul. All good here.*

I mean, maybe that could happen. I've seen weirder things in my life. But it hasn't happened yet, and while I wait to see my Nana resurrected and sent on yet another epic spiritual journey, I remain pissed and resentful that she isn't still on this one with me.

In keeping with the Changer death-is-no-biggie philosophy, Nana, like all Changers who "graduate beings," is to be celebrated, not mourned, in a quiet, positive, respectful gathering. No tears, no drama, not even a wake. If it were up to me, Nana would have a jazz funeral, like the ones in New Orleans, where a uniformed band marches behind her casket, horns blaring out "Just a Closer Walk with Thee," then happier, snazzier tunes as the ceremony progresses, and a second line forms, and everyone hollers and wails and dances and sweats like their pants are on fire.

But no. None of that for Changers. It would be deemed inappropriate. Disrespectful to the other billions of lives that have come and gone before hers. *In the many we are one*, in life and in death. Along with a lack of pomp and circumstance, Changers bury their bodies old school. That is, no draining the fluids, no applying superglue or pancake makeup and embalming Nana with carcinogenic chemicals so she can be "viewed" by friends and family one last time, and no burying her inside a giant steel reinforced coffin, or concrete vault, which supposedly stave off decomposition longer. No cremation, either, which requires a ton of fuel and releases even more carbon and mercury into the atmosphere, not to mention leaves you with material that doesn't exactly replenish the earth from which it came. (Even if it might've been nice to scatter Nana's ashes somewhere she loved, like along the coast of Florida, or even upstate New York, where she raised Dad when his father was still alive.)

So, following Changer tradition, we had a small gathering at our house this morning to honor the completion of Nana's current slate of lives. Tracy and Mr. Crowell came, and Destiny too, to keep me company. Mom's brother and his wife, Uncle Troy and Aunt Misty, flew in from Atlanta. And a friend of Nana's came up last minute from Florida, an old guy who looked like a bald Santa, and who told me to call him Milty—and who apparently had been (mostly unsuccessfully) wooing Nana for years when they lived in the Pickwick Place retirement community together.

Dad said something bland and extremely brief about his mom, his hands starting to tremble slightly at the end. I sat just far enough away that I couldn't really hear what he was saying. When he composed himself, he told guests (speaking more loudly) to enjoy the spread, and to fuel up for the afternoon. People laughed, hugged, ate, and drank. Benign classical music streamed in the background. Nobody was dressed up. I basically camped out in the window seat with Destiny, and stared at the chair Nana used to sit in when she drank her instant coffee. Her wheelchair was still in the foyer, folded into itself and leaning against the wall.

Destiny kept trying to cheer me up—"She's in a better place? Yeah, not really. I know"—but I just wasn't feeling it. I appreciated her trying though. Tracy came over too, just sat beside me, silent for once. But nothing, nobody, could make me less depressed. Not even the dog.

After the short reception, Destiny had to get home because her family was leaving town for the holidays, and the rest of us piled into two cars and drove an hour to this property adjacent to a nature preserve (not too far from Changers Central), where the Life Cycles Changers burial service met us with Nana's body inside a nondescript-looking electric van. Next to the truck was a barely dug oval hole in the ground, with a bunch of shovels sticking out of it like toothpicks on a platter of hors d'oeuvres.

We all started digging out the mound under which Nana, or at least her body, would spend the rest of eternity. Well, at least until microbes finished converting her body into compost. It wasn't scoop a couple shovelfuls of dirt and then you're done, like you see in the movies. A man and a woman from Life Cycles pitched in, but it took pretty much all of us working in nonstop rotating shifts to finish the hole (even though it didn't have to be as deep as a traditional grave).

Mr. Crowell took off his button-down shirt and dug in

a white T-shirt and khakis. Tracy even changed into pants (*pants!*) for the occasion. When her brow beaded up with sweat from laboring, Mr. Crowell gave her a cloth handkerchief from his back pocket to wipe herself. Dad seemed to be the only one who didn't take a break. He said nothing the whole time, just did the labor, machinelike.

After an hour of digging, the Life Cycle dude said it was good, and opened the rear of the van, where Nana was inside a biodegradable wicker casket, almost like a structured burlap sack, which was much smaller in size than the usual coffin. It was, in fact, just a little bigger than Nana herself.

Dad pulled the casket out first, and we all joined in the further it slid out of the van. Soon all of our hands were lifting Nana and walking her over to the edge before gently lowering her into the hole we'd all just worked so hard to dig. She looked like a cocoon once she was a few feet under us. Nobody said anything. We all just stood there and looked into the hole, thinking our own thoughts, panting and sweating a little, even though it was kinda chilly outside. Mom hooked an arm around my waist and rested her head on my shoulder.

After a couple minutes of towering over her like this, Dad quietly picked up a shovel and started stabbing the dirt pile next to the grave and backfilling the hole. I don't think I'll ever forget the shriek of the shovel and then the slapping sound of the dirt crumbling over the top of the wicker casket. Dad did about five solo scoops before we all grabbed our shovels and joined in.

My back hurt, my feet hurt, my hands were developing blisters, but I wasn't going to stop. *Scoop-drop-scoop-drop*. The harder I worked, the less I felt like crying. *Scoop-drop-scoop-drop*. I just kept shoveling harder and harder, this time not taking a break either, working beside Dad until Nana's grave was piled a little higher than the earth around it.

It took way less time to cover her up than it did to dig the hole for her.

It's after dinner now, and I can hear Mom and Dad arguing in the kitchen. Then I hear Snoopy's nails clicking against the wood floor as he scuttles down the hall toward my room and noses through the door. He jumps on my bed, and I hug him, kiss him a dozen times on the head between his eye and ear. Just about the softest place in the world.

He endures this for a little bit before I release him, and he curls himself into a ball at the end of my bed and exhales. I envy him (all dogs, really). It must be nice not to know the specifics of what's wrong, even though I'm sure he can sense something amiss in the house, the absence of Nana, with me, Mom, and Dad shuffling around like zombies since she left—and now, the yelling.

"I don't care about your rules anymore!" I hear Mom scream, as I decide it's probably best to close the door to give them their privacy. And by "their privacy," I mean I don't want to hear whatever it is they're arguing about. It's weird. I can't remember them fighting so much before this year.

"They're not *my* rules," Dad says, like he's talking to a child. "These systems are for the benefit of every single human on this planet."

"A little lofty, don't you think?" Mom snaps back. "Did you ever stop to consider the master plan of your master race isn't actually effective?"

"Goddamnit!" Dad yells then, more out of control. "You know you don't believe that. When are the two of you going to stop being so selfish?"

"I'm giving it to her."

Mom begins angry-marching down the hallway toward my room then, so I pull the covers over my head and pretend to be sleeping. I can hear the door creak open, and picture her staring at me for a few seconds while deciding whether I'm really asleep. I hear her quietly walk toward my bed, pet Snoopy, and then set something on the desk next to me. She turns out the light, closes the door.

I wait until I can hear her go into their bedroom. It sounds like Dad is still in the kitchen, likely at his laptop doing Changers Council work. It's all he does anymore.

I lie still another minute for good measure, then get up, click on the light, and look for whatever it is Mom has left on the desk. It's an envelope, with *Kim* written in Nana's handwriting on the outside. I grab it, but stop short of ripping it open. It's been a crap day already. What if this is more bad news?

Curiosity wins. I go ahead and break the seal, noticing that it seems like the glue's already been unstuck before.

A black-and-white photograph tumbles out onto my blanket. I pick it up, hold it close. It takes awhile to focus and adjust to the light, but a face comes through, clear as can be. It kind of looks like Chase. As in, *my* Chase. Only . . . *what in the . . . ?*

The photo seems to be taken right around the same time as the other photo Nana gave me a couple years ago. I look back into the envelope, and there's also a letter, dated a few days before Nana had her stroke, the handwriting crooked:

Sweet Angel,
   I don't know how much time I have left here with

you. I really wanted to see you through your Cycle and be there at your Forever Ceremony, but it's looking like that isn't going to be possible. I can feel the days slipping away and while I don't love it, there is nothing to be done, so I may as well enjoy what I can while I'm still here.

With or without me, I know you are going to find your way and make the right decision. You are an incredibly special person, and I'm proud to have known you through a handful of your lives. I could not have asked for more from a grandchild.

The reason I'm writing you this letter is because I wanted to share something important with you. Your father didn't want me to tell you, but I'm too old for statutes and protocol, and besides, I am still his mother and he is not in charge, much as he'd like to think he is.

What I hope to do is offer you some comfort. Which is more important than rules any day. I couldn't help but notice how sad you've been since your friend Chase passed. It was a terrible thing that happened, and I can see you tearing yourself up with guilt. That, however, is a useless emotion, a giant waste of time and energy. Guilt serves no one and changes nothing. If you don't take my word for it, I'm confident you'll discover that on your own someday.

Guilt is especially useless in your case, because your friend Chase isn't truly gone forever.

I suppose they don't want you to know this because it might change how you act during your Cycle, or influence your decision about your Mono, but in actuality there is a system, a method to all this madness.

Your Chase was a recycled version of many other Chases throughout the centuries. If you take a look at the enclosed photo, you will see that I was the Chase V for a year during my Cycle. And when I didn't choose Chase as my Mono, he was released back into the universe, free to be inhabited by a new Changer just beginning his or her Cycle at some point after me.

Which means that Chase, as an identity, will return. That identity will go on and on, until somebody selects it as his Mono, and completes a lifetime as that V.

I'm sure this is confusing, my love. And more than a little unnerving. I'm still debating whether I should tell you even as I'm sitting here writing. But it's no accident you felt so drawn to this boy, and likely no accident that he protected you the way he did. And it is no wonder you feel his loss so keenly. But you don't have to. Chase will live on. Somewhere. Somehow.

And one day, eventually, we will all know what it's like to be somebody else. To live as another, feel their pain, their joy, make their mistakes, celebrate their triumphs. It really is a gift we've been given to see and experience so much. A gift we must share. Because it does matter, Kim.

What you do matters.

Imagine how different the world is going to be once we reach that place. When there is no difference left to fear. No outsiders. No "other."

I'm not afraid of leaving because I have so much hope for that future—your future.

So, I'll leave you to it, Angel.

If you're reading this, I've likely passed. But please

don't be sad I'm gone. I'm exactly where I'm supposed to be now. And so are you.

I love you more than you'll ever know,

Nana (and Chase, and Emily, and Jamey, and Lynette)

CHANGE 3-DAY 106

For the curious, here's what the Internet says are signs of major or clinical depression:

Fatigue and/or loss of energy every day
CHECK
Feelings of worthlessness or guilt almost every day
CHECK
Insomnia or hypersomnia
CHECK (the second)
Diminished interest or pleasure in almost all activities, almost every day
CHECK
Recurring thoughts of death
(Not mine, anyway)
Weight loss or gain
(Betch, please)

I've basically had all of these for the last two weeks (maybe longer). Am I depressed? Let me ask Dr. Internet.

Common causes of major or clinical depression:
Grief from losing a loved one
(Try two)
Social isolation
CHECK
Moving

CHECK
Personal conflicts in relationships
CHECK
Major life changes
(Where do I even start?)

Hey, Changers Council, a tip from me to you: in addition to your *Bible*, you need to publish your own mental health evaluation guide. Because far as I can tell, every Changer is going to tick hella boxes on these Static forms. Major life changes? What would I even tell a shrink about that? *Well, I've swapped gender three times, changed races twice, discovered I'm tasked with making the world a shiny, happy place for all of humanity, and, oh yeah, I'm being bullied at school for being fat. You got a prescription for that?*

If I'm honest with myself, my life has been a blur since closing night of the play. Mom is "closely monitoring" the grief situation, and I love her, but nobody should have their mom for a therapist. During the whole holiday break, I've essentially slept 75 percent of the time, occasionally waking up to eat, followed by overwhelming feelings of guilt and sadness, and then more sleep. I have no energy. I care about nothing. I mean, I do *abstractly*. I care about Nana, and Chase, and Snoopy, and starving refugees. The basics. But my teeth haven't seen a toothbrush in days, and my wardrobe of Goth chic has devolved into genuine ambivalence. I could probably stand a shower. Or so I've been told.

Here's the conversation that goes on when I do "join the living," as Dad passive-aggressively puts it every time I manage to drag my grubbiness into the kitchen in between sleeping jags:

"How bad does this have to get," he asks me, but it's

really directed at Mom, "before we start thinking about sending you back to the RRR?"

"This is what grief looks like, Will. You're sick of dealing with it, so we're just going to ship her away to become someone else's problem?" Mom counters, as though I'm not there. (Which I'm not.)

"This feels like something a professional would be better at dealing with," Dad clarifies, trying to sound measured, though his irritation seeps through.

"I *am* a freaking professional!" Mom shrieks, glaring at Dad like she wants to stab a rusty fork into his skull.

Meantime, I just sit there silently eating my cereal, a bagel and cream cheese, burnt toast with peanut butter, a cut-up apple, or whatever it is I've somehow mustered the energy to prepare, before I toss most of it into the garbage and head back to my bedroom to go back to sleep.

CHANGE 3-DAY 108

Destiny keeps bugging me to come out with her and DJ tonight. There's a twenty-four-hour New Year's Eve–into-Day screening of black-and-white noir films from the 1940s in downtown Nashville. Something the old me (well, the *new* old me) would have really dug. But now? Under these circumstances—i.e., having to watch my two friends fall deeper in love by the mushy minute, and given my busy sleeping/corporeal neglect schedule—I'm just not sure I want to ring in the new year sitting ringside at everyone else's joy.

Nor am I sure I could even physically leave the house at this point. The thought of it is unbearable. It's like I'm made of molten lead. Every movement feels like bench-pressing a Buick. I only showered this morning because Dad threatened to take away my laptop if I didn't, my laptop streaming being the only thing that puts me back to sleep or brings me any comfort, my glowing drug of choice.

Mom invited Tracy and Mr. Crowell over for dinner and to "watch the ball drop."

"The ball has already dropped, Mom," I say when she comes into my room. But she is not having it, as she flings open the curtains to allow the last of the low winter light to violently assault me in my bed.

HISSSSS, I recoil like a rabid vampire bat.

"Funny," she says, picking up some dirty dishes and clothes.

"I'm not trying to be funny," I say.

"Well, you need to come out and make an appearance, at the very least. Even if you don't stay up with us until midnight."

Which I don't. Stay up till midnight with them. Nor even make an appearance, unless you count floating down the hall like a ghost, trying not to see or be seen by any of them. Of course, Tracy is like a purebred spaniel, and the minute she hears the floorboard creak, she whips her head around and tracks me to the kitchen.

"Hi, stranger!" she chirps.

"Some might say you're the strange one," I say, popping a bag of popcorn in the microwave and pressing *Start*.

"That's not what I meant."

"No duh."

"You're not being very nice," she says.

"Sorry."

"You don't seem sorry."

"Whatever."

Tracy just stares me down while the microwave fan blows hot air at my face.

"Is this because I'm with Mr. Crowell?"

I stifle a cruel laugh.

"I can see how it might look like I abandoned you. But I haven't. I'm here," she adds.

"Oh, you're here alright."

Tracy sighs, regroups. "How can we help you when you won't let us?" she asks, completely sincere. She seems genuinely upset, helpless even. I can relate.

"It's not you. It's me."

"Do you want me to make you an appointment with Turner?" she suggests.

This time I laugh out loud. "Ah. No."

"Please, Kim. I want to do something. I need to do something. Geez, I'm your Touchstone. It's my job to help you navigate all this."

For a second I feel for her. She really got the booty end of the Changer stick with me. I'm sure she thought that at some point during my V's we'd be braiding each other's hair or making handmade soaps in the garage, and instead she's dealing with a Changer who was abducted, then plunged into a one-two punch of grief, not to mention one who isn't going to win any congeniality contests any time soon.

"Don't worry about it. I'll be fine," I lie.

Beeeep, the microwave is done.

"Jumbo pop?" I ask, pushing the steaming bag in her direction. "I changed my mind."

Tracy comes over to give me a hug, but I dodge her, dump the popcorn in the trash, and slink back down the hall, feeling my horribleness bubble up inside me in a whole new way.

It's getting late, but I can still hear the four of them chitter-chattering in the TV room. According to the digital clock on my desk, it's three minutes to midnight. It's dark in my room, but I've left my blinds open. After a bit, I can hear Mom outside my door, lightly tapping.

"It's almost time. Happy New Year, Kim," she says softly. "I love you."

"I love you too," I manage, praying she doesn't come in.

I listen. She goes back to the TV room. Two minutes to midnight. I scooch up on my pillows, stare out the window into the blackness. And wait.

One minute.

Waiting, waiting, waiting, watching the clock. And . . . another year clicks past. As another has begun. Just like that.

Not that Static years mean that much to me. Lord knows I'm eagerly counting down the days until C4–D1. Two hundred and fifty-seven days to go, to be precise. I'm keeping track on the calendar on my desk; every check is one day less I have to be Kim Cruz in this world.

BAP, BAP. The noise makes me jump. Gunshots.

BAP, BAP, BAP. A few more shots fire. I have a PTSD moment where I'm sure the Abiders are outside my window, coming to slaughter my family and drag me back to their Changer torture chamber. Then I realize it's just some partiers shooting into the sky to celebrate the new year. What idiots. Don't they know those bullets are going to come plummeting back down to earth even faster than when they were shot? They aren't going to vanish into thin air. They have to land somewhere.

CHANGE 3-DAY 110

For some reason I felt like going outside today. No idea why. It just happened.

So I walked out of my room and went to the foyer, pulled some boots on, leashed up Snoopy, yelled, "I'll be back soon!" and opened the front door.

Mom came rushing out, Dad behind her. They were looking at me like Victor Frankenstein when his monster first reanimated.

"So great to see you up!" Mom says, overly cheerful.

"Where you off to?" Dad asks at the same time, trying to be nonchalant, for fear of scaring me back into my cave.

"Don't forget this," Mom says, handing me a lavender-scented plastic poop bag.

Ah yes, a tote for the crap of life. I'll take two.

Snoopy tugs me out the door, and the minute the cold pricks the skin on my cheeks, I reconsider my big outdoor plan. Winter is the worst. Still, Snoopy has business to do, so I press on down the block, letting him stop and sniff hedges, signposts, curbs, crumpled cans, way more frequently than I usually allow. He lifts his leg on a mailbox. Then a bush. Then he circles, squats, but . . . false alarm. We cross the street, and he suddenly cops a squat and poops, I pick it up, tie a knot, and hold the bag as far away from my body as possible on our way back to the house.

The sky is ice blue, cloudless. It looks frozen. Like those plastic cooler packs filled with chemicals. My eyes ache from the midday sun. And from the cold. A kid who looks like Ethan is skating in his driveway on a homemade ramp. I nod as I walk by. He doesn't nod back. *Brat*. I consider throwing Snoopy's poop bag at him.

Back home, I instead toss the poop in our trash bin, open the front door, unhook Snoopy and hang his leash on the coat rack, then slink back down to my bedroom, hoping not to be noticed.

"SOMETIMES I JUST WISH I MARRIED SOMEONE *NORMAL*!" I hear from the TV room. It's so loud and startling and foreign, I think it's got to be the television. I stop in the hallway, still and quiet, and listen for more . . .

It's not the TV. It's Mom.

I hear crying. Two types of crying. One I've heard before (Mom); the other decidedly less familiar (Dad). I tiptoe back to the foyer, loudly open the front door again, and yell, "We're back!" then SLAM the door shut behind me. I practically run straight to my bedroom, in no way wanting to see whatever horror show is unfolding between the two of them.

I sit on the bed. Nothing. Nobody's coming. Nobody's hollering. And then I realize.

I'm not normal.

Oh God. *I'm* making her life worse. More complicated. She deserves to have it easier than Dad and me. Obviously she regrets marrying a freak and now regrets having to raise his freak offspring. Can't say I blame her. If I could choose normal at this point, I sure as shinola would.

Now I notice my chest has started fluttering, and my heartbeat is ramping up and heading out of control. There's nothing I can do to slow it, let alone stop the racing. I try deep breathing, but I can't catch even one breath, much less take a long, controlled one.

I stand up and walk back and forth in my room. Listen for a few seconds. Pace again. Suddenly I have the idea to dive under my bed and fish out my big canvas duffel bag (with *ETHAN* stitched onto the side). I unzip it and put it on the mattress. It's staring at me, like a gaping whale mouth, when I start mindlessly grabbing clothes from my closet and stuffing them in. Pants, T-shirts, underwear, socks, sweatshirts, sweaters, my PF Flyers. Enough clothes for the better part of a week.

Then I scan the room for other essentials. The things you don't realize you need until you don't have them. A book, alarm clock, phone charger, laptop charger, my favorite pillow. My puffer jacket, knit gloves, a hat. Then I go into the bathroom, shove some toiletries into my backpack, with my schoolbooks already in it. What else? Laptop. Phone. Wallet. Bus pass. That's about it.

For what though?

I don't really know. I just know I need to get out of here. Now. I zip up the duffel, then the backpack, and quietly open my door, checking both ways down the hall. Nobody. Listen for a few more seconds. Nothing. It sounds like one of them is in the bedroom and the other is still in the TV room at this point.

I realize it's too risky to hump all this stuff down the hall and out the front door, so I get the brilliant (if I don't say so myself) after-school-special-inspired idea to lower my bags out the window and go around and get them once I'm outside. That way, if Mom or Dad does spot me, they'll think I'm just headed out for a walk again, cured at last of my depression.

I open the window, stuff my duffel through. Then carefully lower my backpack behind the bushes below. I look back toward my door and realize Snoopy has been sitting there staring at me the whole time I've been creeping around. I know it's impossible, but something in his eyes makes me think he knows what I'm doing.

I give him some cuddles, and he just gazes up at me with that sweet unconditional love. It breaks my heart, and I almost reconsider leaving, but then I hear Mom's voice again, the word *normal* ringing in my ears like an alarm. I decide to climb out the window too.

Before I leave, I find a piece of scrap paper in the waste bin, and quickly scribble:

Mom and Dad,
   I'm sorry, but I had to get out of here.
   Don't worry, I'll just be at a friend's house for a few days until school starts.
   I'll call you to touch base soon. Seriously, don't worry. I have my phone. I just need some space.
Best,
Me

It's only after I've been sitting on a downtown N14 bus for fifteen minutes that I figure out where I'm going: RaChas Central. I don't know if they're in the same location anymore. I don't even know if I can find that place. I do know that I'd caught a bus to Lower Broadway the afternoon I met Chase at the Country Music Hall of Fame and he took me to meet the RaChas for the first time.

I can tell I'm getting closer as the buildings appear older and more tightly packed. I take out my phone and check it to see if Mom or Dad has texted. They haven't. They must not have gone into my room yet. I guess that's good.

When the bus stops, I recognize the honky-tonk bar where I'd asked the bouncer to point me in the direction of the Hall of Fame. My bags feel especially heavy as I navigate through all the tourists and head into the warehouse district. I walk by some dudes working on cars in the street, then pass an old brick storefront where a line has formed outside. Seems like people waiting for free food or something. After fifteen more minutes, I sense I'm at last on the correct block. I drop my duffel to rest for a minute, and really give the buildings a once-over.

THERE, I see it, the old converted warehouse with the rusted iron façade. The joint looks abandoned. Kind of the point, I guess. Safety in obscurity. I pick up my bag and run over, the duffel bouncing against my hip.

I knock on the iron door. Wait. Nothing.

Knock again, louder. Wait. Nothing.

How can this not be it? Or maybe everybody's out? Or maybe they moved. It wasn't exactly the kind of living arrangement that seemed to come with a lease.

I feel like I'm about to lose it, and slide down the iron door and onto my duffel, where I decide, *NO, you wimp, you're not going to cry*. That's too easy, too basic. Enough with the tears already. I tilt my head back against the door, close my eyes, and press my scalp hard against the cold metal.

Then I hear footsteps, loud heavy boots on concrete. A punky girl in a rabbit-fur cape appears, blocking the sun so I can see her. She looks at me, then proceeds to let herself in through the iron gate.

"Is this—" I start to say, but remember at the last second

to cut myself off so as not to give anything away that I'm not supposed to. "Uh, does Benedict live here?"

She looks at me for a second, up and down. Checks out my bag with *Ethan* embroidered on it. My backpack. My shoes. Then seems satisfied. She nods at me to follow her in.

"Bienvenido! Willkommen! Namaste!" Benedict shouted, hugging me the moment I entered the main loft space and dropped my bags on the floor.

The embrace was not a symbolic one. He recognized me from my meltdown performance at the last Changers Mixer. Said he understood everything, whatever it was, tell him or don't tell him, deal with it or don't, but a Changer who doesn't wish to cling to the orthodox Changers path is always welcome at RaChas Central. I could stay for as long or as little as I needed.

He gave me the tour: the kitchen ("We job-share food acquisition, prep, cooking, service, and cleaning"); the bathrooms ("If you're looking for gender-segregated toilets, you've come to the wrong place"); the sleeping area ("I think Judy's going to be in Myanmar for another month, so feel free to bunk here"); and finally the work space.

"Some of the crew is—like you—still in school, so quiet time is between five and seven, and you can sign up for tutor help Mondays, Tuesdays, and Thursdays. We don't give a flying rat's ass whether or not you Chronicle while you're here, but graduation's not the worst objective. There's no Internet, but there's a Starbucks a few blocks east, and we set up a tent on their roof where you can borrow a connection when you need it."

It was all a bit overwhelming. Okay, a lot overwhelming.

A life so different from any I'd lived or even really known. I spun around, trying to absorb the scene. It was then that I spied the framed photograph leaning up against the brick wall in the corner, melted wax all around it, a couple candles still burning. There was also a glass of water, a bunch of coins, a bowl of noodles with a couple flies buzzing. A plate of chocolate cookies.

It was a photo of Chase, as his second V, the one I last saw him as in that basement when Elyse and I yanked off his hood. I couldn't help but gasp. I felt like I'd been kicked in the ribs.

"One last thing," Benedict said. "We don't have any rules around here. I mean, you know how we feel about rules. But there is one tenet we all try to live by, and it is inspired by the writing of one of the most revered Radical Changers of all time, the legendary and inspiring Kate Bornstein. And that rule is: don't be mean. Got it? Just don't be mean." Benedict bored his eyes into mine.

"I can do that," I said.

"Good. Oh, wait, there's one more thing. Not a rule. A suggestion. Don't bring in found furniture from the street. At least nothing with fabric. We've been battling a bed bug problem."

"Got it, no prob."

"Everybody!?" Benedict shouted suddenly, and about half a dozen RaChas came out into the main room for the announcement. "This is—wait, what do you want to be called?"

"Uh, Kim is fine," I said, regretting it as soon as it came out. "For now."

"This is Kim!" Benedict called out. "Make Kim feel welcome!"

"Welcome!" they all shouted.

And oddly, it actually felt like I was.

When I finally checked my phone later that night there were, as predicted, about ten messages from Mom and Dad, beginning angry, then softening as they progressed unanswered. The last one read, *I'm not mad, I swear. I just need to know you're safe. —Mom*

I typed back, *I'm safe. All good. Love you.*

Two of three parts were true.

CHANGE 3-DAY 113

The bus ride from Chez RaChas to school felt like it took a hundred years. I guess every journey on a bus that lasts longer than five minutes feels like a hundred years, but with the added miles, plus all the stops on the local, and the complete lack of suspension jiggling my boobs like a drink in a cocktail shaker, my new commute was particularly brutalizing. On the plus side, the distance gave me ample time to think, and because no one ever expects you to be in a good mood on a city bus, my depressive tendencies went completely unnoticed. I imagine it's what living in New York City must feel like.

So far, bunking away from home has been mostly awesome. It is unnerving occupying the same physical space as Chase once did. Literally walking on the same floor, lounging on the same couches. I feel his energy in every corner, and that has been good and bad. I feel closer to him than I have in months, but I can't seem to shake the guilt Nana told me to get rid of. It may be a useless reflex, but it's one that sticks to your heart like tar to feathers, so I expect guilt and me will be partners in mutual abuse for a long while.

Speaking of Nana, knowing that she too was some sort of version of Chase in a former V has exploded my brain, the way talking with Michelle Hu about astrophysics does. I wish I could tell Michelle about us, about the whole alternate universe of Changers. I don't doubt she could handle it. Damn, she probably already intuitively understands more about it than I do. Michelle seems intellectually and emotionally unflappable. I guess that's a quality you want in your future great scientists, which she intends to be.

During one of our nightly chats over dinner, Benedict reemphasized (likely for my benefit) that we should feel free to tell like-minded, trusted folks about who and what we are. That by hiding our truth in the shadows, we condemn ourselves to marginalization. Only, when it comes down to it, he hasn't told anybody either, not directly. Chase getting killed rattled him too. I think he's afraid if he comes out, the Abiders will swoop into RaChas HQ and release a poison gas that chokes us all out. Not to mention, uh, that when somebody found out who me, Elyse/Destiny, and Alex/Theo were last year, we ended up locked in a basement.

"Of course, denial is its own poison gas," Benedict added ruefully. (After which several other RaChas shouted, "Secrets kill!")

Which brings me to my parents. I told them after one night exactly where I was staying. With the Tribulations, they've suffered enough fear about my well-being. It was a really hard conversation, but I made them promise to give me the distance and boundaries I need to work through my issues, language Mom instinctively understood and respected. As long as I was eating well and being looked after and cared for by my peers (and staying in school!), she was down for the new experiment in apron string–cutting.

Dad was ... Dad. Angry. Punitive. He blamed Mom. He blamed me. He blamed the Tribulations.

"Who he really blames is himself," Mom tried to explain over the phone. "He just doesn't know it yet."

Mom had already apologized about the argument I'd overheard before bolting through my bedroom window. She guessed, correctly, that her "normal" comment was the final blow that toppled my neurotic house of cards. I told her I knew she didn't mean it. It's what she needed to hear, even if I still wasn't sure I believed what she was selling.

"I don't even subscribe to the concept of normal," she explained, beyond sincerely. "I was just so frustrated with your father, with his, well, it doesn't matter. I don't need to trouble you with that. I guess I just snapped. I never meant to hurt you, or even him. Maybe him. I don't know. Marriage is complicated."

"It's okay, Mom. We all say cruel things to the ones we love."

"Petunia, if I ever thought you would hear any of it . . ." Here she began weeping. I could hear the snuffling over the phone, the scrap of a Kleenex across the mouthpiece, the loud blowing afterward.

"Mom, I have to catch the bus."

On the way to school, I tried ringing Kris. He's been MIA for days, whiling away the hours conferring with the flower that is Rooster, no doubt.

"I'm hunting your bony butt down the second I get to class," I threatened into his voice mail. "Which at the pace of this bus I'm sitting on should be in about seven hours."

Turns out Kris wasn't in homeroom. But Mr. Crowell was, and it was obvious he'd been put on Kim Cruz suicide watch, because he paid more attention to me than Narcissus did to his own reflection. But Chloe was not about having me get any more of the spotlight than her.

"Have you gained weight?" she snarled when I stood up to leave after the bell rang. "Eating isn't a hobby, you know."

I ignored her, pushing past the clot of kids at the door

and into the hall where I finally spied Kris moping near his locker, the door ajar, shredding his previously taped-up photos of shirtless Justin Bieber and Amanda Lepore with giant scissors.

"Where have you been?" I asked, sidling up beside him. "And what's with the *Mommie Dearest* hysteria?"

I bent to catch his eye, but he wouldn't meet my gaze. He just turned back into his locker, reached both hands in, and heaved all the contents inside onto the hall floor.

"Monsters!" he screamed. "All of them!"

"Who?" I pressed, worried now. "What's going on with you?"

At that Kris doubled over and began choking out half-sobs, half-wheezes. I noticed for the first time that his eye was bruised and his forehead had a long scratch that bled into the hairline.

"Who did this to you?" I shouted, going straight into mama bear mode. "Jason?"

"If only," Kris said. "I did this to myself."

He then slid to the floor and spilled the whole story. How Rooster cheated on him. And Kris got drunk. And he drove off in his dad's Jetta to confront Rooster but didn't get very far because he hit a lamppost at the end of the driveway. And his father saw the whole thing and wanted to kill him.

So as long as the ish was hitting the fan, Kris decided to confess to his dad that not only was he gay, but he liked to wear dresses and mascara ("I was drunk, remember?"), and that sometimes he wished he'd never been born a boy in the first place. After which his dad informed him that "no son of mine" would end up "an abomination" like that, and until he sorted out his "sick life," he needed to "get the hell out of my house."

"Damn," I said, sliding down beside him. "I'm so sorry, Kris. You know it isn't true, right? You're not sick. You're not an abomination."

"Whatever. What I am is homeless. I didn't even have a chance to pack my jodhpurs."

"And Rooster?"

"Rooster is dead to me."

"You don't know. Sometimes people just need a breather."

"He had sex with my gay conversion therapist."

"Okay. Rooster is dead. Got it." I glanced around. The bell had long since rung and the hall was empty save us and a janitor lazily pushing a broom. "I have a solution," I said brightly.

Kris raised his brows half-heartedly, like, *You? Mope girl?*

"You can come live with me."

"I'm not about to crash at your folks' place when your grandmother just died—"

"I'm not there," I interrupted, to which his brows went into full on *whaaaaa* position? "I had my own drama. I'll tell you more later. But I'm shacking up downtown in a warehouse with some really cool anarchist types, and I know they'd welcome you with open arms."

"Open stinky arms, no doubt."

I smiled. "Oh yeah. It's a funk fest. But the people are kind. It's even in the rules: you can't be mean."

"Perfect," Kris said, rolling his eyes. "I'm never mean."

But I could tell he was relieved. "Just make believe you're in a musical," I advised.

"Oh girl, I always do."

CHANGE 3-DAY 117

Now that I've been back in school almost a week, the friends-and-family plea bargaining has really ramped up. Kris decided he'd rather stay with Lady Chardonnay, one of the queens from the Carousel, whom he calls his "drag mother." Probably for the best, since I hadn't really thought through how I would explain Benedict the first time he launched into one of his Changers diatribes, not that he and Kris wouldn't have tons in common. They do both love an audience. Anyhow, Kris has been reaching out a lot more, loving me in my "queer activist" phase ever since flying the suburban coop.

In addition to the flurries of Snapchats from Kris (most of him pretending to hump on inanimate objects), there are daily (pointedly not pushy) texts from Mom (Dad less so), and then tonight, I got my first uninvited visitor when Tracy unexpectedly showed up at RaChas HQ after dinner.

I was scraping burnt brown rice out of our one battered stew pot when Benedict comes up behind me and says, "Kim, you've got an admirer." I swivel around from the sink. And there she is. Pert and put-together Tracy idling in the middle of raggedy RaChas-ville, her arms curved and held slightly aloft like a ballerina's, trying not to let her skin touch any surface.

"Hey, stranger," I call out, plunging my arm elbow-deep into the greasy-sudsy dish water. I feel happy to see her, though part of me wishes I didn't, I don't know why. "I'll be done in a minute."

"Would you like a cup of Rooibos tea?" Benedict asks her. "While you wait?"

"Thank you, that'd be lovely," Tracy replies.

"Honey?" Benedict says.

"Excuse me?" Tracy sounds a little jumpy.

"Honey, for your tea." He gestures to the communal dining table, where the last dishes from the night's meal have just been cleared. "From local urban hives."

Tracy nods just as I am drying my hands on a dish towel. I head over to her. "So how the hell did you find me?"

Tracy smirks, her eyes darting left and right, so as to keep our business private.

"You can talk freely here," I say loudly, and she winces. "That's what I love about it—no rules to constantly have to keep track of and worry whether you're violating."

Benedict comes back over and places a steaming cup of tea in front of Tracy, who recoils when his eagle-feather necklace accidentally brushes her arm. "I don't bite," he says, chuckling, real close to her face. "Despite what you might've heard."

Tracy seems so rattled, I sort of feel bad for her.

"In fact, I think you'd find that if we sat down and talked, our ultimate goals are more aligned than you think," Benedict adds. "We just have different ideas about how to achieve them."

"How do you presume to know what my goals are?" Tracy asks.

"Well..." Benedict starts, looking to me almost for permission to engage. I keep my face blank, and he continues, "I would assume that as a high-ranking Touchstone in good standing with Southeast Changers Central, your goals are probably pretty aligned with Turner the Lives Coach and *The Changers Bible* in its most recent iteration."

"So you're speculating about my professional goals. Not my personal ones," Tracy says tightly.

"I didn't realize there was a difference with 'in the many we are one' Changers," Benedict counters, smiling.

But Tracy doesn't take the bait. "I do believe we as Changers are slowly and steadily making the human race better with each generation. The mission remains and always has been imperative."

"I can't argue with that. But if you are so sure of your mission and its general rate of success, then why be ashamed of who you are and how you are going about it?" Benedict asks. "Why not step into the light and shine as brightly as you can?"

Tracy stiffens. She didn't come here to debate Changer theory.

"Is there anywhere we might go to talk?" she asks me. And then to Benedict, "The tea is wonderful, thank you." (Not that she's touched it.)

"I believe it's wrong for these kids to have to hide and lie for four years of their lives—the most formative years of those lives, by the way," Benedict says, not getting the hint. "It sets a bad precedent and, from what I've witnessed, is ultimately traumatizing to a good number of them. Many of whom end up here at my door, I might add."

"Well, when it is safe, we will come out," Tracy says.

"It won't *be* safe until we do!" Benedict raises his voice, relishing the moment.

"Guys, come on," I insert. "Not the time or the place."

"She's right. I didn't come here to argue," Tracy concedes. "I just wanted to check up on somebody who is extremely important to me."

"Be my guest," Benedict says. "In the many we are one."

Tracy can't tell if he's joking. She watches him go, waits until he's out of earshot, and then whispers, horrified, "How can you live here?"

"It's cool," I say.

"It's filthy."

"Depression and cleanliness aren't exactly bosom buddies," I say wanly.

Tracy forces a close-lipped smile. "These people are dangerous."

"These people are *us*."

Tracy rolls her eyes. "You know what I mean. This is going to end in tears. Or worse. You of all people should know you can't just go around," and here she starts imitating Benedict's voice, *"Whatever man, it's cool whoever finds out whatever, whenever."*

I laugh. Her impression is fairly spot-on. "It's not exactly like that," I say. "More like, RaChas aren't all freaked out by the idea that people may start finding out what Changers are. We're not ashamed."

"*We?*"

"They, me," I say, annoyed. "You shouldn't be ashamed either, by the way."

"I'm not."

I decide to take Tracy over to my bunk so I don't have to listen to her clipped whisper-talking anymore. I climb onto my bed, and after initial hesitation, she reluctantly follows me up, her patent-leather flats sliding off on every rickety ladder rung.

"How do you do this every night?" she asks, struggling to hoist herself up.

"First off, I don't wear shoes to bed."

Tracy scans the room, the piles of unwashed blankets, the festering coffee mugs, the stacks of journals, edges damp and yellowing, the open box of kitty litter. "Maybe you should. Or, possibly, a hazmat suit."

She manages to get a knee on the mattress, then dog-crawls to the wall. We sit there for a while in silence, side by side with our backs against the brick, our feet dangling over the side.

"Well, I'll admit, you *do* seem somewhat less down since I last saw you," Tracy says with a sigh.

"I am." Though in truth, I haven't really considered the notion until now. I haven't really had the *luxury* to consider it, what with school, homework, the long commute each way, my new RaChas collective chores. You don't realize how much parents do for you until they're not there to do it for you.

"That's good, that's really good," Tracy says, sniffing the corner of a sheet.

We tumble into silence again. Not a familiar state where Tracy's concerned.

"Soooo," I say. "Thanks for coming by to check on me, but I—"

"I'm pissed," Tracy blurts, cutting me off. Then turns to face me, sitting cross-legged. "I feel I have to tell you that."

"Okay," I say. "Why are you pissed?"

"Do you know what this is doing to your mother? You are breaking her heart."

And ... what do I say to that? On the one hand, Tracy's probably right, this has to be hard on Mom, but on the other

. . . well, what does Mom always say to me about feelings? Nobody can make you feel anything. It's your choice how you react to the things people do and say.

"Does that even register?" Tracy asks.

"Of course it does."

"Well?"

"Well, what?" I ask, peevish.

"I just can't believe how selfish you've become. There, I said it."

"You did, didn't you."

"Look, she's just really worried about your health and safety, and this radio silence might feel good to you, but it's flat-out unkind to her. What did she do to you to make you feel you can treat her this way?"

"Did she tell you what she said?"

"Said? About what?"

"How she wishes she'd married someone *normal*? You know, as in, not a Changer. As in, someone not like me?"

Tracy seems stunned, but she recovers quickly. "I'm sure she had her reasons. That can't be the whole story."

"Trace, what reason could there possibly be that makes it okay?"

"Tempting as it may be, you can't punish your loved ones for their mistakes. It's like drinking poison yourself and expecting *them* to get sick."

"Nice bumper-sticker psychology, Tracy. Wait . . . did she send you?"

"Your Mom? No, I came here on my own."

"I don't believe you."

She sighs long and heavy. "We both thought it was important to put eyes on you."

"Well, you've put eyes on me," I say. "Satisfied? Do I look

okay? You can report back, you've done your job, I'm fine."

"Okay then," she says, "if this is how you want it."

"It is."

At that Tracy starts to try to leave, but she doesn't know how to climb down the ladder—front or backward. She tries front first, and then when that orientation reveals itself as perilous, she maneuvers around and begins backing herself down.

After considerable struggle, which I try really hard not to enjoy, Tracy's on the ground looking up at me. Probably expecting me to do the right thing, like I always do: admit I'm wrong, learn some sort of lesson, apologize, and move on, promising to be a better person the next time around. But I do none of that.

Benedict suddenly appears, holding Tracy's coat out for her.

"If you need anything," she says up to me, "you know where to find me."

She punches an arm through the first sleeve, then the second. Smiles brusquely at Benedict, turns to look at me once more. Then she marches toward the door, her flats click-clacking on the cement the whole way out.

"You did the right thing," Benedict says, looking up at me approvingly. "You just need to do you."

Whatever that is.

CHANGE 3-DAY 117, PART DEUX

It was only an hour after Tracy left that Destiny showed up at RaChas HQ, also completely unexpectedly.

Benedict led her to my bunk. "You're quite the popular one tonight," he said to me, giggling at some inside joke that he and Destiny had somehow managed to formulate between the front door and the bunk room.

"Girl, look at you!" Destiny sang, hurling herself up onto my bed. (Considerably more nimbly than Tracy.)

"How the hell did *you* find me?"

"What do you mean?"

"My Touchstone just left."

"Cray," she said, lying next to me on my pillow. At which point we started gabbing like girlfriends, which of course we are. (Well, in these V's at least.)

She's falling harder and harder for DJ. He is the best, he is so smart, he is the kindest, most considerate person she's ever met. Thanks so much for dragging her to the play after-party that night. There's a soul connection between them, like she's never felt before. Plus, he's good in the sack.

Ewwwww. Literally the last thing I wanted to hear. Maybe not as bad as thinking about my mother and father "in the sack." Or Tracy and Mr. Crowell. But definitely a close third-to-last.

"Life, man," Destiny said then, taking a deep pull off her e-cig. "Life is freaking beautiful."

"If you say so."

"Why you gotta be such a downer all the time?"

"Well, excuse me," I said, "if I'm not feeling the 'life is beautiful' mythology right now."

She sat up, blew the vapor out her nostrils in two skinny white mushroom clouds. "Look. I get it, you miss your grandmother, that was a blow. But she lived incredible lives, for a really long time too. She had a really good run."

"I'm just not there yet," I said.

"Even your grandma told you herself not to be sad. She knew it was coming; she was ready to go, you know? That's kind of lovely, if you think about it. We should all go that way."

"It's not just her," I said petulantly.

"Well, what is it, then?"

"It's everything. Chase, my parents. Goddamn ME."

"Oh, we're back on that again?"

"Yes, WE are. If by WE you mean I, because even Benedict, King of the RaChas, who's basically blind to people's external appearances, was practically slobbering all over you."

"Kim, come on. I'm on your side."

"Yeah," I said, regretting the following words before they even came out of my mouth. "Easy for you to say, when you look like you do, and you're starring in the greatest love story ever told, and your entire world is one giant confetti bomb of fabulousness."

Destiny looked a little stunned.

Great, I was batting 1.000 on hurting people who'd come a long way just to make sure I wasn't dead.

"That's not fair," she said after recovering her composure. "You know I'm not about that."

"Then why does it feel like you are?"

"Man, you gotta get over yourself. It's not always going to be this way. You of all people know that. So why don't you try to figure out what it is you're supposed to learn from this stage, muddle through it best you can, and then you'll be ready for the next one when it comes."

"Wow, somebody memorized *The Changers Bible,*" I spat.

"Wow, somebody turned into a major dick."

It was a stare-off. And then Destiny silently climbed off the bed and left.

Just like that.

I get it. Nothing's much more pathetic and disappointing than a martyr. The biggest turn-off there is. Taking something ugly and making it even uglier.

And yet I can't stop feeling certain it's the cards I've been dealt that are the problem here. It's not me. It's not my fault. Why can't anybody see that but me?

CHANGE 3-DAY 124

Nobody would ever call RaChas HQ boring. The Radical Changers are definitely bucking the usual sit-around-in-smelly-packs-in-the-park-with-your-mangy-dog-on-a-rope-and-ask-for-a-dollar-anarchist-slash-gutterpunk routine. I mean, something's always going on here, whether it's making sure Changers who are still completing their Cycles are keeping up with work and staying in their various schools (or are getting an equivalent legal education, like when Chase's parents let him homeschool); or doing Abider research and recon in case the Council isn't; or Dumpster-diving items that can be sold on eBay to raise funds. RaChas are some busy little beavers. (Contrary to the Changers Council propaganda that they're nothing but a bunch of layabout, unrealistic rabble-rousers.)

When I come home from school today, and there's a ginormous flurry of activity around the back table, which was covered with files, old books, photographs, etc., I don't think much of it. Benedict is deep into some paperwork when he suddenly slaps the table, hard, immediately quieting everybody in the loft.

People seem stressed, kind of rattled. Confused. But I can't engage because I have an essay to write and craptastic trigonometry to do, and am coming off yet another *blah* day at school. I shuffle down the hall to my bed, figuring I'll try to get some work done there before it's time to help prep dinner.

After about an hour, Benedict comes in, plops down on a chair between the bunks.

"Can you believe all this?" he asks me.

"What?"

"This eugenics stuff," he says.

I have no idea what he's talking about, but I've been getting used to Benedict slipping into self-righteous, pissed-at-the-world jags like Chase used to, so I just close my pencil in my notebook and wait.

"Haven't you been even a little curious about what we've been working on this week?" he asks.

"I, I—" I start. Because I don't know. Am I curious? Not really. I'm trying to be the kid in the bubble, plod through my days, and "just do me," as Benedict keeps saying I should.

"Do you know about eugenics?" he says, impatient.

"Isn't that what the Nazis did?"

"Yeah, but it was first coined in the UK, before them, by one of Charles Darwin's cousins, whom we have reason to believe was a Changer."

"Wow. Is he in the book?"

"What book?"

"The book of famous Changers in history."

Benedict laughs. "I don't think there's such a thing."

I feel dumb, so I keep quiet. *Was Tracy just messing with me? Because that's not like her . . .*

"Anyway, he's the guy who invented the whole concept of 'nature vs. nurture.' He also conducted all this research into genetics, and was a proponent of the wealthy classes reproducing amongst themselves, to pass on the best genes to improve the overall quality of British society."

"That's kind of messed up."

"Yeah. I mean, by all accounts, the dude was brilliant,"

Benedict says, leaning back in the chair and tipping it onto two legs, "but obviously the implications were pretty scary."

After about thirty seconds of mulling it over, I say, "Isn't that kind of what the Changers Council is doing, though? But in reverse? Intentionally muddying the gene pool? Making it so that eventually, in thousands and thousands of years, everybody will be a Changer?"

"Pretty much," Benedict says. "There's a good and bad application of almost every discovery."

"So what's the problem?"

"What we're worried about is, well, we just hacked into a new area of the Changers mainframe and found evidence of gene-selection research they're doing over there . . . And it's starting to worry me that all of this could tip into the bad application again, as far as what that ultimate population is going to look and be like."

"Hmm," I say, because—*see above*—I don't really want to get into all that. I'm just trying to decipher the cosine law here for the trig quiz tomorrow.

Benedict pitches forward on the chair and stares at me, his orange mess of bangs flopping into his eyes. "Chase always said you were like this."

Ouch. The Chase card. "Like *what*, exactly?"

"Unwilling to engage," he clarifies nonchalantly. "He believed you definitely have the smarts, but not necessarily the fire."

I can't believe this shizz is happening right now. I mean, I appreciate Benedict's taking me in, and what he's doing for a lot of Changers. But I don't need to be hearing about Chase's disappointment in me FROM THE GRAVE. Nor do I need yet another parental figure beefing with me about my failing them all the time.

"I didn't realize being politically active was a prerequisite for crashing here," I snip.

"It's not," Benedict says, somewhat defensively. "But at some point this stuff has got to get you pissed off."

"Oh, believe me, I'm pissed off."

Benedict stands up, sits down again. Then stands up, lightly punches the side of my mattress, and turns like he's about to walk away. But he stops himself. Says with his back to me, "I wanted to wait for the right time to tell you this, but what is the right time, when it comes down to it?"

"Tell me what?" For some reason I feel sick to my stomach.

And then Benedict turns around and proceeds to reveal precisely what went down with Chase and the Tribulations last year. And my bubble explodes as if hit by a surface-to-air missile.

CHANGE 3-DAY 125

There is no ignoring the truth once you hear it. No matter how hard we humans might try, distracting ourselves with alcohol, drugs, sex, ice cream, reality television, or whatever denial-abetter of choice.

I failed my trig quiz this morning. After Benedict prepared a giant overstuffed truth burrito and force-fed me the entire thing in one sitting last night, pretty much everything else evacuated my cerebral matter. First and foremost the sine and cosine laws.

Let's see if I can recap.

I had sex with Audrey. I being Oryon, and the sex being last year, because—let's be clear—there is no way Audrey is having sex with Kim Cruz. Enough said.

Anyway, afterward, as has been not only Chronicled, but also played over and over in my head no less than a thousand times, Aud found the bracelet she'd given Drew, freaked out, and fled my apartment. She called or texted Jason on the way, because while I'm sure he was the last person she wanted to see then, he was the only one who could come rescue her, since there was no way she was asking her parents to pick her up from her traumatic first (post)sexual experience with the black kid she made them invite over for dinner a couple months prior.

Jason obviously DID spot me when Audrey got in his car, because, as Benedict explained, Jason and Audrey's church and camp are part of the main nest that the RaChas have been tracking and investigating over the last couple years. Jason, now knowing generally where I lived, probably tipped off his church elders about my whereabouts. While Jason might've just been trying to "teach me a lesson" for messing around with his sister, the elders in his church are—unbeknownst to many of the congregants—affiliated with the Abiders movement, and thus quietly recruiting the younger members, grooming them into cells to do their bidding.

In her vulnerable state, Audrey might've blurted something to Jason about Oryon being somehow related to Drew, or at the very least that Oryon might've lied to Audrey in order to get her in bed, so he had no problem turning me over to the rest of his youth group at the church, who, with the encouragement of the elders, assembled a trio of thugs, jumped in a pickup truck (not much good happens when a mud-splattered 4x4 chases anyone/thing), and staked out where Jason had picked up Audrey the night before, hoping for me to come by, which I obviously did when taking Snoopy out for his morning walk. Walked right into their trap.

Chase, Benedict, and a couple other RaChas were taking turns monitoring online church communications that day (as they had been for some time), and something about the situation that Jason and his buddies were opaquely joking about online made Chase think that it could possibly be me who was just picked up, to be taught a "lesson about dating our women."

Chase went ballistic and was about to storm into Central High and pound Jason to a pulp himself (again), but after Benedict convinced him that Jason probably didn't know much beyond his small role in the kidnapping, and it wasn't worth getting arrested for just yet, Chase instead funneled his rage into two days straight of twenty-four-hour recon, eventually figuring out a way to break into the Changers mainframe. Chase apparently used keyword searches of personal details he knew about my life and somehow managed to decrypt some of my Chronicles, then read my desperate, by-the-minute communications about where we were being held.

It wasn't so much my paltry Chronicled details about the angle of sunlight, and the hallway and cinder-block walls, that led Chase to me, but more that he was now *certain* of the connection between Jason's church and the Abiders. So, with another day of scouring real estate records, Benedict and Chase were able to find evidence of a handful of church property holdings in the countryside, where we were likely being imprisoned.

At that point, Chase and Benedict contacted the Council, turning over all of this information. They naively hoped, Benedict explained, that the Council would act immediately and make use of their deep connections in law enforcement to rescue the three Changers who were hostages in an Abiders cell.

Now here's the hard part to swallow. I can barely think it, much less Chronicle it, because it seems so unbelievable. The Council thanked Chase for all of his hard work, told Benedict and him that they would "take it from here."

And then: nothing.

As in, while the three of us were locked away in the dark, eating stale bread crusts and generally being terrified of imminent execution, the Changers Council not only knew about it, but didn't think it necessary to notify our beside-themselves parents and loved ones, while they were supposedly "completing additional research and determining the prudent course of action."

Another day went by. Nothing from Turner or the Council brass. In fact, when Benedict and Chase tried to go back to Changers Central to force another meeting, they were denied access unless they promised to provide detailed information about how Chase broke into their system. Which, Chase gave up immediately, over Benedict's protests.

And yet the Council did not keep their word. The RaChas remained locked out.

"I'm going public with the fact that you know where they are," Chase threatened loudly outside Changers Central.

The Council's hand forced, a plan was finally hatched. Chase was given a GPS device, a smoke bomb, and instructions on how to put himself in a situation where he knew he'd be kidnapped by the Abiders. After which, the Council tactical team would storm the nest and free us all.

Problem was, no one realized how badly the Abiders would beat Chase before tossing him into the basement with us. Maybe the Abiders knew who he was, or suspected what he was doing. Or maybe his size and strength made the goons especially brutal. Knowing Chase, he probably egged them on. He was never one to back down from a fight.

Benedict never found out exactly how Chase got himself abducted, but it was the blip on the GPS from his tracker that enabled the Changers tactical team to launch a surprise attack and at last bust us out.

Benedict also said that he tried to find out what exactly happened to Chase, but that in all the commotion and chaos in the weeks following the incident, his body disappeared, and Benedict never could get the true, full story. There was nothing beyond the official Council obituary, which said that

Chase suffered bleeding in the brain and died en route to the hospital, after the brave act of saving his fellow Changers during an unfortunate incident of Abiders-related activity, which had been, dismayingly, occurring more frequently across the world in recent months.

I had only one question for Benedict once he stopped talking: "So, if Chase hadn't threatened them and been willing to get himself kidnapped, the Council wouldn't have done anything to save us?"

He didn't seem to want to answer me. With all the politicalization, there was still kindness in his heart. But since honesty is the kindest act of all, he eventually answered softly, "In their defense, they didn't know for sure you would be killed. But, yeah, I think they were ready to sacrifice the few to save the many from possible exposure."

And that was all I needed to hear.

CHANGE 3-DAY 130

My mind won't stop processing. Chewing over the facts. The consequences. The lies.

Chase really did sacrifice himself for me. More than I even dared suspect.

And he read some of my Chronicles. Did he see how I felt about him before he died? Was I a jerk in them? People are always jerks in their diaries. Could he read between the lines?

If I want anything in this world, I want him to know how much I loved him before he died. Isn't that what people always say? Make sure you tell them you love them; you never know what could happen.

Morbid. But not wrong.

I wish he could read me now.

I love you, Chase. You are the family I wish I had. My twin. You made me feel everything. Even when I didn't want to. You believed in me. I didn't deserve it. Not any of it.

How do you thank someone for saving your life? Chewbacca became Han Solo's forever first mate in *Star Wars*, but I'm not going to have the luxury of serving Chase forevermore.

I would if I could, Chase. If I ever meet you again, I will. You won't shake me next time. And know this too: I will make this right. Your life won't have been lost for no reason. I see now what I need to do. I see it all.

CHANGE 3-DAY 143

Tonight was the Polar Ice Ball. Because my life is nothing if not careening all over the spectrum.

"More like polar-izing," Kris quipped when none other than Jason and Chloe were elected king and queen of . . . I never know what. The night? The other students at the dance? The high school social universe? Chipotle?

"Now she actually *is* an ice queen," Kris snarked as he, Michelle, and I stood in a huddle watching King Jason and Queen Chloe peacock up and take their place onstage under fake-snow bunting and sheets of twinkly lights. Jason couldn't help yelling, "Oy! Oy! Oy!" and flexing his bicep when the student council president draped his sash over his suit, his homies in the crowd "Oy-oying" right back at him.

For her part, Chloe flashed her newly whitened teeth and held her posture pageant-straight, getting swathed with sashes nothing unusual to her. She even discreetly shimmied a shoulder just enough to hitch the sash into a more flattering angle. You had to hand it to her—girl was a pro.

"And now our king and queen, along with their court, will take the floor for the first dance of the ball!" the emcee announced, as the first bars of "Crazy" by Aerosmith began to play over the loudspeakers.

I guess we were all supposed to circle and watch them like it was a wedding or something, which feels like the wrong message to send to teenagers, but what do I know?

"This *song*," Michelle moaned.

"Mama's nerves," Kris shuddered. "I'm going to go force the deejay to play some Pussy Riot or Prince."

"I'm going to go find a sandwich," Michelle added, as the two left me alone.

I couldn't stop studying Jason since he took the floor. Of course he couldn't dance like a normal human. For a guy like Jason, dancing would always represent some assault on his masculinity, so instead he hurled himself around like he was at a punk show, ramming into other kids and generally being the giant a-hole we know and despise. Or I do, anyway. The rest of the student body has more tolerance for his agro-macho crap, most of them cowed by his hostility and alpha-male posturing, afraid not to at least *pretend* to like him. I wonder how long that particular magic trick will work. Probably a long time, if corporate America is any indication.

I watch Chloe trying vainly to catch Jason's attention. This is supposed to be their shining moment; there are even spotlights dipping in and out, illuminating their faces. But he won't play along, so she just kind of sways in circles in his orbit, trying not to get snapped like a sapling tree. Soon enough Jason inexplicably bails from the dance floor altogether, and my eyes follow him with laser focus as he struts to a dark corner of the auditorium, takes something from his jacket pocket, and drops it into a drink.

Did he really just do that?

He sniffs the cup, taking care not to put his mouth too close, then grins. It seems our rapey jackhole has graduated from assault to drugging. I give a quick survey of the scene, hoping to spot Kris or Michelle, or even Mr. Crowell (who was chaperoning), but I can't find any of them. I feel sweat beading down my back as I continue to track Jason. He's heading right toward Chloe, who has also exited the dance floor and is sitting sloppily cross-legged on a folding chair, trying to keep her sash from falling off.

I don't have a plan, but I make a beeline for Chloe, and as I do, I notice Audrey is doing the same from another side of the room. We arrive at Chloe's chair at the exact same time, Jason lagging a few steps behind, stopping to take selfies with a gaggle of sophomore admirers.

"What the eff are you even doing here?" Chloe snorts, eyeballing me and my ensemble—a full-length black velvet dress from the thrift store, and my Doc Martens. "Huh, Fat Elvira?"

"Hey Chlo," Audrey steps in, "let's go freshen up in the ladies'."

"I'm already drunk, dummy," Chloe shoots back, rattling a plastic cup with only ice left, then tossing it on the table in front of her, the ice skittering across the white tablecloth like dice.

"No. I mean let's really . . . Uh, I need to talk to you. In private."

I can tell Audrey is nervous, even more nervous than I am. She must have seen her brother dose the drink too. Or maybe she just knows her brother well enough to sense tonight can't end well, not for Chloe anyway, who remains clueless about her sociopathic crush.

"Oooooh, baby! Just what I needed, I'm soooo thirsty," Chloe swoons as Jason swoops in and shamelessly hands her the drink. "What a thoughtful big brother you have, Auddie."

Auddie?

"Let's blow this lame party," Jason says, only just then noticing me. "Who invited Chingy Chong?"

Audrey steps in and yanks the drink from Chloe's hands, then immediately drops it on the floor, splashing it all over. "Sorry, my bad," she tries, her face red and hot. "I was thirsty too."

"And spastic, you retard," Chloe says, leaning back and laughing.

Audrey doesn't laugh. She seems terrified of catching Jason's eye. But I do look him in the eye, and I see a sinister flicker. It quickly dissipates as he says, "No prob. More where that came from. Let's go, ladies."

"We should stay," Audrey says.

"What the eff for?" Chloe asks, standing up and clutching Jason's arm for support. "I'm good to go. Let's party. Woooo!"

Of course she "woooos." How have I never heard her "woooo" before?

"Chlo, I think you should go home," Audrey tries again. "It's been a big night."

"Speaking of big," Chloe cuts her eyes my way. "Seriously, why are you still here? This isn't the zoo."

"Sea World maybe," Jason chimes in, cracking Chloe up.

"Because I'm a whale?" I blurt then, stunning them both into momentary silence. "I just want to make sure I understand the joke. Because I am as big as a *whale*?"

"Who the hell do you think you are?" Jason says after a beat, the pilot light of his rage lit anew. He leans toward me, scrunches his nose like a weasel. I notice Audrey flinch, bracing herself.

I stand stock-still. I do not flinch.

"Who am I? I'm the girl who knows all about you, Jason. I know who you are. I know what you are. And someday, someday soon, so will everyone else. A reckoning is coming, King Jason. And I am the girl bringing it. That's who the hell I am."

For a second, nobody says or does anything. It's just a mutual hate-off, and only then do I realize I'm not scared. I feel solid, strong. My body an ally, a physical manifestation of the power I sense welling up inside me. I am not some fragile twig. I am a fracking tree trunk, and it's going to take more than one demented wannabe Abider and his would-be girlfriend to knock me down.

"She's cray," Chloe, addled, whispers to Jason, breaking the silence. "I think I want to go home."

"Yes!" Audrey chimes in, sensing an opening. "Let's all go home."

Jason doesn't move. He keeps staring me down. Eyes locked on mine. Waiting for me to break. "Do whatever you want," he says, finally looking away. "I'm going to find Baron and get hammered." Then he spits tobacco juice on the floor, and waltzes away as if nothing has happened.

"I need to get my purse," Chloe says to Audrey. "Meet you out front?"

Audrey nods, but I notice she is sizing me up, her expression gentler, in fact, almost familiar. "Sooooo, that happened," she says with an awkward shrug.

"Yep."

"Dances, man."

"Always drama at the dance," I say, wondering whether she's thinking of kissing Drew—kissing me—two years ago.

Audrey gives up a little laugh. "Well, I should go. Need to shovel the Polar Ice Queen into her carriage."

"Sounds like a smart plan. I should go too. My friends are waiting."

But neither of us leave. We just stand there enjoying each other. And then, I have the strange urge to kiss her again.

I lean in slightly, and—I swear on a stack of Changer Bibles—Audrey does too.

CHANGE 3-DAY 144

"Man, I was THIS close," I say, and recline on the couch, kicking my boots up on the coffee table with an emphatic double-thud.

"Better luck next time," Benedict replies, sparking up a joint.

"If there *is* a next time. Damn, I could kill Kris."

If he hadn't pogoed over and yanked me onto the dance floor with him after somehow manipulating the deejay into cueing up "Another One Bites the Dust" by Queen, I really think Audrey and I might've kissed in that moment last night. As in, girl-on-girl, in the middle of the high school dance, lip-locked, just like that first dance freshman year, when we were both balls of want and confusion.

Benedict takes a deep hit, blows it out after a few seconds. He appraises the joint then lazily passes it my way, suspecting I'm not interested since I never have been before.

"You know what?" I announce, thinking, *Why not?* "It was a major night."

Benedict looks a little surprised that I'm reaching over and taking the smoke from him, pinching it between my thumb and forefinger.

"What? I'm safe and staying in for the night," I argue. "It's legal in a bunch of states, not to mention some other countries. And the shizz hasn't hit the fan in any of those places. The stoned masses aren't roaming the streets overthrowing the establishment. Why the hell not?"

Benedict just rolls his eyes and waves his hand in front of his face. "I'm not your mother, dude," he says, smirking.

I slowly bring the joint to my lips, feel immediately that it's damp with his saliva—*gross*—but I forge ahead. I look down my nose, cross-eyed, at the little white thing, as I take a puff... and immediately start coughing.

Benedict giggles.

Which prompts me to try again, this time really concentrating on getting some to stay down in my lungs. It burns my throat, but once it's in feels better, as I stifle an intense impulse to cough. I hold the smoke (this is way harder than Destiny's vaping contraption), and wait to see if I feel something, before exhaling it all in a spate of spastic hacking.

I pass the joint back to Benedict, and look around the room, blink a few times to see if I feel any differently. And ... waiting ... still waiting ...

"I don't think I did it right," I say.

He takes another hit himself and hands it back to me. I go for it again, this time managing to get more into my lungs before the urge to cough forces me to expel it.

I look around the room again, and wait... *Whoa*. Is that it?

Something is definitely creeping over me. Feels like when I got my tonsils removed, just before I fell asleep, and the doctor was telling me to imagine I was on a tropical beach with the ocean gently lapping beside me. A pleasant sort of dizzy nothingness, but it also feels kind of hysterically funny.

Which makes me laugh.

And then Benedict laughs.

And I laugh even more.

"So what the hell?" he says after we wind down. "This is Jason's sister we're talking about, right?"

I nod yes.

"You are messing with fire, boss."

"She's totally different from him," I declare, my tongue seeming to loosen from its usual taut connection with my brain.

"Is she?" Benedict asks, but it's more of a statement than a question.

"Yeah," I say, suddenly feeling kind of philosophical. "Not on the surface, maybe. But what's the surface anyway?"

"Kimbo, there is no way that girl was going to lean over and kiss you right there in front of her whole world order."

"You weren't there," I say. "She was stirred inside, she sensed something inside of me. Like she knew."

"What it was, was, you were standing there finally claiming your space and not backing down from those ass-hats. Confidence and inner strength are universally attractive to people. It's primitive. Triggers our instincts to follow the leader."

"Maybe," I mutter, leaning back on the couch again and gazing up at the immense, dusty, rusty, rattling industrial heater mounted on the ceiling above us. I envision the centuries-old metal brackets suddenly snapping, sending the whole thing violently crashing down on our heads and snuffing us out. But, unlike every other time I've anticipated some random tragic event, I'm not worried. I feel all Zen, like, *Whatever happens happens.*

"You recognized you," Benedict adds then, busting me out of my tumbling-heater vision. "So Audrey recognized you. The you inside you."

This stuff is strong.

We fall silent. Me thinking about Audrey, how maybe she had just been hurt one too many times in her short life—by Drew's abandonment, Oryon's disappearance, by her brother's terrifying aggression, her family suffocating and judging her all the time. By average, hateful, cruel high school life. Maybe Audrey just couldn't deal, so she gave in and took the popular route, something no one would question.

OMG! I just realized the whole scenario is exactly like what happens in one of Audrey's and my (well Audrey and Drew's) favorite eighties movies, *Some Kind of Wonderful*. When Amanda Jones starts out saying, "I'd rather be with someone for the wrong reasons than alone for the right," but then figures out that life's actually better when you do the *opposite,* and she tells Keith to run off and give Watts the diamond-stud earrings he had bought with his entire college savings. God, I love that movie.

Audrey's Amanda Jones! Oryon is Keith! Jason is awful rich, spoiled, loathsome, rapey Hardy Jenns. And I'm Watts! The tough tomboy rock-and-roll drummer with the cute short haircut and red leather–fringed fingerless gloves, who wins love in the end. Wait, that means I win love from myself as another V. Maybe the analogy is breaking down a bit. I blame the weed. I mean, I don't feel, like, really high, whatever that is. I have nothing to compare it to. I don't know. Am I high? HAHAHAHAHA.

[Note to self: Look up whether eighties visionary film director and writer John Hughes was a Changer. Wait, before that, another note to self: find out if it's even true that there's a guide to famous Changers to look things up in.]

Where was I?

"So," I say to my left, but realize Benedict isn't sitting beside me anymore. I have no idea how much time has passed since he was.

I spot my laptop, the corner sticking out of my backpack. I flip it open, start a new e-mail, and without really thinking, begin typing:

Dear Audrey,

I know this is going to sound crazy. Wow, how long have I wanted to say that to you? Anyway, so, this is Kim. Kim Cruz, from school. I hope you got home okay last night. That dance kind of went off the rails, huh?

Anyway, I don't know how else to say this, but it felt like we had a connection last night. Like we've known each other for lifetimes. (Do you believe in that stuff?) I've never felt that about anybody before, which I figure is really rare, so why not just nut up and tell you?

The thing is, we kind of have known each other for lifetimes. Maybe not lifetimes. Well, for me they are.

If you're still reading this, which I would understand if you're not, but bear with me, because here's the thing: I've been at Central longer than just this year. In fact, I have been in your life over the last two and a half years. I've seen you through a lot of ups and downs, a close friendship with a girl who moved away, and then a relationship with a guy who also left school, suddenly, last spring. I know all about Romeo & Juliet. (Boy do I.) Cheerleading. Your brother. Your mother's cooking.

For two years I feel sort of like I've been your invisible protector. (From this guy named Kyle, which is a whole other story.) Anyway, I've loved you every step of the way.

I know you didn't ask for this. It's just, there are things in the universe we can't explain. Actual magic that brings people into each other's lives for a reason. Like I've been brought into yours.

Again, I understand if you want nothing to do with me after reading this. It is admittedly cuckoo for Cocoa Puffs. But what do I have to lose at this point? I can't help but feel that you felt this THING last night between us. You sensed that history too.

So if you did, can you let me know? Maybe we could spend some time together. Trust me, it wouldn't be the strangest thing that ever happened.

&(^^%%!%$#*(&**&#$^$%#&))*(&)*^&^>??
?!?!?!!!!?*

What am I doing why am I writing this I must be freaking insane in the membrane. She is going to think I'm bonkers and never want to talk to me again don't press send don't press send don't press sendddddddd.

I tilt my head from the glow of the screen back up at the heater. My eyelids droop as if ten-pound weights are glued to the lashes. All I want to do is curl up and sleep for seventy-two hours on this crusty couch beneath the noisy heater, suddenly the coziest place ever. I push my computer off my lap and onto the cushion beside me, flop my neck on the pillowed armrest, and close my eyes. I feel all glowy-orange inside, some kind of wonderful indeed.

I open my eyes. It's dark. Calm. For a flash, I think I'm in my bedroom at home. But then I hear the heater rattling above me, and the reality of where I am hits me anew. I lay there blinking into the blackness for a few minutes, listen for movement or voices. Everybody must be asleep, or out for the night. I don't even know what time it is.

My head is pounding. Pounding worse than the time Jason plowed me over at football practice last year. I put my hands on either side of my head and press hard, but it doesn't alleviate the pain even a little.

Now I remember: Benedict's weed.

I sit up, realizing my stomach muscles are a little sore too, like I'd been doing sit-ups in my sleep. My eye catches a glint of light off my laptop, which is sitting closed on the coffee table in front of me. It's then I remember the crazy-rambling confessional I vomited out to Audrey last night. Thank G I didn't push *Send* on that madness.

I open the screen and my laptop wakes up. I see that it's 3:42 a.m. Also: the e-mail's not there. I click through all the open windows. Nope. Not in any of them. I scan the dock: it's not collapsed there either. I check the *Drafts* folder. The *Trash*.

Did I dream I wrote the letter? (Jesus, why do people smoke that stuff?)

Confident that's the case, I click the *Sent* folder. And . . .

Oh

My

Freaking

At the top, there it is: *Sent* to Audrey's e-mail address at 9:43 p.m. last night.

Whoa. Wait.

There's no Internet here. I have no clue how this could've happened. I check the *Sent* folder again, just to be sure.

Yep, still there, off into the wild blue yonder at 9:43 p.m. I click and quickly reread the letter. It's worse than I remember.

There's no way that in my stupor I figured out how to use my phone as a hotspot and connected my laptop to send the message out via cell service. The only person here who could've done all that is . . .

Benedict. (Arnold.)

SPRING

CHANGE 3-DAY 163

Day 13 (not including weekends) of Audrey avoiding me. It seems like it'd be a really challenging feat, given we have the same homeroom and Honors English together, but you'd be surprised how slippery Audrey is when she wants to be, and worse, how ever-present Chloe is, stuck to Audrey's side like a pair of Spanx. Not that I mind. I still haven't figured out how I'd explain the e-mail beyond the obvious, *I was totally high when I wrote that.*

Today, though, in the cafeteria, I thought Audrey might've glanced in my direction over Kris's tiny head as we sat at our usual misfits, gays, and awkwards table, which is one over from the Asian table, where I do sometimes sit, especially when Kris has lunch detention.

"He begged me to take him back," Kris was saying with no small amount of relish about Rooster, as he cheekily stuffed the last bit of his cheese stick into his puckered pie hole and wiped his lips with a paper napkin.

"What'd you say?"

"*I've moved on, I learned how to get along,*" he sang, wadding up the napkin and tossing it onto his tray, then searching the front of his halter top for crumbs to brush off.

"It seemed like you really loved him. Are you sure you don't want to reconsider?"

"One of us needs to have pride, girl." He jabbed a thumb toward Audrey, Chloe, and the smattering of Chloettes who were touching up their makeup in cell phone cameras before heading to class. "And it clearly isn't you."

"Are you kidding me?" I scoffed, as Jason and Baron sidled over to the bitch-squad table, Jason planting a shoe on the bench with his crotch on full display and uttering something SO hilarious that they couldn't keep from LOL-ing enough for the whole cafeteria to hear and stroke his wretched little ego. *"I am so OVER that mess,"* I added, imitating Chloe's voice and tone so perfectly that Kris high-fived me across the table, even though it was a sports gesture, which Kris usually avoids like full-fat milk.

I decided to change the topic: "So, how's it going at Lady Chardonnay's?"

"It's okay. I mean, I'm really lucky she's letting me crash in her cloud, but if you can believe it, I miss home."

"I actually can believe it."

"Well, at least you're welcome back whenever you want," he said, seeming glum (for him). "My parents haven't even tried to find out whether I'm safe. I mean, I'm sure they're checking my school attendance, but besides that? Not so much."

"That can't feel good. I'm sorry."

He glanced over at Chloe again. "Those slags have no idea what it's like to be on their own. Speaking of, how's it going in your dirty little queer collective? And by *dirty* I mean, seriously, get some Febreze or something, because you smell vintage. And by *vintage* I mean not gently used."

"It's good. I guess. Kind of the same thing you're saying. I mean, I used to have hours to sit around and disappear into one of the many screens at my disposal. Now with chores and homework and commuting, I'm lucky if I can return a text, much less get my chat on—"

"Yeah, but . . ." Kris interrupted, "no curfew!"

"And nobody asking how I'm feeling all the time. Looking at me like I'm a jumper on a ledge just because I'm not Suzy Smile-a-lot."

"I met her once. Total bore."

"No sense of humor. Which, weird."

"Given the smiling."

We both giggled as the bell sounded, ending lunch period. Kris leaned across the table to try to slap my butt, but missed.

"I'm too sexy for my body," I sang, and bussed my tray.

"Join the club," said Kris.

It started pouring just as school let out. I was trudging through the deluge in the direction of my bus stop when the ol' familiar terror-inspiring roar of Jason's Mustang growled behind me, and before I could do anything about it, I was completely doused head-to-toe by a dirty gutter-water wave, courtesy of his wide tires.

There was no way it was an accident.

I squished my way to the strip mall to find a place to drain my shoes and dry my hair in a bathroom, and noticed the Toot N Tote-um was open. When I came out of the bathroom, still blotting my face with scratchy recycled paper towels, I practically collided with the owner of the shop, the one who got me and DJ arrested for shoplifting (which we didn't do) last year. I had tried to avoid the place on principle ever since, but any port in a (literal) storm, right?

"Are you buying something?" he asked, seemingly already angry.

"Uh, no," I replied. "I just came in to get out of the rain on the way to the bus stop."

He gave me a once-over, absorbing me in all my pitiful sogginess, then handed me a cup. "Hot cocoa machine over there," he said brusquely. "Complimentary."

"Thanks," I said, not sure what to do. I didn't want to be a traitor to my former, racially profiled self. On the other hand, free hot chocolate . . .

I poured half a cup—seemed somehow less traitorous—and stood outside under the awning for a while, staring into the water-slicked parking lot, the same place I used to skate last year with Jerry from time to time. No skating now, per the five new signs that read, *NO SKATEBOARDS City Ordinance,* posted around our usual spots. So I guess it wasn't only me who had changed.

As I was wondering where my old skateboard even was, a figure in a red and black rain parka and wellies appeared, exiting the hair salon and cutting across the parking lot toward me. The gait seemed familiar, like . . . *No, can't be. Wait, it is* . . . It was Audrey, every step splashing water into messy rings around her feet. Then I noticed Jason's car parked in front of Subway. Of course.

There was nowhere to go, so I stood my ground, figuring Audrey would whip right past, ignoring me per usual. But she kept coming at me. Closer and closer, until we were toe-to-toe. She pulled the hood from her head, shook off beads of water, then looked left and right to make sure nobody else was within earshot.

"We should talk," she announced flatly.

I stood dumbstruck, kind of in shock she was actually acknowledging my existence, post-e-mail-gate.

Then she launched into it: "I don't know what the deal is with you. I'm not sure I *want* to know what the deal is with you. But that e-mail you sent me was totally out of line, and to be honest, creepy as crap. I don't know what you were talking about with some moment you imagined we shared at the dance, and I have NO idea what you're talking about as far as being in my life for three years, or whatever that was."

Here she paused, staring at me for some sort of reaction. Which I wasn't going to give her, at least not until I figured out which way this was going to go.

"Anyway, my friends think that you have an unhealthy obsession with me," she went on. "I'm not going so far as to say that, but maybe you're confused, maybe—"

"Maybe what?" I asked, almost daring her to say what I knew was coming next.

"I think you might be struggling with some mental or emotional issues, and I really hope that you are getting the help you need."

BOOM. There it was.

"Look," she added then, reaching to touch my shoulder in the most condescending manner fathomable, "I don't really know you, you don't really know me, and whatever happened that night at the dance, let's just put it behind us and chalk it up to one big misunderstanding about other people's business. It was between my brother and Chloe, and they're grown up enough to figure it out for themselves."

I started laughing.

Which seemed to make Audrey indignant. And surprised that I was refusing to settle into my place in the social hierarchy.

"News bulletin: those two are probably never going to grow up," I said. "But that's beside the point. You saw what Jason did to her drink. And so did I."

"I don't know what you're talking about," she lied, her face flushed.

"Okay, whatever," I said, utterly disappointed in her. "And listen. I was totally high when I wrote that e-mail. One of the guys I live with"—here her interest piqued, like, *You live with guys? More than one? Wait, what?!*—"we were messing around, and I told them what had happened the night before at the dance, and we were all just typing random stuff into my laptop . . ." It didn't look like she was buying it. "And one of the guys pressed *Send* after I passed out, and I didn't realize it until the morning, and by then of course it was too late. And since at school you've been avoiding me like HPV, I haven't had a chance to explain what happened, and then I kinda forgot about it, so whatever, it's done. Move on."

She stared at me. "I don't believe you."

"Well then, we're both lying, aren't we?"

Lightning flashed just then, followed by one of those earth-shattering thunderclaps, which meant the storm was close by and there was no way I was getting out of there anytime soon. All of it made me want to call my mom. For a ride. A shoulder. A comfy bed. A home-cooked dinner. To be around somebody who tries her best not to judge, and succeeds most of the time. I missed my family. I missed a lot of things.

"For what it's worth, the Audrey I thought I knew stood up to people like Chloe," I started, unsure of what I was even doing. "The Audrey I thought I knew was always herself. The Audrey I thought I knew wasn't afraid of looking dumb when she danced, or challenging the status quo, or loving a guy her parents didn't approve of. So maybe you're right. I *was* confused. I never knew you at all."

At that, Audrey appeared both wounded and utterly baffled. She pulled the hood over her head, and for a blink I wished I could have gone back in time and kept my mouth shut, but then Jason exploded through the Subway doors with a pair of foot-long sandwiches in clear plastic bags, and spotted the two of us.

"Come on," he called to Audrey.

It looked like there was a tear on her cheek. I'm pretty sure it wasn't a raindrop.

"I'm just saying, you might want to ask yourself why you always do the easy thing now," I added, likely plunging the knife deeper. I didn't care.

"I said, come on!" Jason yelled, and Audrey stepped back out into the storm.

CHANGE 3-DAY 164

I'm minding my own business, heading to trig, when four Central letterman jackets suddenly block out the fluorescent light above my head. And there he is, something wicked this way coming—Jason marching up and proceeding to corner me beside a cluster of lockers, his buddies forming a semicircle intimidation wall around me so I can't escape.

"I know you're in love with my sister, Obeast," he seethes.

"I didn't know you had a sister named Obeast," I throw back, not feeling scared of him, even though I probably should be. I try to squeeze myself between two of his henchmen, but they don't budge. The other two tighten formation while the rest of the school population just saunters by, paying no mind to what's going down behind the jock curtain.

"Audrey told me how crazy you are," Jason says with that stupid ugly smirk of his.

I smirk right back.

"This isn't a joke, zipperhead," he says, just as the assistant principal comes out of a door across the hallway from us.

"No kidding," I say, seizing my opportunity and slamming my books loudly enough onto the floor to catch the assistant principal's attention. The menacing lettermen from hell scatter like marbles, as does Jason, but not before he leans into me, his breath hot on my neck. "I've made people disappear before," he hisses. "And I can do it again."

"That is some crizazy shizzay," Destiny says after I tell her about Jason's big-boy move on me this morning. "I want to pound that punk's face in, and I've never even met him."

We are Skyping for the first time in too long, me poaching Internet on the roof of the Starbucks near RaChas HQ.

"I'm really sorry," I say.

"For what?"

"Being me."

"It's okay. You don't have to keep apologizing."

"I know," I say. "It's just . . ."

"It's just what?"

"I should've acted better."

"Save it for your headstone," she teases.

"DJ looks really happy whenever I see him at school."

"He *better*. I mean, look at me." She strikes a cheesy duck-face pose, cracks up. "He says he's been looking, but he never sees you."

"I'm stealth."

"Seriously, why don't you find him and hang?" Destiny asks.

I don't know how to answer. The word *shame* pops into my head. "It's complicated. We went through a lot together. I don't know. Oh, dang," I say, catching the time above Destiny's face. "I gotta go, my mom's meeting me downstairs in a minute."

"You're seeing her?"

"I miss my Mommy," I say. "Waaah."

"Later, tell her hi for me."

"K, love you."

"Love you more."

When Mom pulled up and parked in front of the Starbucks, I almost didn't recognize her, even though she was rolling in our same old family car. She looked weary, pale, and, like every grizzled cop in every detective movie, "too old for this crap."

I met her at the door and she kind of lunged forward and hugged me immediately. Hugged me hard and didn't let go for a really long time. It'd been a couple weeks since I last saw her for what had become our designated, Tracy-negotiated appointments. I don't know why I was being so stubborn about moving back home. Half of me wanted to tell Mom to start the car and let's hop in, pick up a large pizza, and bring it back to the house to eat in front of the TV while we watched old *M*A*S*H* episodes. But the other half of me felt like I still had something to prove, if only to myself, and that there was no way I was going to let my NON-NORMALNESS infect her space anymore. (*Yeah. Not over it.*)

Sometimes I worried that Mom was being so cool about me living with the RaChas because it was actually a relief to have me and my bad attitude gone. But then I'd see her on these visits and swear I could actually hear her heart breaking when she looked at me.

After we got our lattes to go, we met Tracy for dinner at this hole-in-the-wall Cuban place downtown, best fried plantains anywhere. Over the meal, it was the usual conversation among us, real polite, catching up on everybody's lives. Even Snoopy, who has taken to sleeping by the window I crawled out of six weeks ago. (If *that* doesn't make me feel like a monster . . .)

Mostly they asked me about school, how I was doing, how's Kris, how's Destiny, how's PE, did I have enough clean clothes, was I getting enough to eat, was my cell phone working, did I need more funds added to my bus pass, and so on.

When the check came, Mom said, "I was reading over

your Changers packet the other day and noticed your V's birthday's coming up soon."

"Sweet sixteen!" Tracy clapped.

"So?" I asked. "That's just BS paperwork for school records."

"Par-tay!" Tracy said, still clapping.

"More like, li-cense!" I countered. "I never even got my learner's permit."

"We'll do that over spring break if you want," Mom said. "Last year was kind of, well, you know . . ."

"It wasn't the best time to be thinking about learning to drive," Tracy finished.

"Yes, not exactly the best time," Mom said.

"I'm not really in a party kind of a space," I mumbled, like Charlie Brown with a rain cloud over his head.

Mom ignored my sourness, pressed on: "Dad and I bought you a gift we'd love to give you. And if you feel like taking a few of your Static friends out to a movie or dinner or concert or something, we'd like to offer that as an option."

"It's okay," I said. "Life is the only party I need."

Tracy rolled her eyes, sensing shades of Benedict-speak.

Mom nodded, said "Okay," and signed the credit card slip, but she seemed deflated, despite trying to keep up appearances.

"I've got to pee," I said, wondering why they were suddenly making a big deal about Changers Council–assigned milestones, which only exist for show. "I'll meet you outside."

We said our goodbyes to Tracy in the parking lot. Then Mom and I strolled in silence to the car. She put her arm around me, and I put my head on her shoulder, and we walked like that for a while.

"How's Dad?" I asked, soon as we reached the vehicle and climbed inside.

"Ahhh. He's not having the best time with all of this," she said, "to be perfectly candid. But I'm handling it, so you don't have to worry."

"Is he still mad at me?"

"For what, sweetpea?"

"Leaving."

"Oh, no," Mom said, but I could tell she was covering. "He's just at one of those, I guess you could say crossroads in life, where you take stock and try to figure out what comes next."

"Isn't that kind of like all of life?"

She adjusted the rearview mirror. "I guess so."

"You don't have to protect me from the truth, Mom. I can handle whatever. I mean, if I've learned anything, it's that existence can be incredibly complicated, so like," I stumbled a little, "I'm perfectly able to hold two conflicting concepts in one brain. Or more than two. I mean, obviously."

Mom smiled, but her sadness still bled through. We pulled up in front of RaChas HQ.

"You're a smart little bug," she said, setting the emergency brake.

"Are you okay?" I asked her.

"I'm the one who should be asking *you* that."

A couple of dodgy guys walked by the door, kind of peeked in, then moved along.

"Are you sure I can't convince you to come back home tonight?" she asked.

Yes.

No.

"Not yet."

CHANGE 3-DAY 189

I know it's been awhile since I've Chronicled. I can't even remember when the last time was. Although I could do with a little less lentils and brown rice at every dinner, life at RaChas HQ is actually kind of a relief where Chronicling's concerned. I don't feel the usual Changers Council pressure to do it as much as possible, much less every day. Some of us do, some don't; and still others do it sporadically. It's so nice not to have the spirit of my future Mono staring me down with the (not so) implied threat of, *Record every minute detail so you can CHOOSE WELL,* when it comes time to declare at my Forever Ceremony.

I mean, show me a Changer who manages to Chronicle every day during their Cycle as mandated, and I'll show you ... Oh, duh: Tracy. Speaking of Trace, her main matrimonial squeeze was sweating me today in homeroom. It's my grades. They suck. No surprise, given my living arrangements, mood swings, PTSD, and overall evolving worldview.

Mr. Crowell delivered our midterm grades today, making a little speech (in his "we're all in this together" way) about how we juniors needed to start considering college applications, something he would be pleased to talk through if anyone had any queries, especially about scholarships.

Not only are PSATs coming up, he said, but the importance of grades during the second semester of our junior year "should not be underestimated."

"Which is why I'm implementing a Study Buddy program in homeroom," he said, explaining that kids who were currently "excelling" would be paired with other kids who were currently "underperforming," the former helping the latter with organization, time-management, note-taking, or whatever it was that might be plaguing the strugglers' performances.

"Look at it as just, you know, a strategy-sharing opportunity," Mr. Crowell continued sheepishly. "Sometimes I find it's helpful to hear what works for others as we're developing our own systems and techniques for success."

Ew. Since when has high school become a corporation? Oh, right. Since everything did.

Mr. Crowell, in pairing up the class, was really trying to match people who weren't already friends. His best couple? Chloe and stoner skater Jerry, hands down. The most shocking aspect being that Chloe, with scarcely two brain cells to rub together, actually managed to make it into the "excelling" group. Second place went to Kris, who got one of the Chloettes ("I'm going to flip this script and teach this chick about avant-garde theater," he whispered), and then I of course got . . .

Audrey.

I mean, really? I'm sure Mr. Crowell thought he was helping, but I wish he had just put me with someone like meek Madison from the front row. She would've been ideal. As in, I'd have said, "Let's not meet up but say we did," and she would've nodded her head, and nobody would be the wiser. But no. I'm with the person who wants to see me the least in the world right now, if her continued duck-and-weave behavior over the last few weeks is any indication.

As soon as Mr. Crowell announced the pairings and the required meeting outside of school, there were groans all around the class. Chloe whined aloud to her neighboring Chloette, "Jerry, really? How am I going to function with a contact high?" while Jerry loudly kissed his hand, slapped his butt, and then blew the kiss across the classroom in her direction.

Audrey, whom I could see only from behind, seemed to sink in her chair and exhale loudly when Mr. Crowell called our names, subtly glancing up through his floppy bangs to gauge my reaction. I kept chill, mostly to placate him. He's a good guy, means well. He didn't have all the information, so I couldn't really blame him.

"Can we swap partners?" this girl Sara asked.

"It's not Secret Santa, Sara. You can't trade for someone else. And if you think you can just blow off these study sessions without my knowing," Mr. Crowell yelled as people were beginning to do the rude thing of packing up while the teacher is still talking, "then you are wrong! I will require proof of your meeting—a photo of the two of you together somewhere, preferably off-campus. And then a file card with three things you know now about your partner that you didn't before."

At this the entire class began grousing aloud. "A photo of me and Wiz Khalifa? I *die*," Chloe snarked as the bell rang. At which point Jerry picked up his skateboard, grabbed his backpack, and blew by Chloe as she exited, yelling, "On like Donkey Kong!"

"Well?" I said to Audrey as she gathered her belongings. There were just a few of us left in class.

"I guess we're doing this," she said. She seemed preoccupied—but oddly, not by this.

"You want to go to Starbucks after school?" I asked. "To get it over with?"

"Sure," she said, rushed. "Sounds good."

"What time? Is four okay? I have to catch a 5:05 bus."

"Okay," she said, heading out the door. "Wait, the one by school?"

"Yeah." *You know, the one where you and Oryon interviewed Mr. Crowell for the love-themed issue of the* Peregrine Review. *And where you and Oryon met up before you went back to his apartment and—*

"Kim," I hear Mr. Crowell saying. It's just the two of us in the classroom now.

I shake off the memories of that night. That life-altering, amazing, messed-up night. "Yeah?"

"Are you okay?" he asks, perching on a desk beside me. "I've been concerned about the grades situation."

"I don't know if Tracy filled you in on all this, but," I double-check to make sure the classroom is truly empty, "the Council provides official transcripts for our Monos to use to apply to colleges, so none of this really matters."

He looks taken aback, gathers himself. "It's not really about the grades per se. I'm more concerned about the habits you learn along the way, and your grasp of the material, you know? The bigger concepts."

I try to think of a polite way to tell him I don't need a Static's help with "bigger concepts." "I know what you mean," I say, "but I don't think a study session with Audrey is the solution."

"I just figured it might be a nice ice-breaker."

"Well, you got the ice part right."

He snorts as I shift my backpack to the other shoulder. I feel exposed in front of him, and I just want to go. I don't want to have to confront my ugly, naked history in the glaring light of my high school homeroom.

"Tracy said you've been having a rough go of it," he says then, not giving up. "She guards your privacy of course. And maybe it's not my business. But you should always remember how loved you are. By so many. And from where I stand, you have weathered way bigger storms before this."

"Climate change, Mr. Crowell. It's no joke."

He snorts again. "That's it right there. You haven't lost your sense of humor. A sense of humor is a life raft, Kim. You can save yourself with it."

"Thanks," I say. "I'll consider it."

Audrey blows into Starbucks five minutes late. I'm holding a couple cushy leather seats for us in the back by the restrooms.

"Howdy," I say, soon as she dumps her stuff on the other chair.

"Hey."

"So . . . this is awkward."

"I know," she agrees, somewhat relieved.

"Can I get you a drink?"

"Uh, sure, I guess." She reaches for her wallet.

"On me," I say, then head over to get in line and order for us.

Once I come back and set the drink in front of her—soy cappuccino with one sugar—Audrey says, "Thanks. Wait, is this soy?"

I nod my head in the affirmative, and just sort of stand there with my iced coffee.

"How'd you—" Audrey starts, then stops herself, puzzled, but less ragey than she was at our Toot N Tote-um showdown.

I don't say anything, just take my seat and diligently

pull out my planner, open it on my lap, keeping it official.

Audrey sips her coffee, and by the way her lips flinch ever so slightly around the hole in the plastic lid, I can tell it burns. She puts the drink down, opens up her planner too. Like she's supposed to.

"So," I say, "what's the secret to your success?"

Audrey makes a face. "Study Buddies have got to be the lamest thing ever invented."

"I know, he's off his rocker," I say. "But I'm sure Principal Redwine is hounding the teachers to get all of our scores up."

"How'd you know how I like my coffee?" she asks suddenly.

"Sorry?" I say, completely off-guard. Trying not to make this tip into yet another conversation about my SAF (single Asian female) obsession.

She waits.

"I guess, well, like I was trying to tell you," I stammer, girding myself, "I, uh, I just pay attention to things. To people."

"That's a nice change of pace," she says, sounding more like OG Audrey. "Most people I know are only concerned with themselves and what they want."

"Maybe you know the wrong people," I say, all easy-breezy. Not invested.

She sucks in her cheeks fish-face style, managing to look adorable. And I am reminded why I haven't been able to forget her.

We nominally go over our study schedules, with me explaining that I usually get all A's and A-minuses, but that my living situation changed last semester, which has affected my ability to get my work done well, and on time. She's extremely curious about my troubles at home, the "anarchaqueer freegan space" I'm crashing at downtown, and how my parents are even letting me do this. Audrey's parents, she explains, "would not be down with that sort of thing."

Understatement of the freaking year.

Aud's ease around me appears to grow as the first hour passes, and then we're approaching the two-hour mark. I try to remain detached but warm, and stick to the task at hand. I don't try to tell her about herself anymore. I mean, I hate when people try to tell me about myself, so why would she want to hear it?

I realize I've missed my bus, and we haven't even done our sharing exercise yet. "Okay, so you have your first fact about me: I'm not living at home right now," I say. "What else do you want to know?"

"Well, unlike some people, I don't know *anything* about you," she replies cautiously.

I don't want to upset the carefully stacked apple cart, so I don't pick up the trail she's seemingly laying for me.

"Fine," she resumes after a few moments, "what's your favorite movie?"

"That's impossible. How am I supposed to narrow it down to one?"

"Just pick one."

"Okay, how about *Some Kind of Wonderful*?"

"That's a good one," she says, sort of side-eyeing me.

"What's your last question?" I ask quickly.

"Besides your parents, who do you love most in the world?"

"Do they have to be living?"

"Yeah."

"Is it weird to say my dog? He's really been there for me in ways people haven't."

"That's not weird," she says. "What's his name?"

"Elvis," I lie, because of she's made Snoopy's acquaintance. "Okay, you have your three."

"Now you ask me," she says, adding sassily, "if there actually *is* anything you don't know."

Again I refuse the bait. Just feels wiser at this point to let that wayward e-mail fade into oblivion. I try to think of things I don't know about Audrey. There aren't a lot. "Uh, how about . . . Okay, where do you want to live when you're older?"

"I haven't really thought much about it. Outside Tennessee, I guess," she says, kind of sadly.

"I mean, if you could like live anywhere, where would you want to be, even if it's just for a while?"

"I guess I'm really curious about New York City. It just seems like you can slip into the chaos and be whoever you want to be."

"That's cool," I say. "Who do you want to be?"

"What do you mean?"

"You said *be whoever you want to be*. So, who do you want to be?"

Audrey knits her brow. It seems like she's going to confess something, but instead, she takes a big gulp of her coffee and answers, "It was just a metaphor."

"Yeah, I know," I deflect. "So. What kind of toothpaste do you use?"

"Ooh, deep," she chuckles. "Colgate."

"Okay, and big finish: besides your parents, who do *you* love most in the world?"

I hear the blood *whoosh* to my skull. It starts pounding like the surf. Audrey is staring at me, her eyes narrowed, not answering, not answering . . .

"Crap, I need to catch the next bus," I blurt, then start frantically stuffing my binders back into my bag.

"Wait, we still need to snap a photo for Mr. Crowell!"

"Okay, okay," I say, zipping my backpack. "Let's do it outside."

The sky to the west is bright orange, the clouds blowing past fast and furious, the sunlight breaking in and out as if being turned on and off by a switch.

"Let's not have ourselves in the shot," Audrey suggests.

"Oh, so you're ashamed of being seen with me?" I tease. Damn, I wish I didn't just say that. "I'm not even on social media," I add.

"It's not that," she says. "After what we were talking about, let's not make it about us, you know? Let's make it about the experience."

"Give me your phone."

The sun is nearly gone now, but what light remains is casting long shadows everywhere, including up against the side of the boring-ass-same-as-every-other Starbucks, making it look somehow new. We stand side-by-side, inching closer to the building so the shadows jutting out from our feet creep up the gray stucco wall. Hers is thinner and taller, mine shorter and rounder.

I open the camera on Audrey's phone and frame the shot perfectly—only our shadows are visible, plus the lower half of the Starbucks sign—so Mr. Crowell will know that we were together off-campus. I snap the first, but then Audrey's shadow suddenly pumps a fist in the air like Judd Nelson at the end of *The Breakfast Club*, so I snap another.

"Now we've fulfilled our duty," I say, handing her phone back. "You want to e-mail that to Mr. Crowell? You can tell him you scared me straight and it'll be all A's henceforth."

"Well that was easy," she says sarcastically. "But yeah, I'll send it tonight."

"Study Buddies for life."

"Long live Study Buddies."

For a second it feels like old times.

"See you around," I say.

"Yeah, see you around," she echoes, as I turn toward my bus stop.

CHANGE 3-DAY 191

When I got home from school this afternoon, Benedict and a few members of the crew were crowded around a computer, as Wylie the dreadlocked IT whiz madly pecked at the keyboard.

"Kim!" Benedict yelled, waving me over. "We're finally launching."

"Sweet," I said, kind of wishing I were coming home to some apple slices with peanut butter and lemonade like Mom used to make for me sometimes, instead of yet another rebel plot to subvert the establishment. "Launching what?"

Wylie tipped the display so I could see a little better. It looked like a bunch of gibberish to me, html code and whatnot, but at the bottom of the page was a tiny thumbnail photo of Chase, as his first V.

"What are you doing?" I asked, now genuinely curious.

"Taking WeAreChangers.org live," Benedict explained. "Finally honoring everything Chase stood for, what he died for—what we *all* stand for."

I thought back to Chase telling me about the website that the RaChas were intending to launch right around the first time he brought me to HQ. It was meant to introduce Changers philosophy to the world, to take action that the Council could not control nor have any part in. And do it in a way that didn't put any actual Changers at risk, which sounded like a difficult needle to thread. But that was the last I remembered hearing of it.

"How are you getting Internet?" I asked (selfishly, if I'm being honest—what a privilege it'd be not to have to rip off Starbucks for wireless).

"Wylie cracked the gallery next door's WEP Wi-Fi password. But nobody can use it except when they're closed."

"Sweet," I said. "When's it launching?"

"Tonight, at 11:01, or 12:01 on the East Coast. At which point, we shall hide in the shadows no longer," Benedict said, and then added as though beginning a ghost story, "because those who lurk in darkness can never light the way."

(Where does he come up with this stuff? And so much of it . . .)

"Uh, isn't it sort of . . ." I started to ask, then thought better of it.

Sensing a challenge, Benedict cocked his head toward me, asked, "What?"

"Nothing."

"What?" he goaded. "Just say it. What?"

"I was just going to ask, isn't it sort of dangerous to be coming out like this? I mean, with the recent Abiders stuff?" I mean, I would know.

"It's not like we're putting our faces and names out there—yet," Benedict said defensively, like I was intimating he hadn't thought this through sufficiently.

"No, I'm not saying—"

"Once people's eyes are forced open, I believe most will choose acceptance," he declared, louder than he needed to for me to hear. But there was something else in his tone, like maybe even *he* didn't completely buy what he was selling.

"Is there anything I can do to help?" I asked by way of changing the subject.

"I think we're in good shape," Wylie said. "I just have to

iron out a few of the widget issues, and then we'll beta test for a couple hours, and hopefully be set to launch by the deadline."

"Right on schedule," Benedict echoed, clapping Wylie on the shoulder.

"What are you doing with Chase's photo?" I asked.

"We're including a memorial to him on the site, kind of like an altar where we'll keep a cybercandle burning for him forever."

I nodded my head. But inside, I wasn't sure how I felt about that particular aspect of the endeavor. I don't think Chase would've wanted his face splashed across 100 percent fair trade T-shirts like Ché Guevara, so hopefully this wasn't going to tip into that territory.

I went to the quiet zone to try to get in some studying for my last two finals before spring break. I opened my books and put some headphones on, but there was a lot of noise and activity all over HQ, and it was hard to concentrate. So much for pulling the grades up this term. Sorry, Mr. Crowell. *#StudyBuddiesFail*

When I came back out to the main space a few minutes before midnight, it was oddly hushed. Benedict and the rest of the RaChas were hunched around Wylie, all of their faces aglow from the monitor. I joined the scrum to look closer at the screen, and I could literally smell the tension in the air. As in wet dog b.o. wafting off each and every one of them. I smelled my own armpit as a self-conscious reflex.

"It's go-time," Benedict said under his breath.

Wylie looked back at him and nodded. Pressed *Enter*.

People slapped hands, clapped. And then . . . we waited.

The site looked the same as it did a second before—a giant modified Changers emblem with many arms and legs circling da Vinci's *Vitruvian Man*, more arms and legs than on the regular Changers emblem (the RaChas thereby essentially seizing and reappropriating the emblem for these verboten purposes—Turner the Lives Coach is not going to like this!):

Only now the site we were looking at was apparently live and public for anybody in the world to see. Wylie clicked back and forth between windows, e-mailing cryptic press releases to many news sites, blogs, and social media platforms.

Benedict asked me for my laptop, to check what the site looked like on a different computer. I gave it to him, and he logged on to the pirated Wi-Fi using the password Wylie read aloud: *"L-I-F-E-I-S-A-R-T."*

"I'm in," Benedict said, pecking *w-e-a-r-e-c-h-a-n-g-e-r-s-dot-o-r-g* into my browser. He studied it for a second, refreshed the page, then refreshed it again. Looked at the site that kept coming up. Spanning the entire home page was the normal eight-limbed Changers emblem. Benedict looked confused. "Wylie, did you leave the old emblem up by accident?"

"No," Wylie answered, still shooting off press releases. "Why, what do you mean?"

Benedict brought my laptop over, and Wylie looked at it, started clicking around the website on my track pad. Or trying to.

"No," Wylie said after a few clicks.

"What?" Benedict was starting to lose his cool.

"No, no, no." Wylie went back to his own computer, pecking and typing madly.

"What the hell is going on?" Benedict asked. "Answer me."

Wylie dropped his head on the keyboard, mumbling, "They got us, they hacked us."

"Who? What?"

"The Council. Who else?"

"How?"

And then the whole HQ erupted into hysteria and havoc for at least the next hour, while Benedict surveyed the damage and Wylie tried to figure out how the Council had managed to jam the new website, and had put up their own version of it, which looked at first glance like a promotional site for a new reality TV show.

Benedict was devastated. Not to mention deflated, dejected, and disheartened. I have to admit, I was fairly gutted myself, as were the others, being faced with (more) evidence of just how far the Council's fingers are capable of stretching when it comes to protecting the mission.

Somebody floated the idea that the art gallery next door could be a front for the Council, a way to keep tabs on RaChas activities. Somebody else started sweeping the crannies of HQ to make sure it wasn't electronically bugged. Benedict triple-checked with each of us that we hadn't inadvertently Chronicled anything about the launch, just in case the Council was monitoring our Chronicles. As the mood devolved even further, and all of us grew even more sleep-deprived/suspicious, somebody suggested there could be a mole inside the RaChas, one of us who's feeding every new development directly to the Council. Now I'm paranoid I shouldn't even be Chronicling *this*, after the fact.

A heated argument started over by the couch, and somebody got pushed. I couldn't even see who it involved.

"Enough!" Benedict yelled, and everyone snapped to. "We're not going to stand for this. And we're not going to be defeated by it, either."

People were listening, though nobody seemed to have much faith left. My eyes were blurry and they stung, and I had a math final the next morning, but I was curious about how Benedict was going to respond to being foiled and betrayed by the Council yet again.

"Screw the tech overlords, we're gonna kick it old school," he started, slowly and tentatively, but somehow invigorated. "If they won't let us express ourselves freely in the greatest public forum in existence, then we'll use our bodies, our mouths, our legs, our arms, our fists, and take our mission to the streets."

Wylie hopped up from his desk for the first time all night, suggesting to Benedict, "Maybe we don't talk about anything in detail until we figure out if there's a leak?"

"Oh, we will root out any leak, be it next door or closer to home," Benedict said calmly, peering around the room. Then continued, "Because nothing is going to stop change. Real change, the change we need, the change we deserve, will not come from waiting for power to be given. It will come when we *take* it!'

It was as if Chase were speaking through Benedict. I remembered words just like those coming out of his mouth when he first discovered the RaChas mission and started hanging around HQ. Back then I was terrified of breaking the rules. But this time I felt camaraderie, and a sudden swell of pride. In Chase. And in myself. We were part of a club, of the long line of all the underdogs who ever stood up to a much more powerful force in the name of doing something they believed in. Right or wrong.

A nascent, possibly ill-advised plan was hatched (I'm not going to go into it, just in case), and then we all zombie-walked to our bunks and crashed. Statics would find out who Changers were, even if it wasn't going to be through a measly website. The RaChas were going to make sure of it.

And I would be standing among them.

CHANGE 3-DAY 192

Destiny and DJ are making out in her car in the parking lot when I roll up on them, rapping on the window, loud.

"The hell?" DJ hollers, jumping back from Destiny.

"Condoms save lives," I mutter, opening the door and sliding into the backseat. "And prevents them, FYI."

"What's up?" Destiny says, retying her ponytail in the rearview.

"I don't know. What's up with you guys?" I ask.

"Oh, you know, nothing," DJ replies. "You're clearly not interrupting anything." He leans over and pecks Destiny's cheek. "Call you later. Bye, Kim."

"Bye, Deej," I say, as he double-takes at my use of the nickname, then hops out of the car and heads back up to school to meet his mom.

"I'm not your chauffeur," Destiny turns and says to me then. "Get your arse up here, Sir Kensington."

I climb over the backseat, purposely bumping her shoulder with my butt on the way.

"Can we eat somewhere downtown?" I ask, hoping to bum a ride to HQ after.

"Sure."

We buckle up and head out, listening to the old-school hip-hop station, which only comes in closer to town. Something about the city outside my window makes me change my mind about dinner.

"Can we go somewhere and chill for minute instead?" I ask.

I direct Destiny to a clearing on the bank of Cumberland River just across from downtown. She finds a spot to park where we can see the water flow past, and we roll down the windows, take off our seat belts, and stretch our legs across the dash and out the windows. They dangle like we're children in too-big chairs, as we inhale the breeze, cool and damp off the river.

I tell her about last night, about what the RaChas had been planning to do, going public with the website. And how the Council prevented them from doing it. "Prevented *us* from doing it," I correct myself as it comes out.

Because there is no "I" vs. "They" anymore. And then I want to tell her way more, even as I'm not sure whether she wants (or needs) to hear it.

"There's some other stuff," I say.

She whips out her e-cig.

"I thought you were trying to quit."

"It sounds like I'm going to need it," she says, clicking it on.

"I don't have to tell you. Say the word, and I'll shut up right now."

She's quiet while inhaling, then blows the vapor out the window. "No, I should know. I mean, obviously I want to know. Knowledge is power, right?"

So I tell her. Everything. About how the Changers Council was aware we were being held in the basement, way before we were actually rescued. How they didn't do anything at first, and seemingly toyed with the idea of sacrificing us so as to keep things quiet. How maybe Chase didn't need to die. How we didn't need to be in there as long as we were, our folks didn't need to suffer heartrending worry, and Alex didn't need to lie in a coma for months while waiting for his next V.

I spill and spill, until I look over and notice that Destiny is shaking.

"Are you cold? You want to put the windows up or—"

"I'm furious," she says, spitting the words through her teeth. "No wonder you were so freaking pissed at the world. The whole time they're supposedly nursing us back to health and teaching us to deal with our trauma, they've been lying to us? Our parents endured all those extra days of worry when the Council could've told them where we were, so at least they'd know we were alive? What kind of jacked-up type of empathy is that supposed to be exactly?" She grinds her teeth, squeezes her eyes tight. "Why didn't you tell me sooner?"

"I didn't want to burden you."

Destiny cuts her eyes at me like a switchblade.

"I don't know, I've just been processing everything in my own time," I say. "It's all so confusing, trying to make sense of it. It's a giant mind-frack, is what it is."

After a beat, Destiny says, calming herself: "If you understand, things are just as they are. If you do not understand, things are just as they are."

"Damn. How many years is it going to take me to unravel that one?"

"However long it takes you," she says. "Do your parents know?"

I shake my head.

"My folks are going to be pissed," she says. "Like, demand-an-emergency-meeting-with-Turner mad."

"Are you going to tell them?" I ask, momentarily panicked I've said too much, stirring up a storm when it was none of my business to get in the mix. But then I remember Destiny's Zen saying from two seconds ago and realize, the Council put themselves in this situation. If there's a handful of pissed-off parents they now have to deal with, concerned—with good reason—that the Council doesn't have the best interests of their children at heart? That's on them.

"I guess I don't know if I should," she says.

We fall quiet as the sun starts to dip below the water, the bleating of the cicadas filling in with their shrill, desolate song.

"The RaChas are planning a demonstration," I say after several minutes. "A visibility march down Lower Broadway, all along the Honky Tonk Highway from Rosa Parks Boulevard to this river we're looking at. They're coming out. And I'm going to be there."

Destiny raises an eyebrow, sucks on her e-cig like it contains the serum of eternal life, then breaks into a magnificent, dazzling grin. "Like, *out* out?" she asks.

"Like, no-going-back-in out."

"Exciting . . . terrifying," she purrs.

"I don't know what's going to happen afterward."

Our eyes lock for a few beats, and then she says: "I'm in, baby."

We slap hands. "Wait, what about DJ?" I ask.

"DJ," she says flatly, "will have to adjust. Because you and me? We're ride-or-die."

"Things are just as they are."

"Until they aren't."

CHANGE 3-DAY 193

If you'd told me when I woke up this morning that I'd end the night splitting cheese fries and a Cherry Coke with Audrey while "Car Wash" played in the background, I'd have said, *Keep smoking, Benedict,* because the odds of me and Aud whooping it up on a girls night out seemed about as likely as Jason taking up needlepoint.

And yet.

I guess it's true what they say about confidence. All that *Fake it till you make it* bumper-sticker philosophy seems to genuinely work on most people. It's like that old psychology study where they made unhappy people smile, and the very act of smiling tricked their brains into thinking they were feeling better. It really is that simple in some ways. Not the deep stuff. That remains a convoluted murky mess, and I guess holla for that, because without it we wouldn't have Basquiat or Emily Dickinson or My Chemical Romance. But still, it's a comfort to realize I have a modicum of control over my mood, if nothing else. *[Insert ☺ here.]*

This afternoon I was sorting through my locker, filling my backpack with all the supplies I'd need over spring break, when the bitch squad happened to be passing by. I could sense something odd in their energy, something amiss, like maybe one of them forgot it was flat-iron day or whatever simple-minded club they invent every week to reinforce their already abundantly clear conformity. As I was packing up, I could hear the whole rift unfold, front-row seats to girl vs. girl implosion.

"You betrayed me!" Chloe shrieks.

"You don't understand," Audrey replies, her voice warbly.

"You knew how I felt about your brother. How could you?" Chloe whines back, really turning up the drama to telenovela levels.

"You were supposed to be her best friend," one of the Chloettes hisses then, obviously thirsty for the job.

"*Yeah*," adds another. Because, *Yeah*.

"I told you that in confidence, and now the WHOLE SCHOOL KNOWS!" Chloe bellows, really going for her Oscar nod.

And natch, all I can think is, *Knows what*? That she had a nose job? That she is as petrified of difference as she is of gaining two pounds? That she is Camille Paglia's worst nightmare?

"I didn't tell him anything," Audrey sighs.

"Well, I happen to know you did," Chloe snips back.

"Just forget it."

"I will NEVER forget!" Chloe seethes, placing her own embarrassment in the same league of tragedy as, like, 9/11. "You are dead to me. I'm out!" She flips her hair, huffs, "Let's go," to the Chloettes, and the remaining squad scurries behind her, leaving Audrey alone and, seemingly, friendless.

"She's going to make an excellent Real Housewife of Nashville," I call down the hall, slamming my locker shut. "Or heartless dictator," I continue, as Audrey turns my way. "Depends on where she settles down."

Audrey slinks back toward me, releasing her bag on the ground, where it lands with a thud. "I guess you heard all that."

"Hard not to. If it makes you feel better, I don't think I know what the WHOLE SCHOOL KNOWS. So there's that."

Audrey can't help but smile. "She was just being dramatic."

"Nooooo . . . *really*?"

Now Audrey is giggling. And I struggle not to float to the ceiling. I pick up my bag, double-check my lock is tight. I notice she's watching me closely, with what feels like curiosity, a big step from her usual fear/avoidance of Kim Cruz.

"Got big plans for the break?" she asks, trying not to seem too interested.

But I know better. I know how much she hates being home with her family, how she feels like a three-headed alien in the middle of a Norman Rockwell painting, how she probably had her whole vacation scheduled around Chloe, and now she was staring down the barrel of so many empty hours, and would do almost anything not to have to fill them with Jason and the rest.

I also know it would be un-Changery of me to take advantage of that intimate knowledge, to pull a *Groundhog Day* on her and seduce her with what I already know are her favorite things. That such techniques, and heck, even our resuming a real friendship, are strictly verboten by the Changers Council. Add to that how manipulative it is to exploit her vulnerability in a time of need.

Ah, screw it. "You want to go out tonight?" I ask. "As friends?"

I swear she blushes. "Man, you really are bold. Kudos on the big balls."

"Just thought you might dig a night at the Bowl-Me-Over, the premiere karaoke/disco/bowling venue for karaoke/disco/bowling enthusiasts of all ages." I smile. (And like those chumps in the experiment, I feel good.) "They also have food."

Audrey cocks her head. Expels the longest sigh I've

heard in my lifetime. Maybe she's remembering Oryon, and the aborted bowling date he/I was meant to take her on before it all went pear-shaped. Or maybe she was doing the social calculus of what exactly would happen to her standing if she were somehow spotted out in public with me, Kim Cruz, chubby likely lesbian and stinky radical who may or may not have a mental imbalance.

"Just the two of us?" she asks at last.

"And every song the Bee Gees ever wrote."

And that was that. She said yes, and we made plans to meet up later, and when we did it was rocky at first, but there is no discomfort so grand it cannot be subdued by the sights and sounds of middle-aged white Americans performing karaoke.

Audrey and I found ourselves laughing at the same absurdities, like we had so many times before, and I could tell after a surprisingly short time that she was startled by how easy it was to hang out with me. I wasn't actively trying to use our history to ingratiate myself, but I couldn't exactly pretend I didn't know what would tickle her, or thrill her, or gross her out. The thing is, I've always felt I've known who Audrey is. I knew the second I saw her in homeroom on C1–D1 as Drew.

"You going to go up?" she asked, pointing at the queue of singers idling behind the mic.

"Oh, I'm going to go," I said, pulling my shoulders back. "I have a signature song."

"You do not."

"Watch me, girl. Let me show you how it's done."

I high-stepped it to the deejay, wrote down my selection, and took my place in line. And okay. I was lying, 1,000 percent. But I was so buoyant, so out of body with hope and joy and promise and warm memories and the realization of a year-long dream, that if she had dared me to break-dance in my bra and panties I would have thrown down a square of cardboard and started back-spinning, because so help me Gods, that's what love does.

I was with the girl I loved again. I was capable of anything.

Before I knew it, I was up next. My heart rate was elevated, but I felt in control, ready. The first lines of the background vocals blared from the speakers and I lifted the microphone and . . . went for it: "*If you change your mind, I'm the first in line, honey I'm still free. Take a chance on me . . .*"

That's right, folks. I was singing ABBA. Really, it was more than singing. I was *owning* ABBA. I had zero shame. I was large and in charge, ticking my hips right and left, shimmying my shoulders, making that grubby bowling alley stage my bitch.

Okay. In retrospect, the lyrics may have been a tad too spot-on. But I was past the point of caring. This was the new Kim Cruz. The one with nothing to lose. The one who stood up to Jason, who survived, who was loved by the friends she did have, who was learning to love herself, damaged or not.

As I kept singing and twirling and stomping around the stage, my inner diva gloriously unleashed (Kris would be kvelling!), I saw Audrey undergo her own transformation, moving from stunned, to uncomfortable, to grudgingly respectful, to warily standing, to contained dancing, to *actual* dancing, flinging her body around with an abandon I hadn't seen since that night she watched me when I was Drew, playing drums with the Bickersons.

By the end of the song, the entire crowd was with me, belting out the words, a chorus of broken hearts, all begging for another chance. I exited the stage to rousing cheers, the whole bowling alley whipped into a Swedish froth, courtesy of the apparent new Karaoke Queen.

"Holy Toledo!" Audrey gushed when I finally made my way back to our seats and scooched into one, fanning myself with the laminated snack menu. "That was off the chain!"

"Thank you."

"Why didn't you sing in the school play? You didn't even audition."

"I don't really sing," I said, "I was just inspired by the moment."

Audrey smirked. "Bowling alleys are known for their inspiring qualities."

"And their immaculate restrooms," I batted back.

"And their comfortable footwear."

"And their fine cuisine."

"And their homey smell."

"And their flattering lighting."

"And their beer farts."

I busted out laughing. "You win. Want to split an order of fries?"

As we ate, we talked about classes, the unseasonably warm weather. We avoided anything fraught, only touching briefly on the subject of Chloe, whom Audrey was clearly loath to discuss.

"Someday you'll have to tell me what you did to make her so mad," I said.

"I did her a favor. She's just too dumb to see it," Aud replied, dropping her gaze in a way I knew meant she was thinking about her brother—the glaring, devastating liability of Jason.

"I know you'd never hurt her on purpose," I offered.

Audrey shrugged. "Is that a good thing?"

A few rounds of bowling, one cheeseburger, a plate of nachos, some chair disco dancing, and three claw arcade games later (no fuzzy bear prize, dang it), the time came to call it a night. I had my usual bus to catch. We said our goodbyes in the parking lot, which stunk faintly of sewage and carton cigarettes.

"I wonder if they do weddings here," I joked, trying not to inhale.

"Or baby showers?" Audrey countered. It seemed like she didn't want to leave.

"I, for one, had an incredible time," I said.

"I did too!" Audrey said brightly, her surprise showing.

"Maybe we can do it again."

"Oh, well, I have family coming from out of town this break. They want to see the Grand Ole Opry, and do all the touristy stuff downtown. So . . ."

"I wasn't talking about this week."

"Oh." She was embarrassed.

"I have some obligations myself," I explained, trying to take the sting out.

"Of course."

"I'm glad we did this. We've done the impossible, and that makes us mighty."

"*Serenity!*" Audrey squealed, recognizing the line. "Who was in charge of canceling that?"

"Life is full of inexplicable decisions." Recognizing a good exit line when I see one, I gave a small bow and left.

But not before I hugged her goodbye. Just a quick, friendly squeeze, nothing desirous or needy. (Her hair smelled like mangoes.)

CHANGE 3-DAY 195

Mom won't stop weeping.

"Here, Connie," Dad says, passing his cloth hankie.

"It's all good, Mom," I add, carrying my duffel and books past her and down the hall to my bedroom, Snoopy watching the whole procession with a combination of excitement and annoyance.

"They're happy tears," Mom snuffles, blowing her nose with gale force. "I'm just so happy you're home. And on Easter Sunday."

"We don't celebrate Easter, honey," Dad quickly corrects, never one to let a chance to be a holiday Grinch slip by.

"I know, but it finally f-feels right," Mom sputters, the crying ramping up yet again. "My baby has come home. We're a family again."

Yup. The band is officially back together. After my karaoke triumph and my reunion with Audrey, such as it was, I went back to HQ and told Benedict that I thought it was time for me to move along. I won't lie, Tracy's nudging helped, texting me daily quotes about the love between a mother and child, and e-mailing videos of baby animals and their mommies cuddling in the wild. You see enough newborn elephants curling their whiskery trunks around their mamas' legs, and you feel like leaping back into the freaking womb.

So I leapt. I was in a better place now. With Audrey, obviously. With Nana's passing. With Chase's too. But also with myself. I was less depressed. The fog had lifted enough for me to see some horizon, and while Kim is probably never going to be America's Sweetheart, I wanted to kill people a lot less, and this I counted as a good sign.

When I broke the news, at first Benedict was, per his irritating custom, judgmental in his nonjudgmentalness. "If you're certain this is the path you need to walk, then you absolutely should go where you belong," he said.

I just miss home, dude. I'm not joining Hitler Youth.

He added some other stuff about staying on track, and not allowing the comforts of domesticity to quash my nascent politicalization, and keeping my eyes on the RaCha prize, and I listened, but, I explained, the work I was most called to do right then was make things right with my folks.

"I'll be at the demonstration," I promised.

Which delighted and satisfied him enough to help me finish packing my bag while I texted Mom to come get me. She was there to pick me up before I'd even reached the curb out front. It was almost as if she'd been circling the block, waiting for the call.

As we drove home, I sensed she was laboring not to spook the exotic bird. She didn't ask questions or gloat or make mention of my appearance or attire. She let me control the radio. When we pulled into the garage, I immediately spotted a vintage orange Vespa scooter with a matching orange bow on the handlebars. My Kim Cruz birthday present. Damn. They must've *really* missed me.

"We can get your permit now that you're back," Mom said.

"Cool. Thank you."

And then the happy tears started. And they haven't really stopped.

***

I've been back half a day, hiding in my room for much of it, and it feels like I never want to leave again. My room feels cleaner, brighter. All my stuff is where it always was. Even my alligator pencils are lined up exactly the way I'd arranged them. Nothing touched. A shrine to me.

That's not weird or anything.

I check Skype to see whether Destiny is avail. No dice. That's right, she and DJ were planning to take a road trip to Dollywood for the weekend. (I hope they send me a photo of them eating a giant turkey leg and a funnel cake.)

I text Kris to see if he's around. He texts right back, and I miss his face, so I ask him to get on Skype. After much equivocation (he's in his underwear), he finally agrees to put on a shirt and talk to me.

"Guess who's back, back, back," he sings the minute he clicks on my screen and sees me in the bedroom. *"Back again."*

I flip him the bird.

"How goes reentry?" he asks, half-buttoning his silk polka-dot shirt and reclining on a chintz divan, like he's living in a Tennessee Williams play. Which come to think of it, he is.

"Odd. Lotta tears."

"Sister, there should be. That's what family is for."

"It feels bizarre. Like I'm the guest of honor. I want everyone to chill. Stop making so much out of it. Get a grip. Something."

Kris leans forward and presses his nose right up to the camera. "Kimmycakes?"

"Yes?"

"You're being a Regina George."

"Screw you."

"No. You need to hear me. This is your come-to-Jesus moment. Your parents love you. You rejected *them*. How do you think they should feel? What would be an *appropriate* response for you?"

I keep my mouth shut. His voice suddenly grows venomous, angry. But not at me.

"I was kicked to the curb like gay garbage. My parents don't even want to look at me. And I still miss them every day. So maybe you could see clear to giving yours a break for whatever stupid thing they said or did *months* ago and realize for once in your privileged life how lucky you are."

"Are you done?" I ask.

"Yes," he says, popping his collar up.

"I love you, Kris."

"I love you too, dumb bunny."

After Kris and I disconnect, I march straight to where Mom is sitting in the TV room, blotting her eyes, and throw my arms around her waist, just like the baby elephants.

I feel her body melt.

Then I feel the same happening inside my own.

Later, after dinner, I helped Dad clear the plates from the table.

"Thanks for the scooter," I said.

"It was your mother's idea," he answered.

I handed him a dirty skillet. "I know you're disappointed in me. And I'm sorry," I said. "But I really am trying. Believe me when I tell you, you can't hate me more than I hate myself."

I noticed his lips start to tremble. Then his cheeks. He turned around to the sink.

"I didn't die in that basement, Dad," I pressed on. "I'm still here. I'm still alive. I'm still your kid."

I wanted him to acknowledge me, to say something, to yell, anything. But he just clenched his jaw, slipped the skillet into the sudsy water, and left the room.

CHANGE 3-DAY 201

What does one wear to a coming-out protest/visibility march? I must've been standing in front of my closet for a good ten minutes before defaulting to a plain black crew neck and my black stretchy jeans with a hole in one knee. For shoes I dig out my old black Converse hi-tops, a conscious nod to Drew, who started this whole thing.

As I'm tying my laces on the foot of my bed, Snoopy pushed up against my lower back, I notice the memento box in the back of my closet. I finish one double-knot, then the next. I get up and pull the box out, flipping the top open and setting it on my comforter. Snoopy grunts.

I see a stack of Nana's letters, the last one Mom gave me after Nana died perched on the top. The sight of it makes my eyes haze over with tears, but I blink them away, pick up the letter, and examine Nana's shaky writing on the envelope.

I wonder what she would've thought of all this Ra-Chas vs. Changers Dawn of Justice business. Whether she would've been in favor of a visibility march. Something tells me yes. Or at least, if that last letter is any indication, she'd approve of whatever I decided to do about it.

The truth is, all of her encouragement and faith in me is almost too much to carry sometimes. (Now being one of those times.) I don't want to let her down. To be a person she wouldn't respect. To be someone she never thought I was.

I sniff the envelope. Nothing besides that dry-paper

smell. I sort through the photos in the box, a smattering of the Ethan years: Mom and Dad putting up a tent at a campsite in Vermont, with me and Snoopy, just a puppy then, poking our heads out of the flap; a naked shot in the sink as a baby; another of Ethan's elementary school holiday concert, sporting a crooked navy clip-on tie.

As I root around the box, my fingers slide over the friendship bracelet from Audrey. I pluck it out, cradle its weight in my palm, then pinch it between my fingers, the little drum-kit charm dangling back and forth. The memory of the day she gave it to me pops into my head like the photographs I was just looking at. Clear, unalterable, frozen in time. It all seems so long ago.

I decide to put the bracelet on. Just for the day. If I'm going to be marching, may as well take along the beat of my own drum. I also tuck the first photo Nana gave me of when she was a Chase V inside my back pocket. It feels right to carry them both with me.

While I admit my first instinct was to lie to my parents, in the end I decided to tell them the truth about where I was *going*, if not what I was *doing*. (I couldn't risk Dad finding out and possibly tipping off the Council. Then *I'd* be the rat.) When Destiny showed up out front in her car, a little early, I told my parents we were meeting a couple of RaChas for lunch, and then going to listen to some music downtown for the afternoon. (Technically, we would be *hearing* music blasting out of the dozens of honky-tonk bars along Broadway, so that wasn't totally a lie.)

Mom seemed down with the prospect of my hanging with RaChas. I think she credited Benedict and the rest of them with my eventually coming home, plus the shrink in her realizes the more you forbid something, the more enticing it becomes. Dad, however, was his new normal, not particularly cool about anything, including this, but he deferred to Mom before heading into his office to get some work done. Mom slipped a twenty-dollar bill in my pocket while holding me extra tight (her new, stage-five-clinger normal), and whispering in my ear, "Have a nice time, be safe." She waved at Destiny as I headed out to the car.

Twenty bones richer, we stop by the vegan craft donut shop in East Nashville, pick up a baker's dozen to share, and make it to RaChas HQ in record time.

"Maybe no one will even see us out there," Destiny comments about the lack of traffic.

"It's Easter weekend and spring break," I say. "By lunchtime, downtown is going to be jammed with tourists and families. Believe that."

"Awesome," Destiny answers in a way that suggests she is well into her second, if not third, thoughts about the whole coming-out-on-the-street plan.

It takes us a couple spins around the block to find a place to park. Benedict wanted as many shiny Changer faces as possible parading down Lower Broadway this afternoon, so he and his team spread the word that all RaChas-related (and even RaChas-leaning) Changers needed to get their butts down here for the action. Judging by the lack of asphalt, it seemed like his pied pipering might've worked.

We knock on the metal door and Wylie lets us in, leading us back where final touches are being made. I set the donuts on a table, and the box is immediately swarmed.

I read the posters filled with various slogans and the amended many-limbed RaChas symbol. *We Are Changers.*

Changers Happens. I Changed: So Will You. I'm Not a Changer, But My Girlfriend (or Boyfriend) Is. Gender Is a Social Construct: Deal With It. Changer Pride. Who Do YOU Want to Be When You Grow Up? Identity ain't nothing but a number.

And so on. Stacks of pamphlets are rubber-banded together on the table, for each of us to take and hand out to curious passersby.

"Kim Cruz!" I hear from across the room. It's Benedict, motoring toward me, trailed by a scruffy squatter-looking guy juggling a stack of schedules in his arms. "I'm so glad to see you."

"Of course," I say, "wouldn't miss it for anything. Plus, it was an excuse to buy donuts. Did you get one?"

"Nobody told me there'd be donuts," Benedict says theatrically, embracing Destiny and then me. At which point, the guy next to him hands us each a schedule for the day.

"Thanks," I say without looking at him, my eyes anxiously scanning the agenda.

"You are *very* welcome," he says, obviously more to Destiny.

Wait, I sort of recognize that voice. I glance up from my schedule. The face is familiar too. Pale skin, dark green eyes, intense eyebrows. There's more beard scruff than seems familiar, but I swear I—

This can't be happening.

He looks at me, lips parted as if about to say something. I can't speak.

I obviously look like I've seen a ghost (which at this point I'm sure I have), because Destiny asks, "Are you okay?"

"I—I . . ."

"Oh, Kim, this is Andy," Benedict says casually. "He's been crashing with us for a couple nights."

Andy.

My Andy! As in Andy, Ethan's old best friend for life. (For Ethan's life anyhow.)

Andy extends his hand to shake mine. "Nice to meet you, Kim," he says.

"And this is Destiny," Benedict adds.

"Great name," Andy gushes.

I can't do anything but stare at him. I mean, so intensely that I'm sure I'm beginning to give off a creeper vibe. My stomach feels like it's grounded out beside my heels.

I'M ETHAN, I'M ETHAN, I'M ETHAN, I'M ETHAN, I'M ETHAN! is running through my head. *All I have left of you are photographs in a box. Well, until now, that is.*

I can scarcely follow as Benedict rattles off: "Andy's been bumping along from squatter city to squatter city, and he stumbled upon us because he had a messy relationship with a Changer at his school, and it really effed him up, what with all the Council rules about Statics, yadda, yadda, yadda. And he heard rumors about Changers who weren't all about rules and regulations—uh, that's US! Anyway, Andy's got some childhood best friend who moved to Nashville a few years ago, so he's hoping to find the guy—he thinks dude's parents will let him bunk there, since he got kicked out of his house in New York for some, whatever, personal reasons."

"Benedict!" someone hollers from across the room.

"Well, you tell them your story, Andy. Be back in a sec," Benedict says, leaving me to gawk at the kid sans running narrative.

"Well, that sucks," Destiny says to Andy, to fill the space.

"Yeah," Andy replies, a little reticent to pick up Benedict's narrative.

"So what happened?" Destiny pushes.

"Well. This girl," Andy starts. (I'm no doctor, but he still seems majorly confused and perturbed by the whole ordeal.) "She was literally everything to me, and then *poof*."

"Where is she now?" Destiny asks.

"I think she turned into a guy?" Andy says.

ANDY SAYS!

"On the first day of school," he continues, sounding a little rattled, "this new kid comes up to me and seems to know all this stuff about me. So in retrospect, I think that might've been her, but then I guess the parents or Council whatever swooped in, and I could never get any additional information, and it all really screwed with my head."

"It's kind of the rules," Destiny says. "I'm sure she wasn't trying to hurt you."

"The rules are kinda dumb if you ask me," Andy blows back.

But nobody asked you, ANDY.

"So what? You hate Changers now or something?" Destiny says.

"No, no, no way. Now that I'm learning a little about it, I'm totally down with the RaChas mission for sure. Benedict says that you guys could use some Static allies, and that's all I want to be. He asked me to do some recon here at HQ while you're at the march." Andy taps a walkie-talkie clipped to his belt.

I still can't form a word.

I feel completely seen, found out, embarrassed, scared, bewildered, sad. Guilty for bailing on the guy. Being another person who disappeared on him because there was no other choice. But he doesn't even know it. My mind can't get itself around the fact that he's standing right in front of me, knows way more than I ever thought he would—and yet he has no freaking real idea.

For now.

"You usually can't shut this one up," Destiny says, poking me with a bony elbow. "Don't know what's gotten into her. Stage fright maybe."

"I'm fine," I stammer. "Just thinking about this schedule."

"Well, I'm going to set up the waters," Andy says, overly helpful. "Can I get you ladies some?"

"No thanks, we're good," Destiny says, and when he's gone, she turns to me: "Are you into that guy or something?"

Ack! Gag. "No."

"What then? It's like you were possessed the second he showed up."

Because he's the ghost of Changer lives past, Destiny.

I can't tell her. I want to. But not yet. I need time to think. To figure things out, to run some scenarios in my head. To freaking breathe. Past, present, and future are colliding. Here I am, about to "come out" with the truth, or at least one truth, about myself, and yet I can't tell Andy who I am. Nor Benedict who Andy is.

It's like, somewhere Ethan still exists now, as long as Andy thinks he does and is still looking for him. And that somehow feels... *good?* I guess you can't erase fourteen years of a life. Just like I'll never be able to erase a year as Drew, a year as Oryon, a year as Kim. People will always remember who they knew and loved. So long as everyone has their memory boxes, no one ever really goes away.

I notice the troops have started to rally, and hear Benedict yell from atop the dining table, "It's twelve hundred hours," as everybody gathers around him, and he starts to go over the schedule down to the minute (in military time, no less). Andy seems to have nuzzled right in at HQ in the week since I left, sitting beneath Benedict and assisting with whatever he needs handed up to him—maps, pens, schedules, and so on.

And then Benedict yells, "Let's roll!" and . . .

RACHAS ACTION FINAL SCHED.
1230: Depart HQ (bring signs, whistles, water, cell phones)
1300: Convene in parking lot on 11th Avenue (west of train tracks)
1315-1345: Review schedule (Benedict), map & communication (Wylie)
1345-1400: Partner up, exchange phone numbers (if you haven't already done so)
1400-1415: Final preparation, sunscreen, hydration, etc.
1420: Group affirmation hug
1421: Walk as group to Union Station Hotel (bathroom break, all encouraged to go)
1445: Convene on SE corner of Rosa L. Parks Blvd. & Broadway (meet on steps of Customs House)
1500: Display signs, BEGIN MARCH East down Broadway (do NOT block business entrances or traffic)
~1600: Convene at circle at end of Broadway/1st Ave. at river side*

*Note: Please keep moving around circle at all times while demo continues in this location: police can still make arrests, but moving helps.

We reach the river at 1553 hours—a hair earlier than Benedict had planned. We did it. About a dozen RaChas strolled down the sidewalk on Broadway, making noise, handing out brochures, answering questions—and we are now gathered on the appointed little oval of grass, wondering what comes next.

A local news van has set up at the curb opposite, its satellite dish pointing to the sky. A crowd of about fifty tourists are just standing and gawking at us, also seeming to wonder what's next.

"Change isn't strange!" Benedict yells. "Change isn't strange!"

And we all start chanting along, blowing our whistles, a couple dudes banging bongo drums slung around their necks.

"Change isn't strange! Change isn't strange! Change isn't strange!"

A few policemen on bikes circle, making sure things remain safe. Some of the older folks in the crowd begin to whisper in each other's ears. A toddler with a Mylar balloon shaped like a cowboy boot runs up and dances beside us like we're singing the most beautiful song ever. Just then, a news reporter sidles up to the group, calling, "Who's in charge here?"

Benedict comes forward. "I can speak with you," he says, stepping off the grass island and right in front of the camera.

Watching him get ready for his close-up, I can't believe we just walked down the street like we did, proclaiming who and what we are to any and everybody who was interested. Of course, most people weren't. Not really. I imagine they assumed it was just a bunch of kids acting up. Or a political rally for general, run-of-the-mill "change." Which is okay. Because the march isn't for them. It's for us.

"The world you think you know is not the world that is!" I hear Benedict shout into the microphone over our chanting, as the reporter fixes her hair, which has flopped across her face in a balmy gust of wind.

Way beyond them, a clot of white tourists has just emerged from the Hard Rock Café on the corner and moves en masse the way tourists do, in the direction of our gathering, presumably to see what all the commotion's about.

"I'm talking about an entirely different type of diversity," Benedict is saying now, "mind-blowing levels of difference that society is only beginning to comprehend!"

I squint and notice a family inching closer toward us, one member breaking from the pack and pulling ahead, followed by another larger shadow.

I keep chanting, holding Destiny's hand, bouncing my sign above us, staying in constant motion. It's loud, we're proud, and everybody seems to be getting used to it.

Maybe this could actually work in the world. We can all be who and what we are, and it ain't nobody's business if we do...

And then it registers. Who's headed my way. The face at last snapping into focus. The most familiar face in the world.

Audrey.

A corner of her lip is curled up in some sort of profound bewilderment. She's coming right for me, her brother Jason ten steps behind. Her entire extended family trailing after them.

As she approaches, I drop Destiny's hand. I also drop the sign I've been holding (which reads, *I am what I am. And am, and am, and am*). I'm frozen.

Destiny veers around me and keeps step with the group.

"Kim?" Audrey shouts, loud, over the chanting, as I stoop down to pick up my sign, pretending I can't hear her. Audrey rushes over and bends down at the same time, reaching for the wooden handle in the exact instant I do.

"What are you doing? What's all this about?" she asks, then recoils, retracting her hand as though she'd been about to dunk it in a vat of acid. She jolts upright, wobbling as she stands. Her face is pale.

I can tell she's seen it.

The bracelet.

In fact, she can't take her eyes off it.

I would do anything to throw my arms around her.

"Audrey," I say.

She finally looks at me, looks right into my eyes.

"Drew?"

(NOT) THE END

COMING SOON

BOOK FOUR

WEARECHANGERS.ORG

ABRIDGED GLOSSARY OF TERMS

(EXCERPTED FROM THE CHANGERS BIBLE)

ABIDER. A non-Changer (see *Static*, below) belonging to an underground syndicate of anti-Changers, whose ultimate goal is the extermination of the Changer race. The Abider philosophy is characterized by a steadfast desire for genetic purity, for human blood to remain unmingled with Changer blood. Abider leaders operate by instilling fear in humans, for when people fear one another, they are easier to control. Abiders sometimes have an identifying tattoo depicting an ancient symbol of a Roman numeral I (*Figure 1*), the emblem symbolizing homogeneity and the single identity Abiders desire each human to inhabit.

I

FIG. 1. ABIDERS EMBLEM

CHANGER. A member of an ancient race of humans imbued with the gift of changing into a different person four times between the ages of approximately fourteen and eighteen. (In more modern times, one change occurs at the commencement of each of the four years of high school; see *Cycle*, below.) Changers may not reveal themselves to non-Changers (see *Static*, below). After living as all four versions of themselves (see *V*, below), Changers must choose one version in which to live out the rest of their lives (see *Mono*, below). Changer doctrine holds that the Changer race is the last hope for the human race on the whole to reverse the moral devolution that has overcome it. Changers believe more Changers equals more empathy on planet Earth. And that only through empathy will the human race survive. After their Cycles (see *Cycle*, below), Changers eventually partner with Statics. When approved by the Council (see *Changers Council*, below), Changer-Static unions produce a single Changer offspring.

CHANGERS COUNCIL. The official Changer authority. The Changers Council is divided into regional units spread out across the globe. Each Council is responsible for all basic decisions regarding the population of Changers in its specific region.

CHANGERS EMBLEM. A variation on Leonardo da Vinci's *Vitruvian Man* drawing, dating to approximately 1490 CE (*Figure 2*). The Changers Emblem contains four bodies superimposed in motion, instead of two (as portrayed in da Vinci's composition), and appears to the eye as both four bodies and one body at the same time—though all sharing one head and heart. An emblem of the Changer mantra: *In the many we are one.*

FIG. 2. CHANGERS EMBLEM

CHANGERS MIXER. Required events for all Changers to attend, during each of the four years of high school. Council rules and regulations are emphasized at mixers (see *Changers Council,* above). Mixers sometimes require classwork and formal discussions, but mixers are primarily designed to offer more informal camaraderie and problem-solving techniques, both of which help Changers address some of the difficulties that frequently arise during their Cycles (see *Cycle*, below).

CYCLE. The four-year period of different iterations, or versions (see *V*, below) that a Changer goes through between the approximate ages of fourteen and eighteen. One V per each of the four years of high school.

FEINTS. The story a Changer family tells the non-Changers (see *Static*, below) in their lives, to explain each V's (see *V*, below) absence during the following year of school. The specific details for Feints are provided by the Council (see *Changers Council*, above), unless a Changer and her/his parents submit a formal request for an alternative Feint, which is necessary under certain circumstances (i.e., when Statics are especially integrated into a particular V's life, or when a particular Feint will better protect the identity of the Changer and her/his family).

FOREVER CEREMONY. Regional "graduation" events held on the day after high school graduation for every Changer within a designated region. A joyous though private (from Statics—except parental Statics; see *Static*, below) occasion, as each year of ceremonies initiates more and more Changers to migrate into the world and eventually find a Static mate, with whom they will start a family and raise Changer offspring of their own. At the Forever Ceremony, Changers are introduced one by one, and each speaks a little about each of her/his V's (see *V*, below) before declaring in front of both the Council (see *Changers Council*, above) and their community whom they will live as for the rest of their lives (see *Mono*, below).

MONO. A Changer's "forever identity," a.k.a. the V (see *V*, below) a Changer ultimately selects for her/himself after living as each of the four different assigned V's. A Mono cannot be the individual a Changer lived as during the approximately fourteen years before her/his Cycle (see *Cycle*, above) began.

RACHAS. Abbreviation of "Radical Changers," a small but growing splinter group of young Changers who seek not to live in secret, as the Council (see *Changers Council*, above) dictates. RaChas are freegans, anarchist free spirits, living in the margins, surviving on what human society at large throws away. RaChas philosophy calls for living openly as Changers and agitating for liberation and acceptance for all, Changers and Statics alike. RaChas have replaced their former emblem (an ancient Roman numeral IV rotated on its side) with a new image, a modified Changers emblem, (see *Changers Emblem* above) with multiple limbs (*Figure 3*), symbolizing the RaChas' desire to shake up traditional Changers philosophy and call attention to the limitations of the four-V Cycle (See *V*, below; see *Cycle*, above). RaChas have also been known to battle Abiders (see *Abider*, above) and even stage missions to rescue Changers who have been abducted by Abiders and held in Abider deprogramming camps. [*Nota bene*: while the Changers Council is at odds with the RaChas movement, it can also no longer deny its existence.]

FIG. 3. NEW RACHAS EMBLEM

STATIC. A non-Changer (i.e., the vast majority of the world's population). Particularly sympathetic Statics are ideal mates for Changers later in life. Once a Changer has completed his or her Cycle (see *Cycle*, above), s/he will be fully prepared to assess various Statics' openness and acceptance of difference. When a Changer feels certain that s/he has found an ideal potential Static mate, s/he may, with permission of the Council (see *Changers Council*, above), reveal her/himself to the Static. [*Nota bene:* This revelation can occur only after a Changer's full Cycle (see *Cycle*, above) is complete, and s/he has declared his or her Mono (see *Mono*, above).]

TOUCHSTONE. A Changer's official mentor, assigned immediately upon a Changer's transformation into her/his first V (see *V*, below). The same Touchstone is assigned for a Changer's entire Cycle (see *Cycle*, above).

V. Any one of a Changer's four versions of her/himself into which s/he changes during each of the four years of high school. Changers walk in the shoes of one V for each year of school (between the approximate ages of fourteen and eighteen).

Acknowledgments

Thanks are due to several individuals who helped *Changers* evolve from a lightning-bolt idea in the park to an actual book series we are proud to have our children (and others) read. The love, kindness, and support of the following friends, family, colleagues, and representatives can be felt on every page of *Book Three* (and beyond): Johnny Temple, Johanna Ingalls, Aaron Petrovich, Ibrahim Ahmad, and Susannah Lawrence at Akashic Books; Kate Bornstein; Deborah Choi; Consortium Book Sales and Distribution; Tim Daly; Dixie and Matilda; Betsy Brown Eagle; Theo Brown Eagle; our families; Mary Gonzalez; John Green; Ryan LeVine, Karl Austen, and Danielle Josephs at Jackoway, Tyerman, Wertheimer, et al.; Tom Kelly; Téa Leoni and family; A.J. Morewitz and Chris Selak at Lionsgate; Jennifer Mencken and Ben Pivar; Gina Mingacci; Langley Perer and Dawn Saltzman at Mosaic; Alex Petrowsky; Spencer Presler; Amy Ray; Scott Turner Schofield; Zac Simmons at Paradigm; Michael Redwine; Scott Silver; Doug Stewart at Sterling Lord Literistic; Meryl Poster and Tesha Crawford at Superb; Tommy Wallach; Sarah Chalfant at the Wylie Agency.

And to the seventh grader at Middle School 378 in New York City who asked, "Are there Changers in the real world?" We believe so!

ALLISON GLOCK-COOPER and **T COOPER** are best-selling and award-winning authors and journalists. Between them, they have published eleven books, raised two children, and rescued six dogs. The *Changers* series is their first collaboration in print. The two also write for television and film, and are currently adapting *Changers* for television (with Lionsgate TV). The authors can be reached via their websites: www.t-cooper.com and www.allisonglock.com.